BRIGHT OF THE MOON

A DARK-ELVES OF NIGHTBLOOM NOVEL

MIRANDA HONFLEUR

Paperback ISBN: 978-1-949932-23-2

Cover art by Mirela Barbu

Map by Rela "Kellerica" Similä

Editing by Jessica B. Fry

Proofreading by Anthony S. Holabird at Holabird Editing & by Nic Page

AUTHOR'S MAILING LIST

Visit www.mirandahonfleur.com to sign up for Miranda's mailing list! You'll get "Winter Wren" for free.

PREFACE

A little note on reading order: Although *Bright of the Moon* is the second novel in the Dark-Elves of Nightbloom fantasy romance series and can be read as a standalone, if you prefer to read in chronological order, then the events of this book take place before the epilogue at the end of the first book, *No Man Can Tame*.

ALSO BY MIRANDA HONFLEUR

This book is for...

Katherine Bueche, Nic Page, Rachel Cass, Anthony S. Holabird, Wanda Wozniczka, Lea Vickery, Elise Kova, Alisha Klapheke, Clare Sager, Catharine Glen, A F, Andrea Peel, Dana Jackson Lange, Debra Henn, Erin Miller, Fiona Andrew, Joye Stallman, Lisa Witt, Mariana H, Wendi Guerrero, Chelsea Estebanez...

...and everyone else who's supported me and spread the word about my books from the start. I couldn't do this without you, and you being in my corner has meant the world to me.

CONTENTS

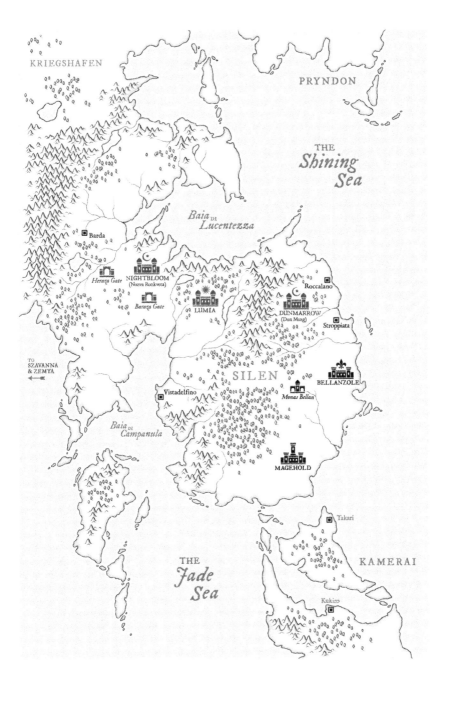

KRIEGSHAFEN

PRYNDON

THE *Shining Sea*

Baia DI *Lucentezza*

Barda

Heraza Gate

NIGHTBLOOM
(*Nozva Rozkveta*)

Baraza Gate

LUMIA

Roccalano

DUNMARROW
(*Dun Morg*)

Stroppiata

TO
SZAVANNA
& ZEMYA

SILEN

BELLANZOLE

Vistadelfino

Monas Bellan

Baia DI *Campanula*

MAGEHOLD

Takari

THE *Jade Sea*

KAMERAI

Kukiro

PROLOGUE

*H*er breath sharp like knives, Bella raced through the stark forest as fast as her booted feet could take her.

Flashes of immaculate white darted through the grove of chestnut trees, glimpses just barely visible in the distance. Low-hanging branches snatched at her dress like desperate hands, but she dared not slow down. Not if she wanted to catch up to the unicorn.

She weaved through the slender trunks, her steps crunching on frozen twigs. Her cloak pulled at her neck, caught on a snow-shrouded bough, and she unclasped it. No matter. The late-winter chill wouldn't halt her flight.

All her life, she'd secretly searched for others like her, who believed in the sharpness of ingenuity over that of the blade. At first, they had been only humans. But when untold numbers of immortal creatures had awoken about a year ago, more hope had blinked its eyes open. A war raged between humans and Immortali. And if unicorns were real, then maybe their mythical powers of peace were, too; she'd meet this one face to face. Here. Today. Maybe it could help spare another Bella somewhere from losing the love of her life to war. At the very least, she wouldn't disappoint Cosimo's memory.

She leaped over a fallen tree. Her boot slid in the slushy deadfall, but she caught herself with a gloved hand.

Precious time. She was losing precious time.

But the magnificent white coat shone just ahead, in stark relief to the withered foliage and ash-brown bark.

The unicorn had stopped. It was waiting.

She slowed, testing her approaching steps cautiously. Chasing it had been one thing, but running toward it now? She couldn't risk spooking what she'd admired for so long. Not now. Not when she was so close and her idol so real.

Tarquin, Luciano, and Mamma would never believe her, but it didn't matter. The only thing the Belmonte family believed in was war. But as "Renato"—her pseudonym and secret political alter ego—she could introduce the kingdom of Silen to an entire society that had renounced war eons before Silen had even crowned its first king. With the help of the unicorns, she could change the course of not only her family but the realm.

As long as she could avoid the assassins chasing the price on Renato's head. The price on *her* head.

Now that she'd slowed, her face burned. She struggled to remain upright as she sucked in breath after life-giving breath. With any luck, her wheezing, grunting, and panting like a constipated barbarian wouldn't frighten it. Writers, perhaps, were not always the best of runners. Or breathers.

But it just watched her, flicking its tail, long, wavy silken hair swaying in the breeze. Although horse-like, calling it—*him*—a horse wouldn't have been right. He had a loose, open bearing, and gave a curious tilt of his head. A slight toss as if to say hello. There was a surprisingly human quality to his body language. Had he intended to lead her here?

She straightened. What did unicorns know of human society, anyway? Everything she'd ever read of them had suggested they were reclusive, isolated, kept to themselves, some even preferring solitude entirely. Wouldn't their communication—verbal or otherwise—reflect that?

Other sources had guessed at telepathic abilities. Had he read her thoughts?

Perhaps the two of them would be able to communicate? All the better. "Hello," she said shakily, cautiously. "I'm Bella."

From thirty feet away, she met his eyes. Bright, alluring violet, magical, as if the most coveted, priceless jewels had been given flesh and intention. Then—

The world blurred around her, a sweep of greenery. Her chest tightened as though she were falling, but her feet found the dirt beneath her.

The unicorn stood before her, his face level with hers, his horn a mere inch from her forehead. Violet. Brilliant, breathtaking violet—

She gasped. An arcane shiver trembled through her shoulders and down her spine. Magic. It was magic.

The horn—long, twining, and sharp—would be daunting on any other creature but the father of peace. Still, she dared not move but to breathe, and slowly, his gaze drew her in.

Those eyes were limitless, the boundless skies of another world, where the wind flirted through the endless summer grasses studded with vibrant wildflowers, where a herd of unicorns swept past, manes swaying, horns gleaming, beneath a warm sun...

Warm... and she was like them, her heart filled with quiet, the kind of peace lost on other worlds, except this one... This one was the dream. Where no one fought, no one killed. Where her family's armies had never killed her only love, Cosimo. Where she'd never been too blind to see it coming. Where battles were waged with words, and victories were bloodless. Where unicorns ventured out of their isolation and met the world with warmth and quiet hearts.

Their dream. Her dream.

If only she could become—

A pinprick heated her forehead. She blinked at deep eyes shrouded with long, dense lashes.

The unicorn stepped back, bowing his head, his gaze never leaving hers.

The tip of his horn was red.

Frowning, she blinked again. Red flowed down the twining horn, a swirl of bright ribbon against pearlescent white.

She raised her fingers to her forehead, and they came away red, too. Blood red.

All her research had said they were peaceful. They were, weren't they? But then, what was this? An accident, maybe? It had to be...

And before her was no longer just the unicorn.

A *herd* of them. *The* herd stood in a meadow.

She swayed, and her weak knees buckled.

There were at least two dozen. How—?

The world blurred around her again. He had to be taking her some-where. But where? She turned in place, spun, but everything only blurred more, more and more and more...

She misplaced a foot and fell, descending like a feather on summer air, gliding down to the forest floor, impossibly green and lively. She fell through piles of leaves and colorful flower petals, through visions of the sun soaring across the sky, and then the moon rising, violet eyes and green ones and blue, her gloves slipping off and flying away from her grasp, the satin petals against her skin and cool grass, the sun, the moon, the sun...

The blur sharpened, slowly, brushstrokes of color coming together into the shapes of chestnut trees and fresh spring leaves in the predawn light, and the magnificent unicorn peering down at her, all of it framed in the most beautiful palette of glowing prismatic hues.

How was it possible...? It was winter after all, wasn't it...?

In this world, it is only a dream. You must make it come true, Arabella, a firm, soothing baritone said to her.

She tilted her head, but something tickled her nose. As she reached up to scratch it, a hoof rose beneath her.

Her arm wouldn't cooperate—her arm—her arm...

Her heart racing, she looked down at herself. At her long, immacu-late white legs. At her hooves.

At her *hooves.*

With a gasp, she backed up, shaking her head. It wasn't possible. A human couldn't turn into... There was no way. She couldn't be—

But you are, the voice said.

Violet eyes. The voice—it was *him.*

Her legs continued to retreat without her volition.

There's nothing back there for you, the voice said gently.

Nothing back there? Her family was there: Mamma, Tarquin, Luciano... Were they all right? Had something happened to them? This wasn't real. This wasn't—

Arabella, come—

She ran.

PAST THE GROVE of chestnut trees and far into the range of the northern Sileni hills, Bella scrambled home, the cold air stinging her teary eyes. This wasn't happening. It was some spell of the unicorn, some illusion, or... or she was still in that dream. It had to be. Merciful gods and empyreal Veil threads, it *had* to.

Once she was with her brothers and Mamma, it would all break. She'd be reminded of the real world, and rooted in it, whatever spell or dream this was, it would end. Unicorns in myths had dazzling powers of the mind. If she believed those tales—and considering she'd just seen a unicorn in the flesh—maybe a trick of the mind was all it was.

Just over the hill, the olive orchards stretched before the Belmonte castello and its city of Roccalano. She bolted among the thin young trees for the open gates of the city. The staccato of hooves against the cobblestone invaded her ears, beat further and deeper. No, it was a dream. The sound was unreal, just as it all had been.

The few citizens outside in the hour before dawn gasped and gaped, jumping out of her way, unlike their usual smiles and warm greetings. Every gape tore at the dream, challenged its fiber. *Maybe it's not a dream.* She shook her head and ran faster toward the castello gates.

Shouts rang out among the guards, but she made it through and into the courtyard bearing Cosimo's sculpture. She charged straight for the nearest door, paying no heed to the chaos building in her wake.

She reached up to knock, but hooves hit the mahogany wood, sending splinters flying.

Mamma! Tarquin! Luciano!

Try as she might, no voice sounded when she called. *Please, someone! Anyone, hear me!*

She hit the door again and again, and if the gods could but spare her a mercy, Mamma or one of her brothers would hear.

A bellowed order—Captain Sondrio and a squad of guards closed in on her with polearms. A stormy scent dominated the air.

Captain, it's me! Please!

But the squad only advanced, and she leaped away from the sage-green *arcanir* blade tips and their magic-nullifying metal. Pottery shattered and flowers crunched beneath her as she scrambled past a window. The shutters hung open, and inside, Tarquin stared back at her, his reddish-brown eyes wide.

Tarquin, she breathed, her heart soaring. Her big brother, her hero, the one who'd always bandaged her skinned knees and wiped away her frustrated tears. He would see her, dispel whatever this was, set everything right. *Help me!*

His hand reached for a sword that wasn't at his hip, not this early in the morning at home.

She tapped the glass, but it shattered, sending jagged remnants flying like daggers.

"Is it Bella?" Mamma's frantic voice called from deeper within the house. Light footsteps pattered nearer, quiet but audible on the thick-pile heirloom rugs.

Darkness passed over Tarquin's face as he shook his head. "Mamma, stay back," he called over his shoulder. "It's one of the Immortali beasts."

Beast...? Mamma! Tarquin, it's me! Couldn't they see through this illusion, or whatever it was?

Mamma stood beside Tarquin, scowling as she clenched a fist. Her reddened eyes teared up nonetheless, a grim match for the dark circles shadowing Tarquin's gaze.

A stab of white-hot pain seared Bella's side.

She staggered backward, avoiding the points of sharp polearms. One of the guards lunged toward her, but Captain Sondrio held out a hand to stop him.

Her stomach clenched. They would—they would kill her.

"Captain!" Tarquin's voice boomed. "To bows! Someone get me a blade and get that beast out of here!"

That beast. *That beast.* This wasn't an illusion or some trick of the mind? She was truly a unicorn after all?

How could this happen? Why?

But as her heart slowed, every hair of her mane stood on end. It was true. Gods above, it was true.

If this was a dream, shouldn't she have awoken by now?

Arcanir. If this had been some spell, the arcanir blade of the polearm would've broken it. Arcanir cut magic, but there had been no illusion to cut.

Below her were still hooves.

Shuddering, she retreated, eyeing the guards, the smashed pottery, the shattered window, and the shards of glass. Fragments of an equine reflection stared back at her. Broken. Everything was broken.

An arrow clanged onto the cobbles just before her. Reinforcements.

She spun, faced with blades at every turn except the exit, and with a wound stinging her side, she bolted for it, back down the streets of Roccalano, weeping.

Whatever the unicorn had done to her, it wasn't some dream or spell that could be easily reversed.

They had always been described as pacifistic beings, ambassadors of peace, so why had this happened? Why had he done this to her? And if everything that had happened was real, then he'd made it clear she'd have nothing to return to.

But he was wrong. As she ran among the olive trees she'd helped tend all her life, the chill air stole away her tears.

She didn't always see eye to eye with her family, but she loved them and they loved her. She'd find a way to get through to them, to make them see it was still her in this body. They would look past the physical and find her in dire need of their help. Together, they'd uncover the answer to all of this, and fix her. She'd find a way to reverse this Change, return to her true form and her normal life.

She'd just have to keep trying… and pray Tarquin wouldn't order the guards to attack with lethal force.

AGAIN AND AGAIN, Bella returned to the castello, at all hours of the day and night. Her family had to know she was missing, but nothing in the myths had suggested humans could change into unicorns. Still, trying to get through to them was the only option she had.

In the short gaps of time she had before the guards charged in, she made a habit of interacting with things they would associate with her—

nosing the courtyard bench where she'd often done her reading, pawing the soil of her small vegetable garden, nudging the unicorn statue Cosimo had sculpted for her, even tapping the windows beneath her chambers. Sparkles among the plants of her garden witnessed her futile attempts—pixies who'd recently moved in—but she couldn't stop now.

Something would inspire the epiphany she needed them to have. It had to.

On her third visit, she stabbed the tip of her horn at a lock, wishing it open, astonished to find her wish came true. Success! It was the heartening sign she'd needed to keep her going. She willed doors open and windows, and arrows not to hit her. That much worked, if not any wish that she be heard or seen as her true self. But she'd go to her chambers, knock over her favorite things. If she just gave her family enough clues, they'd understand it was her.

Tonight, nearly two weeks after her first visit, she willed away a part of the stone fortifications surrounding the castello and walked right through. Once again, she headed for the windows beneath her chambers, hooves clopping softly on the courtyard's cobbles.

All she wanted was for someone to see the real Bella, just one person, and help her become herself again. One. Just one.

No footsteps or shouts sounded yet; maybe the guards hadn't heard her, and she had more time?

She ripped white lilies from the garden and arranged them on the flagstones to spell her name.

Unicorn, an unfamiliar male voice spoke into her mind, *it's a trap. Flee!*

A sparkling little pixie clad in acorn shells, wielding a needle, pushed against her nose. They usually kept to themselves. What was he trying to...?

A familiar scent clung to the air, like the fresh, earthy smell after a storm, but—spiced, somehow.

Go, now! he urged.

She began to back away when metal clinked, and she bucked. Chains wove around her legs. A heavy net landed on her back.

The sting of the metal was instant and painful, burning into her skin like a brand. She screamed. The metal—sage tinted. Arcanir. They meant it to bind any magical abilities she had.

Tarquin! Mamma! Luciano!

The pixie flitted at a guard, lunging at his face, but the guard swept his hand back and forth to hit him.

No, don't! she wanted to scream, but only a sharp braying emerged. *Don't fight! They'll kill you!*

"Capture it alive!" Captain Sondrio commanded.

The chains and the net tightened. Although she leaped and kicked, guards closed in around her, multiple squads pulling the chains taut. The pixie ignored her, harassing the guards' faces.

Stop—please! It's me, Bella! She tossed her head, her horn scraping against chainmail, and one of her kicks landed with a squelching crunch.

A hit struck her back, and another and another. Wooden clubs beat her to the ground. The burning chains closed around her legs and threw her off balance.

She crashed heavily on the cobbles with a thud, pressing the searing metal deeper against her skin. It burned with agony.

A guard slashed at the air with his sword.

The pixie screamed, plummeting to the cobblestones. She opened her mouth, but before she could shout, the guard stomped on him.

Witam! another unfamiliar voice chimed in her mind.

Crying out, she fought and struggled to rise, but the hits didn't stop until she went still, and the burning didn't stop at all, not even for a second. Weights pressed her down, one after another, the guards sitting on her as she rebelled, cheering and laughing to one another.

A small, shimmering pair of figures darted in and stole away the pixie's body. Was he dead? Had he died trying to help her?

Her heart seized. How, how had this happened? Under Mamma's watch, under Tarquin's watch? War was the Belmonte trade, but she'd never known Tarquin or his men to relish violence.

She searched the courtyard and the windows for a sympathetic face. Just one, any one. Her window glowed golden with candlelight, and in it stood Tarquin, his arms crossed, brow furrowed, peering down at her. The way he looked at her wasn't with the warm eyes of the brother who loved her, but cold, hard, like a lone bronze statue in an empty town square. He watched it all. Cold. Wordless. Malevolent.

Her heart beat throbbed in her throat. *He doesn't know. If he knew...*

Her entire body blazed with arcanir, pain so white hot it blinded. With the weight of the guards pressing down on her, she tried to breathe but every breath was a battle, each harder won than the last, until finally the evening sky and all around her turned to black.

CHAPTER 1

Four Months Later

𝒶 screech came from the marsh. Darting beneath the scant light of the stars, Dhuro found the fallen harpy writhing in the murky water and sedges, its broken wings flapping in futility.

And now you die.

Pinning its remaining arm, he slit its throat with one deep cut before burying his *vjernost* blade in its heart. His weapon's sage tint glowed for a moment until the light left the monster's eyes.

As the night breeze swept away its death rattle, he searched for any remaining threat among the marshland's swaying vegetation. One of the dark-elf *kuvari* warriors rose from the greenery's concealment, wiping the blood off her blade in the quiet. Her innumerable braids, beaded with amber, brushed over her shoulder and down her back. Kinga. Cold, calculating, capable Kinga.

She met his eyes across the undulating spikes and, as she sheathed her blade, gave him a slow once-over, twirling a white braid around her finger. Mm-hmm. He knew that look.

"Is that all of them?" his oldest sister and living bucket of cold water, Vadiha, called out.

"Yes, Vadiha," he called back, standing up as he cleaned his blade. As the strongest warrior among Mati's Quorum, Vadiha had been given charge of their home's defense—a duty that required increasingly more attention these days.

"I was asking Kinga." Vadiha approached him and, hand on her hip, sized him up dubiously. "What are you even doing here? Shouldn't you be with the *volodari*?"

"I was," he gritted out. As if his hunt were more important than the battle? He spent more than enough time in the trees. "I was in my hunting blind when I heard the fighting."

Her golden eyes narrowed. "You should've stayed there. As you can see, we didn't need your help."

"You're welcome," he deadpanned, walking past her and shrugging off her oh-so-kind attitude. It wasn't enough that she'd kept him out of their army's elite forces when they'd been at war with the light-elves of Lumia. *No*, she needed to keep him out of every battle and skirmish she could.

He raked a hand through his shoulder-length hair, shut his eyes, and heaved a sigh. Vadiha never missed a chance to shove his face into the sand.

"Dhuro," she shouted.

Darkness, what else? He looked back over his shoulder and grunted.

"Mati has summoned you."

Had she tattled to their mother? At least it gave him an exit out of this pleasant conversation. "Well then, I'd best not keep her waiting." He gave Vadiha a reluctant nod.

Next to her, Kinga raised her eyebrows at him again in that look he knew so well. Nothing stoked the blood of a dark-elf like a good fight. Oh yes, he'd see about that look later. Although he'd spent many years among the humans with his best friend, Dakkar, and his father, he hadn't forgotten Kinga. Not how she'd used him to climb the ranks, and... not how she used to climb him either. All told, life as a volodar hunter in his mother's queendom wasn't bad at all.

With an inward grin, he crept through the marshy rushes, sweeping aside their hollow stems to make his way to Heraza Gate and their home, Nozva Rozkveta.

All women wanted something, whether it was just a night's pleasure or a stepping stone to his mother and the queen's inner circle, the

Quorum. Kinga wasn't the only one, and never had been. No matter what it was, as long as they kept the emotional mess out of it, he didn't care. Considering how brilliantly that emotional mess had worked for his star-crossed parents, as well as for his older brother's decade-long doomed love affair, *that* was just another item on the long list of things he never wanted or needed.

At the Gate, he beat the entry rhythm on the door, and it creaked open.

"Your Highness," two kuvari—Gavri and Danika—said by way of greeting. They barred the stone door after him.

"Do you know where my mother is?"

"At the training grounds, I think," Gavri answered. She'd once spent time as his brother Zoran's lover.

With a nod, Dhuro headed down the tunnel toward Central Cavern. What had that near-decade of emotional aching been for? Zoran had left to become Queen Nendra's king-consort in Dun Mozg, and his so-called beloved Gavri had been left behind. If they'd been wiser, they would've kept it simple.

These days, he stayed out of it. No one took his advice anyway, so it was a waste of breath; everyone seemed determined to learn the hard way. Even Veron had fallen for his human bride, and although they genuinely seemed to love one another, it wouldn't end well. It never did. He inhaled deeply and shook his head as he entered Central Cavern.

Ah, home. He never tired of looking at it. On the stalactites above, bioluminescent mushrooms lit the realm beneath with a lavender glow, mingled with the radiance of the white glowworms. The shimmering tangle of *roza* vines had sprawled and thrived since the Rift, their glittering red blooms dotting the stalactites with crimson stars. Nothing in the sky realm could compare to it, although by now he'd explored every bit of it.

The Stone Singers still worked tirelessly to restore the gleaming, mirror-like blackstone outbuildings, where glistening streams fed fields of green sprouts fighting their way out of the fresh cave soil. Deeper into the heart of Nozva Rozkveta, most of the dwellings along Central Cavern's interwoven pathways had already been stone-sung, and its most precious jewel—the palace—blossomed in black crystal perfection, ringed by the shining teal waterway that tumbled down into the Darkness below.

The black stone paths were empty and quiet today, unlike a fortnight ago when Veron had married his human princess, Alessandra. Although the violence from the human Brotherhood had dwindled to nearly nothing, the Immortal beasts had begun attacking with unusual fervor.

Was that why Mati wanted to see him, to give him a position with the queendom's defense? Maybe Vadiha, for once in her life, hadn't complained about him to their mother. Vadiha had defeated his challenge once, only *once*, and it had been thousands of years ago now. True, he'd barely been out of his adolescent years—forty-two—but the Sundering's petrification had lasted over two thousand years, if the humans could be believed. There had to be some limit to how long her victory could shackle him.

With renewed purpose, he headed for the palace's black crystal spires, passed the four kuvari at the entrance, and strode down the side corridors to the training grounds.

The *vykrikovati* shouts echoed—short, loud, and forceful—and he had to fight back a smile. It had been a long time since he'd been among them, alongside Dakkar, but not long enough that his body didn't remember this. His instructors had made a warrior out of him, out of all the dark-elf children; with every strike, he'd abruptly tensed his abdomen, forcing the shouted breath out to generate as much power as possible. What had been sheer joy as a child had been the terror of the battlefield, as dark-elf legions had struck fear into the hearts of their enemies.

Two glaive-bearing kuvari stood aside as he entered. "Your Highness."

With catlike grace, Mati sparred with the young novices in her white silken peplos, haloed by her voluminous, jewel-beaded cascades of platinum hair. She held back just enough to check the novices' skill, and as expected, they were fierce. After all, this motley troop of youngsters represented the future of Nozva Rozkveta.

Mati met a strike with her vjernost bracers, and a smile cracked her diamond-shaped face. The smile met her amber eyes, and then she turned to him. The sparring stopped, and as she stepped away, the novices resumed their training with one another.

He bowed his head to her. "They look strong."

"They'll get stronger." She brushed his arm and, with her bare clawed feet on the black stone, led him alongside the training rings, amid the novices' vykrikovati and the instructors' shouted encouragement and orders. "The kuvari have informed me you took part in the battle."

Tattling it was, after all. *Thanks, Vadiha.* Mati had said it matter-of-factly, but he knew better than to trust that.

"I did."

If Mati wanted to make a point, then trouncing him here amid the children would accomplish that, far harsher than he'd earned. As their people's best warrior, it would be child's play for her.

"Your ambition is relentless." She paused to watch another group of novices spar.

He joined her. "I take after my mother."

An amused flicker of her gleaming amber eyes, and then she returned her attention to the sparring. "We can handle the beasts. We always have. But while there will be humans above us building the library, we must take additional precautions."

His people had always been skilled fighters; they built their lives around martial prowess. But if more winged creatures like today's harpies attacked, they couldn't keep the land above their domain safe from invasion, not entirely. And all it'd take to reignite enmity from the humans would be one human fatality. Darkness forbid it would be Alessandra.

All he wanted was to live up to Mati's expectations. That meant protecting his—and his people's—way of life and earning his place not as a hunter but as a warrior. If Mati wanted his help in the defense, she'd have it. And then he'd be free tonight to go find Kinga. "I await your orders."

Her even expression didn't waver as she continued watching the novices. A pair of girls sparred, then wrestled each other onto the sand while the instructor barked commands at them. "You're familiar with the unicorn among us."

How could he not be? He stifled an inward half-laugh. She stood out like a unicorn among dark-elves.

"When we exiled the leader of the Brotherhood, he agreed to go quietly." She clasped her clawed hands behind her back, her shoulders stiffening. After the battles the humans' Brotherhood had waged against all the Immortals, no doubt she'd wanted to rip Tarquin Belmonte's head off his body. Exile, however, had been more palatable to the humans and likelier to lead to a lasting peace, especially when the alliance had been sealed by a dark-elf Offering and a human marriage between his brother Veron and Alessandra. "Part of the terms involved aiding his sister, which we do willingly."

Belmonte's sister, a human turned unicorn, was safe here, learning more about her kind from Noc, a fey horse and friend to him and his brothers. The unicorn had saved his brother Veron and had helped stop the war with the Brotherhood, which despite her questionable familial ties, set her apart from the trash Belmonte had led.

"Although she's learned much in her time here, she needs to learn control of her Change. Our scouts have returned with information about a herd of unicorns near Dun Mozg—probably Gwydion's—and we must move swiftly. I'm sending a team to take her there to find the unicorn who sired her."

It wasn't a long journey through the tunnels; he and Dakkar had traveled it countless times. "Dun Mozg isn't far."

"The team will go by land."

Frowning, he tipped his head up. Roza blooms studded the bioluminescent vines sprawled above, consuming the stalactites and the ceiling. It hadn't been so long ago that his people had suffered a food shortage, but with the human alliance, they'd come back from it stronger than ever, and that bounty had been shared with Dun Mozg. The neighboring queendom had no compelling reason to cause them harm. And considering Zoran was king-consort, and Dakkar, not just his best friend but a prince of Dun Mozg, had been fostered here, their ties were nigh unbreakable.

He eyed Mati. She didn't suffer questioning, but if he was to avoid the tunnels, there had to be a reason. It would be better if he knew what he was getting into rather than proceed blindly. And ignorantly.

She sighed. "These beast attacks aren't random. There's a leader, assisted by a dark unicorn. These attacks are their strategy to keep us at bay. They've joined forces to conquer the humans."

A few months ago, he would've said *let them*. But as much as it galled him, when his people had been most in need, it had been the humans who'd lent a hand. And his sister-in-law, Alessandra, wasn't *so* bad. "Why aren't the humans handling it?"

Mati's mouth tightened to a grim line. "They don't know who's in charge. And they must not know."

Then information didn't flow so freely in this new alliance.

"The dark unicorn is Gwydion's responsibility, so he must be made aware. Arabella's sire will likely be among his herd. You will take her there."

He nodded. If that's what Nozva Rozkveta needed, then he'd see it done. With Gwydion's help, these malcontents would be disbanded. Unicorns possessed the rare ability to induce calm, even among a blood-thirsty army of beasts and rebels... *if* the unicorns could be persuaded to enter a conflict. Something Mati was tasking *him* with.

Once he finished this mission, he'd return home and take his rightful place as a *kuvar*. Things would finally be as they always should have been.

Mati cleared her throat. "Whatever Gwydion wants in order to forge the alliance, give it to him. He'll have heirs who take elven or human forms. Seal it with an Offering between you and one of his line."

"What! Why?" he blurted. Darkness, she would sacrifice him to a political marriage as she had Veron. Deep, Darkness, and Holy Ulsinael, of all the—

"Because the leader of this rebellion is *our* responsibility, and he must be stopped before the humans discover he's a dark-elf. And he will be stopped, with Gwydion's help."

His head spun. "The dark-elf rebel leader... Who—?"

Mati turned to him, facing him squarely. "Dakkar of Dun Mozg."

CHAPTER 2

ollowing the squad of dark-elves, Bella trudged through the marshland alongside Noc, their hooves splashing in the fetid waters. Led by Prince Dhuro, they'd been proceeding in the daylight under dense tree cover, but the bareness of the marshes meant journeying by dark, such as tonight, to the unicorn herd.

The dark-elves traveled almost exclusively via their tunnels. It was strange that they weren't doing so now, but no one had thought to tell her anything other than it was time to go. Still, she'd find out one way or another. It had been over four months since she'd seen Mamma. The past weeks she'd spent among the dark-elves after their battle with the Brotherhood, they hadn't exactly been forthcoming, but she hadn't expected them to. Her brother had wanted a genocide. Although she'd been freed and had tried to stop it, she was still sister to the man who'd wanted to destroy them all.

The dark-elves had rightfully demanded Silen exile him. A fighter for as long as she could remember, Tarquin nevertheless had gone quietly into exile. Tender and caring with her, however, he had spent his entire life trying to protect her, looking out for her, and if anyone had told her he'd spend months letting a creature be tortured by his men, even not knowing it had been her in another form, she never would have believed it. Not until three and a half months ago.

When the mercenary irregulars of the Belmonte Company had taken it upon themselves to capture a unicorn, Tarquin had let them, not knowing his missing sister had been trapped in the poor creature. For so long, so many had been killed in the name of his mission to find her while his men had tormented her, not recognizing her in unicorn form. The pixie Witam had come to her aid, and they'd hurt him, likely *killed* him, without a second thought. Countless senseless killings, all for her sake, and it had taken everything she'd had to Change the night of the battle with Nozva Rozkveta, just to try to stop it.

Once he'd learned the truth of her identity, after Princess Alessandra had freed her, Tarquin's warmth hadn't reappeared. He'd castigated himself, punished himself, retreated into himself, and she hadn't known how to communicate telepathically yet. Now, with a little luck, she could enter the mind of almost any being and often receive thoughts that were "loud enough," but back then, everything had been too new.

Now he was gone—who knew where—and she might never have the chance to tell him that she loved him, that she forgave him, and that he could rise above what he'd been if he only wanted to.

Still, she couldn't even hope to look for him until she picked up the pieces of her shattered life and herself. After the months of torture she'd suffered, burning beneath a net of arcanir, beaten by the soldiers, the dark-elves' quiet hospitality had been the breath of life. They'd given her a place to heal, a place to forget, and now a chance at regaining her true form and returning to her normal life. For that, she would be eternally grateful.

Noc flicked his tail next to her, shaking off the stagnant water, and neighed.

I'm sorry, Noc, she said to him telepathically. His friendship was yet another thing meriting her eternal gratitude. He'd been a good listener, a nurturing friend, and a partner in crime when she'd most needed someone, and she only hoped to someday repay a fraction of that compassion. *I'm glad for your company, but you really didn't have to come along.*

He eyed her incredulously, shifting his forelock as he bobbed his head. *My glamour might prove useful.*

True enough. In case of danger, fey horses could cast illusions that might help them. Noc had called them parlor tricks, but he was modest.

Besides, as a newly Changed unicorn, you're little more than a child. You still have a lot to learn, and even if you didn't, I'm not about to leave you in Dhuro's hands.

What's wrong with Prince Dhuro's hands? she joked.

A laugh echoed in her head.

You're being facetious, she chided.

You catch on quickly, youngling. Noc nudged her gently. *As I said, you have much to learn, and Dhuro can be indelicate.*

Hmph. She could handle *indelicate.* But she couldn't argue with Noc's assessment of the prince.

She raised her head and looked to the front of their cavalcade, where a tall, hulking dark-elf led them, his every booted step a vexed assault upon the earth. As he raked clawed fingers through his shoulder-length white hair, his slate-blue skin—a shade or two darker than his brother's—fell into dusky relief against the night sky.

Dhuro, one of the princes of Nightbloom—Nozva Rozkveta. One of the dark-elves' hunters, he'd been absent from the subterranean queendom more often than present. The times she *had* seen him, he'd been training with the queen's guards or his brother, whenever Prince Veron wasn't working on the new library building project with his wife. Although Queen Zara's people appeared very industrious, Prince Dhuro pushed himself. A lot.

Still, she could imagine rabid bears less grumpy than said fair prince. She'd seen him brooding and stomping around, always beneath a black cloud, full of thunder. With a sweet personality like that, his fangs and claws really *had* to be purely ornamental.

Prince Dhuro glanced back over his shoulder.

She ducked her head. Gods above, had she said that to him telepathically? Noc had been teaching her, but she still didn't have a solid grasp of it.

Afraid he saw you? Noc teased.

Her heart beat faster, but she ignored it and pushed the bravado. *I'm rather hard to miss in this form, aren't I?*

Noc whinnied and tossed his head, his laugh echoing in her skull.

Prince Dhuro was undeniably handsome and everything she couldn't stand, which meant he was perfect for her. Ever since Cosimo had been killed, she'd kept her entanglements light, with lovers she could walk away from unscathed. And someone like this bitter prince, so bitter she could never love him, was completely her type.

But there was the small, tiny, *minuscule* matter of her being stuck in unicorn form. That made *entanglements...* difficult. She sighed inwardly.

Noc took another step and stumbled, nearly tripping into the marshy water.

This is ridiculous, she said to him. *I'm going to ask the prince why we can't take the tunnels.*

Queen Zara wouldn't have sent us on this route if there weren't a good reason, Noc replied, struggling out of the dip.

At least then we'll know why we're stumbling all over the marshes. She didn't wait for a reply as she moved up through the cavalcade, nosing her way between horses and dark-elves.

Excuse me, she thought to Prince Dhuro, but he didn't react, so she trotted to catch up to him. *Excuse me!*

A dark look over his shoulder. Gleaming golden eyes raked her over, narrowing. For a moment, the scent of fresh water and mountain stone cut the marsh's odor.

"What?" he said, more of a grunt than a question.

She jerked back her head. His lovely tone really shouldn't have surprised her. *Why aren't we taking the tunnels?*

"If you needed to know, you would've been told," he replied, his voice low. He held her gaze, as if challenging her to talk back.

This terrain is very difficult for Noc and me.

He scoffed. "Don't hide behind Noc. He's been through rougher terrain than this. If you hate getting your little hooves wet, Princess, then just admit it."

Princess? Her eye twitched. Had he just called her "Princess"? *Listen here—*

Bella, Noc interrupted, *don't mind him. He's not—*

"No, how about *you* listen?" Prince Dhuro leaned in, his voice cold. "You got yourself Changed into a unicorn and stuck in your form. We're taking you directly to your sire, whom we should reach in a few days. No one wants to be here, and your complaining won't improve circumstances for anybody."

Complaining? *All I asked for was an answer,* she replied. *But I can see now that verbal communication isn't one of your precious few skills, Your Highness.*

His handsome face contorting, he opened his mouth to argue, but she turned away. He could argue all he wanted, but he could say it to the back of her head.

An arrow darted between them.

Prince Dhuro shoved her aside.

One of the guards drew her sword and batted the arrow away. She shouted something in their language. The dark-elves sprang into action, fanning out and taking cover while Noc sidled up to Bella. Her entire body chilled to ice cold, trembling. No, not again, not like with Cosimo—

"Stay with Noc!" Prince Dhuro gritted out to her before he joined his allies.

Remain in contact with me, Noc said to her. *I'm casting a glamour.*

Doing as bidden, she let him urge her into the shadows, onto dry ground. When he froze, so did she.

More shouts, and metal clanged ahead. Gods above, not again. Cosimo—

Deathly screams, the reek of blood.

No. No, no, no—

What is it? Noc asked. *Are you all right?*

She most certainly was not. Cosimo had died to violence. Witam had died to help her. So many had died to help her during the war with the Brotherhood, and...

I can't let a single person more be killed for my sake. Not again. Not ever again.

Before Noc could stop her, she ran toward the sounds.

CHAPTER 3

With both swords drawn, Dhuro crept through the shadows cast by the scant trees. Steel flashed in the moonlight, and he chased the skirmish. Whoever it was, even Dakkar himself, he wouldn't allow them to endanger this mission.

Blades danced beneath the night sky as Gavri and her squad fought five women—light-elves in familiar brown leathers. What were *they* doing here? Were they from Lumia?

A fifth lunged at him—a man. Dhuro parried and counterattacked with his second sword, cutting the light-elf's thigh. Blood spattered the mud.

The light-elf hissed with retreating footwork before advancing once more with renewed vigor. As they fought, massive shadows blotted out the moon.

Cries rent the air.

Powerful gusts pushed against him from flaps of enormous feathered wings. Griffins descended, ear-splitting screeches ringing from their eagle-like heads.

"Gavri!" he shouted, blocking a strike from the light-elf.

"I know!" With a sharp vykrikovat, she slashed down the arm of her opponent, who rolled away with a yelp.

A huge beak snapped shut next to Dhuro.

He lunged aside, facing off against the griffin and the light-elf, who smirked.

Although their talons were dangerous, griffins had weak spots at the wing joints and neck. He could handle this.

The light-elf's gaze flickered to his abdomen. With his vjernost blade, Dhuro blocked the strike and then evaded the swipe of talons.

The ground thundered with galloping hooves from behind him. Now what?

He pivoted and leaped away as the stark-white unicorn raced toward them. Arabella Belmonte.

Darkness, what was she thinking? These griffins would tear her apart—

Stop! her shrill cry commanded.

And everything on the battlefield froze.

The light-elves, the griffins, his forces. Him.

Shit.

Leave! she ordered.

The light-elves backed up a few steps, their faces contorted, eyes wild. They mounted the griffins. With a few beats of their massive wings, the griffins took flight, soaring into the dark sky.

The light-elves were gone.

Blinking up at them, he stood, unable to move, to speak—Darkness, barely able to *think*. His people only eyed him, no doubt feeling the same.

He and his forces were frozen in place.

What had this fool of a unicorn just done? If any more enemies emerged, he and his people could be killed.

You can move now, she said, slowly approaching them, her hooves clopping in the shallow water. *Can't you...?*

If he could move, he wouldn't be standing here doing his best impression of a rock.

Her head bowed low, she inched closer, blinking over large, shining eyes.

Gods above, you can't move, can you? She looked over her shoulder at his people, and then back at him. *I'm sorry, but I don't know how to undo it.*

She'd charmed him and his team, leaving them exposed and unable to defend themselves, and she didn't know how to undo it.

Deep, Darkness, and Holy Ulsinael. She had the Darkness's own good fortune that he *couldn't* move right now.

Noc, he thought, *if you can hear me, for the love of all things dark, talk some sense into this unicorn.* He'd tried to speak the words, but all that had emerged sounded like a snarl.

Arabella's ears turned back, and her gaze darted about uneasily, but she quickly raised her head and inhaled a steadfast breath.

Noc trotted in behind her, eyeing him with an amused glimmer before facing Arabella. She squeezed her eyes shut, shook her head, and toed the mud.

Noc, Darkness help me, she can undo this, can't she?

Craning his head around, Noc stared at him pointedly. *I can either guide her through this, or commiserate with you. Do you have a preference?*

Dhuro rolled his eyes. At least he could still do *that* much.

Thought so, Noc replied, before turning back to Arabella, who fretted, huffed, and made a great show of trying.

Darkness, was she this insufferable as a woman, too? A woman after Vadiha's own heart, involving herself in others' affairs, thinking she knew better. She made him want to just—

Just...

She peeked around Noc, her sparkling green eyes meeting his, and lowered her head, flicking her tail. With a quick look back to Noc, she approached.

What was the plan? End this idiocy and stab him through the face with her horn?

She stopped just before him, her head—and its pointy horn—a hand's breadth from his own. Darkness, that... that *wasn't* the plan, was it?

Closing her eyes, she rested her face against his chest and took several deep breaths, and for a moment, he could've sworn the sweetness of spring had replaced the marsh's pungent odor.

The top of his head tingled, as if stroked by the gentlest touch, and then his face warmed. His shoulders relaxed, and that touch feathered down his arms, down his chest, his abs... until his fingertips and toes sparked.

She stepped away, and he fell forward, just a step before he caught himself with a hand on her withers. Her eyes met his, but she didn't waver or pull away, not until he withdrew his touch. Making sure he could stand on his own two feet?

Then, without a word, she receded and headed toward Gavri, repeating the same touch and release process with her and then Kinga, Danika, Marysia, and Halina.

Once they were all freed, she returned to Noc, bright eyed, flicking her tail.

Ah, she thought that was the end of it.

Dhuro narrowed his eyes and crossed his arms.

How wrong she was.

CHAPTER 4

*B*ella faced the prince squarely, holding her ground in the sludgy terrain. If he thought he could glare at her and make her feel ashamed for stopping needless loss of life, he was wrong.

The arrow had been aimed at her. Ever since her teens, she and Cosimo had talked of peace and attended secret salons hosted by the nouveau riche intelligentsia on the subject. But after Cosimo had been killed in her family's bloody warmongering, she hadn't been content to merely talk anymore. She'd cried all the tears she'd had to give and then some, and she'd decided to do something about it. To give her all so that another Cosimo would never be senselessly killed, nor another Bella left to grieve his loss. That something had been becoming "Renato," an insider who knew the inner workings and secrets of the Sileni Condottieri.

She'd sneaked information from Papà's correspondence, and later from Tarquin and Luciano's messages and orders; in treatises distributed to the public, she'd thwarted what bloodshed she could and condemned the use of force among the nobiltà.

The Condottieri had doubtless put a bounty on her head. Somehow word of her transformation must have spread, perhaps by members of the Brotherhood who'd seen her that night of the battle with Nightbloom. In any case, these assassins were here on her account, for her pacifistic ideals and actions, and she wasn't about to let them be killed. If Prince Dhuro thought he could dictate their fate, then he was about to face reality.

The other dark-elves took one look at him and returned to their previous path.

Good luck, Bella, Noc said, slowly moving to join them.

Thank you for your help. I couldn't have undone that without you, she answered. She owed that to Noc, and a lot more. In only a couple of days, she'd have the narrow window of the full moon, the night before, and the night after to try Changing into her human form, and Noc had been instructing her on how to do it stably. Hopefully it would work.

Noc bobbed his head before departing.

And then it was just Prince Dhuro, staring her down as though she'd left him bound on an anthill and covered him in honey.

He stalked up to her with quiet fury, his mouth a grim line. "I don't recall giving you permission to charm me," he bit out.

She raised her head. *I don't recall giving you permission to kill the assassins after me.*

He scoffed coldly. "The assassins after *you,* Princess?"

It's Arabella. And it wasn't as though he'd mentioned any other threats. What else could it be but the assassins?

He met her at eye level. "You think everything is about you, don't you, Princess?"

There it was again. Princess! *That's adorable. You've met one human woman who's a princess, and you think we all are. You know, if you want to learn something, I heard there's this library being built—*

He raised a dismissive hand. "Don't change the subject, Princess. You are not permitted to control me or my people in any way. So don't try it again."

She stamped her hoof. *I didn't intend to immobilize you the first time!* It hadn't been a question of intent but inexperience. *I'm not going to allow anyone to be killed on my account. The price is on my head, not yours.*

He tilted his head, peering at her. "There's a bounty out on you?" For a moment, he raised his eyebrows before turning away, a muscle working in his jaw. "You didn't think to mention that vital bit of information?"

She stared into the dark water, finding a shade of her reflection. *I didn't think they'd recognize me. I look, you know, different? And I wasn't sure they'd traced my publications to my identity. But... I suppose they have.*

"Your what?" He stepped into the water reflecting her image and crouched.

Nonviolence, she answered, meeting his gaze squarely. *I published treatises under a pseudonym—Renato.*

He scoffed, rubbing his jaw before giving a slow, disbelieving shake of his head. "Nonviolence? Your people worship war. Your family lives and breathes it for coin."

Then he understood how rampant and close the problem was. She lifted her equine head and sniffed. *I wrote about the alternatives of nonviolence, their potential to resolve conflicts, and their implementation in other cultures, both human and nonhuman.*

"Alternatives?" He sneered. "What alternatives? Asking nicely?"

In an ideal world, yes, that would have been enough. *Perhaps you've heard of this force called magic?*

He froze, his gaze slowly tracking toward hers. "Magic was the Dragon Lords' preferred style of rulership over all Immortals before the Sundering," he said quietly, his eyebrows drawn together contemplatively. "Using magic to usher in peace and maintain it? Not the worst idea I've ever heard. Other than it relying on your kind to succeed."

Her kind? Humans, he must mean. *Clearly someone took it seriously enough to put the bounty on me. And they've found me.*

He shook his head again. "They haven't. Those fighters were light-elves and likely have nothing to do with you. They probably just"—he combed his clawed fingers through his hair—"shot at you first because of your unicorn capabilities. Removing the biggest threat to them before eliminating us all."

Her power... She'd been able to wish things to happen when she'd first returned as a unicorn, and this had been an extension of that power. She hadn't thought of its use in battle, but he was right. It seemed possible that—if she gained better mastery of these abilities, of course—she could stop battles.

A giggle escaped her, but it sounded more like a whinny.

Dhuro quirked a thick eyebrow. "Something funny about this to you?"

She shook her head. *No, just... Unicorns really can stop wars, can't they? With just a thought, they can stop loss of life.*

With a long-suffering sigh, he hung his head. "You're missing the point." He glared up at her with that same grumpy face, then rose and headed back toward the path, with her following. "Don't do that again, and we won't have a problem."

Don't do what again? she asked.

"Use your power."

Never use her power again? She'd most certainly never use it on him and her allies again, but never at all? Not even against their enemies? Not even if she trained more with Noc?

Walking alongside him, she ducked under a low-hanging branch. *As a prince, you must be accustomed to everyone bending to your will. I'm sorry this won't be what you're accustomed to.*

His face twisted. "That wasn't a request. If you don't obey, I'll have to—"

Yes?

His golden eyes flared, bright in the moonlight for a fleeting moment, then he clenched his jaw and looked away.

I'm certain your queen wouldn't approve of hurting me or killing me, so... I don't see how you can stop me?

He shook his head with a bitter laugh. "You're not the first determined woman to step into my path, Arabella Belmonte."

Nor the first to succeed, I'm sure, she replied smugly.

His knuckles cracked as he balled his hands into fists, but they slowly relaxed. "You think that by trying to stop others from killing, you'll be saving lives? You don't even realize what you could've done."

She hadn't intended things to go the way they had, but was he this upset that she'd taken control and *saved* everyone? Despite the enemy light-elves and griffins—*griffins!*—no one had gotten killed. Could he say the same if she hadn't intervened?

"The griffins flanked us as we were fighting the light-elves," he said, nodding to one of the dark-elves as he rejoined everyone on the path with her. They headed deeper into the wilds to set up camp. "After you charmed us all, what would've happened if more enemies had ambushed us?"

If they had been immobilized, and more enemies had...

They could've been hurt or—

Her skin went cold, and she shivered. Although her mouth dropped open, she quickly closed it with a click. *I would've stopped them, too.*

He exhaled an amused breath. "I just spent half an hour frozen in place because you couldn't control your power."

Well, that... That had been different. When she felt strongly in the moment, things just *happened*. Like the locks opening in Roccalano. Impassioned, this time she'd wished the fighting to stop and for the aggressors to leave, and it had happened. But once the danger was over, it wasn't so simple to make her wishes come true.

"If more enemies had emerged, could you have done it again? What if you'd exhausted your power?"

I—

"We could have all died. And you would've been responsible." His eyebrows drawn, he speared her with a piercing gaze.

She shifted her withers. Yes. Things could have gone badly. She'd been so desperate to prevent any more deaths that she could have caused more bloodshed; he'd made that clear to her.

But only a fool could miss what she *had* done. Her charm had immobilized the entire field, and because of it, no one had died. If she figured out how to control it, she, herself, could be an instrument for peace, and she was not about to walk away from that. Before, she'd wanted to reverse her Change, return to her true form and her normal life, but her years as Renato had made her crave the kind of power to stop violence that she had now. She wasn't about to give up on preventing senseless death because the method wasn't immediately perfect.

The answer isn't to give up on trying to save lives. It's to continue improving the method, she replied. That was what she'd do—work with Noc until she *could* control her abilities. She wouldn't charm Dhuro or the other dark-elves again, but once she trained more with Noc, she would use it on their enemies if necessary to prevent deaths.

"Wrong answer."

Wrong? She sniffed. If he was set on taking lives, and she was set on saving them, then he left her no choice but to be at odds. There was nothing left to say to him. She split away to bed down next to Noc.

As she chose a dry, grassy spot, Prince Dhuro approached with a bedroll under his arm. He laid it out next to her, descended, and rolled up his cloak before stuffing it under his head.

What was he doing? She couldn't help but stare.

"You think I want to sleep here, Arabella Belmonte?" He grimaced, jerking his head toward a female guard who gaped at him blankly. "My queen tasked me with getting you to Gwydion's herd, and so shall I do. I'm not about to let you get yourself killed by some human assassins and ruin everything."

Ruin...? But he'd already closed his eyes.

Lying there, handsome and muscle bound, with his eyes closed and —more importantly—his mouth shut, she could almost understand what that female guard saw in him. Almost.

CHAPTER 5

*H*e didn't agree with Arabella Belmonte about much, but at least they were out of those dreaded marshes. Ahead, the Altobelli Mountains towered over green hills, their staggered gray peaks biting into the high-noon sky. He wouldn't relish how long it would take to travel the meandering mountain path, steep, narrow, and rocky.

At least the air at that altitude would be fresh, crisp, a welcome respite from the stink he'd breathed in the marshes. Before the Sundering, he'd spent a lot of time topside, both as a boy with his *ata* and best friend Dakkar, and then as an adult, scouting, hunting, guarding spice caravans. He'd come to know humans well, a few very well, enough to learn never to trust them. Given the Sundering—when humans betrayed all the Immortal races, leaving them petrified for over two thousand years 'til the Rift—it seemed he'd been right after all.

With a grunt, he led the way up, keeping a careful watch for any sign of enemies, whether they be the dark-elf rebels or Arabella Belmonte's alleged assassins.

When she'd mentioned the bounty on her head for her "publications," he'd assumed her little treatises had been inconsequential to most of the human kingdom. Although the peasants who fed into military recruitment would probably entertain her arguments, most couldn't read. And the nobility who benefited from constant skirmishing and raiding should have laughed her little treatises away.

But they hadn't. Someone had cared enough to put a bounty on her head, which meant those "little treatises" had merit, enough to make her a threat to fortunes made by nobles and their instruments of war.

Still, it was not his people's way. Even when it came to his best friend, there was only one answer. Mati's.

How could Dakkar have betrayed his own people like this, leaving them vulnerable to not only losing the humans' help but also potential retaliation? That wasn't the friend he knew so well. But if Mati had said it, it had to be true. It burned like nettles.

He beckoned the cavalcade on toward the mountain path, watching them navigate the uneven rocky soil, and when his eyes met Arabella's, she huffed and turned her head away. Ah, thank the Darkness, she wasn't speaking to him. There was that. The brink of war and starvation, possible death on this mission, and his best friend's betrayal wasn't compounded by her ceaseless complaints. It had never failed to amaze him that human women believed the silent treatment was a *punishment*.

No, the true punishment had been taking her constant barbs and needling. If not for the four legs and horse body, he might have sworn she was a dark-elf woman. Except the sharp repartee that took place between two dark-elves usually led to a clash in the Ring... or the bedchamber. He didn't need that kind of frustration from a *unicorn*. His interest began and ended with women of the two-legged variety *only*, for Darkness's sake.

Guarding Arabella so closely meant those loaded looks from Kinga had gone infuriatingly unanswered.

Whatever. At least Arabella had taken to pestering Noc all day. About what, he had no idea, but better Noc than him.

Blowing out a breath, he set his jaw and moved ahead, scouting their trail. The mountain path felt solid beneath his booted feet, its packed pinkish dirt and rocks a firm foundation. Its width would suit even the more equine members of their group. That was lucky, because if he had to hear *one more complaint* about how difficult the marshy terrain was, he would—

In the distance, a gray mound of stones blocked the path. He squinted, evaluating the extent of the rockfall. Boulders made up much of the mass.

A dead end. A Darkness-damned *dead end.* How many things had already gone wrong? How many more would follow?

Inhaling lengthily, he squeezed his eyes shut and threw his head back, wanting to roar at the top of his lungs, but instead he heaved an exasperated sigh.

"The sky realm hates you." Gavri's voice was pitying.

He opened one eye. "Tell me there's another way through these mountains."

With a tight smile, she gave him the slowest of shrugs.

He groaned. It had to be this route. Any other would take them too far out of their way or too close to Lumia, the light-elf queendom. Mati hadn't wanted them to risk that, and he wouldn't. Especially not after what Lumia had done to his ata.

Darkness, what else? Were the clouds going to open up and pour a storm down on them?

Noc and Arabella approached, and she craned her long neck to see around him and Gavri.

Is this the wrong way? she spoke into his mind, with the barest hint of a lilt.

He grimaced at her. "This is the right way," he shot back, taking a step into her space. "This must have happened recently."

She raised her head, her iridescent horn luminous even in the overcast sky's dimness. *I'm sure you know what to do.* She gave an encouraging nod.

Was it really encouraging? Or just another barb, veiled a bit better than the rest?

He looked away, grinding his teeth together. What he needed to do was to send scouts into the wood to assess the threat level, but after the attack by the light-elves, he needed all the kuvari he had in case of another one. And considering the hostility of Lumia, if the light-elf queendom wasn't *officially* involved, he could provoke conflict with Nozva Rozkveta just by ordering a dark-elf to even set foot in their wood. That conflict would stoke ancient enmity anew.

The only real option would be to trace the foot of the mountain alongside the lake, trapped like a cave salamander against the stone. To attack them, Lumia would have to assume the risk of provoking hostilities. But who attacked first only mattered if someone lived to tell the tale.

The rockslide could have been calculated, a move by Lumia to force them on the path against the foot of the mountain.

Arabella poked his leather pauldron with her horn, nudging his shoulder. *What's the plan?*

He grunted. "Come nightfall, we're taking the lake route."

Gavri, twirling her long braid, paused and opened her mouth, but when he jerked his head toward her, she shut it and gulped audibly before looking away.

No, he did not need to hear about all its drawbacks from her, too. At least once night fell, his people's advantage of seeing in the dark would afford them more warning if Lumia did try to ambush them.

Why are we waiting until night? Arabella asked, wiggling her muzzle in a way that brought to mind wrinkling one's nose. *What are we going to do until then?*

"We're going to camp somewhere safe," he gritted out, nodding to Gavri to lead them back down the mountain, "and ignore any more questions from you."

As he passed her by, scanning the periphery for threats, Arabella snorted. Because of course she did.

The queen who'd granted Arabella protection had given him and his team this mission, and it had been shit from the first day. Arabella not only wanted to pester him with complaints but also to question his every move and demand constant explanations. Those answers required secrecy to protect his people. He wasn't about to prize her curiosity over their safety.

As they made their way down the mountain, Noc trotted up to him and shoved him none too gently toward the stone.

She's just trying to understand you, Noc said to him pointedly, with a misstep that seemed a lot like a hoof attempting to crush his toes.

I don't need her understanding, he answered. This journey wasn't about making friends. He was still bleeding from the ones he already had stabbing him in the back, most of all Dakkar. He didn't need any more, much less some unicorn he'd never see again after a few more days.

She's been asking about you and the others, and about dark-elves, Noc continued, his voice gentler. *Ever since the light-elf attack, she's been contemplative.*

Good. Maybe she could contemplate not interfering next time and risking his whole team's lives.

I think she's been imagining how things could have gone, Noc added.

How things could have gone? What, if they'd all been killed when she'd charmed them?

He scoffed. If she felt bad, then she'd think twice before acting next time.

But she was asking questions about him and his team? He cleared his throat and lowered his gaze to his boots, where the pinkish mountain dust caked the black tips. *What's she been asking?*

What you love to do, what your dreams are—

What I *love to do?* Dhuro blurted.

Each of you.

He raised his eyebrows and swallowed. Of course. Not just him. *What did you tell her?*

That you don't think about what you want but what others need.

He paused. The answer had been like a firm palm to his chest. He didn't think about what he wanted? He'd never quite heard it put that way, but he supposed it was true. He did want to improve the lives of everyone in Nozva Rozkveta as much as he could. Even Vadiha's.

What else had Noc told her about them? The possibilities were many, and a good many strange. He smirked to himself. *Did you tell her Gavri loves that weird tea Alessandra brought from Bellanzole? She takes that stuff with her everywhere.*

Noc huffed, and a laugh rolled through his mind. *That, and butter.*

Who could forget? If no one stopped her, Gavri would eat that stuff by the handful. Literally, with her hand.

His smile slowly faded. *If she wanted to know all those things, why not ask everyone?*

Ask everyone who could've died because of her actions? Noc shook his head.

Breathing deep, he looked away, popping his jaw. He'd laid all that weight on her, and she'd taken it all. All this quiet from her, it hadn't been the silent treatment but reflection. Space. She'd waited, probably hoping he'd cool off, and then when she'd finally spoken to him again, he'd ripped her head off.

He gnawed on the inside of his cheek. So what did it matter if he'd gotten things wrong, if he'd upset her? Once she was with Gwydion's herd, she'd never see him again and would forget all about this.

You're known among the dark-elves for having the emotional range of a cave troll, but I know that you're just hiding behind that, Noc said. *Perhaps we should examine why you've been so cold?*

Dhuro sighed. *No.*

Then perhaps we should examine your refusal? If Noc had possessed more expressive eyebrows, at least one of them would've quirked up judgmentally.

Go away. Dhuro crossed his arms. The last thing he needed was Noc trying to pick apart his past and attempting to make him a kinder, gentler cave troll.

Noc whipped his tail, catching Dhuro in the back. *Just remember, even cave trolls pause in their rage from time to time to give a care about something. You can do at least as well as that.*

Dhuro sketched an amused smile that swiftly faded, then shooed Noc away. Enough of this gooey, sticky emotional mess.

I know that Janessa—

He turned on Noc, glaring. *We do not discuss her. Not now. Not ever.*

It had been over two thousand years since he'd heard her name spoken, and it was too soon. Never again would be too soon, in *that woman's* case.

Arabella passed them by, her head hung low. Noc blinked over wide eyes and, without another word, accompanied her away.

Dhuro smoothed back his hair, watching them walking side by side. Noc gave her drooping head a nudge, and she perked up a little, if only briefly.

Dhuro drew in a deep breath, fighting a twinge of conscience. All this time, she'd given as good as she'd gotten. Things weren't different simply because guilt had displaced her sense of moral superiority.

As long as there were no more charms during battle, it didn't matter what she thought, and he didn't need her to think well of him. If that meant he had the emotional range of a cave troll, then so be it. He just needed to do the job Mati had given him, and do it well. And right now, that meant finding a secure campsite.

The early-afternoon sky had only grayed further, and he wanted some shelter while it was still dry.

Just then, the first droplets of the storm began to fall.

CHAPTER 6

*A*rabella glanced beside her, and that bitter porcupine of a dark-elf was close. Far too close. Huddled together in a mountain cave should've been better than being out in the storm, but if it meant getting some distance from him, then the rain, the thunder, and the lightning began to feel inviting. And the sooner the other unicorns could help her get her powers under control, the better.

Noc took the rare opportunity to nap, leaving her to stand around, unsure where to rest her gaze.

Arms crossed, Dhuro leaned against the stone, his head bowed, staring intently into the space before him. Eyes couldn't strangle anyone—she was fairly certain—and yet anyone who'd intrude into Dhuro's line of sight right now wouldn't be ridiculous to wonder. Occasionally he tapped a claw against his bicep but one look at the slope of his eyebrows on his shadowed slate-blue face would dissuade anyone from asking him what bothered him.

Was he still angry over her charm during the battle? Maybe his dark mood had nothing to do with her at all, but she was certainly taking the brunt of it.

In the heat of the moment, she'd misunderstood, and he knew that. She'd tried to make peace between them, but she wouldn't force her presence on him. If he didn't want to forgive, then the remainder of this trip would feel all the longer, but that was his choice.

All eyes meandered to the outside from time to time, just as hers did, anxious to get out of these tight quarters, no doubt. The sun was setting, and it would soon be dark. Dhuro and his team had taken so many precautions, but if his reaction after the ambush had been any indication, they hadn't known about the bounty out on her.

So which enemies had they been so prepared to face? He wouldn't tell her anything, but she'd have to find out, somehow. If only to know what she was walking into out there. All he'd said of their attackers was that they were light-elves and had nothing to do with her. This enemy of theirs had to be problematic, something they wanted to hide. Something she'd uncover, if she had anything to say about it.

Even more curious had been the griffins' involvement. From everything she'd learned, griffins were high mountain creatures, and light-elves made their home in the lowland woods. The peculiar partnership had to mean more, especially since it had etched that ever-present furrow on his brow even deeper.

When darkness finally settled outside, Dhuro jerked his head to the dark-elf with the long braid—Gavri—and she gathered the team.

Bella nudged Noc awake. *Seems we're heading out.*

Noc nodded sleepily, then as the dark-elves leaned in together, he turned an ear toward them.

Can you hear them? she asked.

He craned his neck toward them a little, but when they dispersed, he made a show of looking around.

Dhuro narrowed his eyes at him before tipping his head in the direction of the exit. "Time to go."

Although he faced Noc when he said it, those golden eyes stole the briefest of glimpses at her before he strode away.

She shifted from hoof to hoof, turning to Noc. *Well?*

Something about watching out for the light of the crystals. They must be wary of light-elf attacks, since they use crystals for illumination in the dark. We are very close to Lumia's territory.

Lumia? These might be the answers she needed. She followed the dark-elves out alongside Noc. At least it had stopped raining. *Is it a particularly aggressive queendom?*

Noc hesitated, picking his way carefully through the rocky dirt. *There's bad blood between Nozva Rozkveta and Lumia. At the end of their last war, the light-elf queen killed Queen Zara's partner, Mirza.*

Bella's heart fumbled a beat. Queen Zara's partner? *Was he Dhuro's father?*

Yes, Noc answered somberly.

Dhuro had lost someone to war, too. Someone he'd loved. Being so close to Lumia had to put him on edge, worry him, just like the sounds of battle always reopened her anguish at losing Cosimo. Every time, it was as sharp, as deep, and as devastating as the first time, darkness and numbness stretching for months, for years.

No, she wouldn't dwell on that right now. Whenever those dark feelings resurfaced, she tamped them down, focused on what she could do to *stop* that kind of violence as Renato. It didn't always work, but she had gotten better with practice.

How did Dhuro bear the loss of his father? Did he have someone he shared the burden with?

She gulped a breath. This wasn't about what scars they shared.

Whatever he'd been hiding, was Lumia somehow involved? The attackers had been light-elves, after all. Was there another war brewing? If so, how did taking her to the unicorns figure into it?

That night of the battle, when she'd charmed everyone, had come with a realization: Unicorns could stop wars.

It was clear from Dhuro's every stomping step that he'd like nothing more than to paint the mud red with his enemies' blood. But Queen Zara, perhaps, had another strategy in mind to deal with threats to her queendom. Would returning a wayward unicorn to the herd grant the dark-elves some sort of favor? If unicorns could stop wars, then their support would be a useful tool for anyone to win. But what would the bargain be? Surely returning a fledgling such as herself wouldn't be enough to buy a tool like that. There had to be something else, something immensely valuable on offer, but what it was would for now remain a mystery.

Skirting along the base of the mountain, the dark-elves ringed her, a few leading the way. Their wary eyes traced the woods, pausing at the night's sounds. Owls hooting, wolves howling, the wind rustling the trees. Even if the final bargain would involve more important trades, they did protect her. More than simply helping her find her sire, they guarded her. Perhaps she was their way in with the unicorns? An overture to negotiations?

That's why.

Noc turned his head to her abruptly. *What?*

Her breath caught. *Oh, I... Um...* Sometimes she still didn't manage to keep her thoughts to herself.

What did you mean by that? he pressed.

Nothing, just an idle thought I meant to think to myself. I'm sorry! She laughed self-consciously.

He half-laughed. *Don't be so hard on yourself. You're still learning.*

She bobbed her head, although she didn't agree. Because of her stance on the mercenary business, all of her family relationships had relied on her ability to keep her thoughts private. And because of her writings as Renato, when she'd spoken to strangers, her family's *lives* had depended on it. Becoming a unicorn hadn't only taken her body from her, but her mind, too. Her privacy. Perhaps even her ability to keep her family safe.

As a human, unicorns had seemed so magical, so wonderful, this symbol of peace, these magnificent beings.

In some respects, becoming one was magical and wonderful. Speaking into others' minds, charming violence away, stepping into a world most humans hadn't even dreamed of...

Yet with every new blessing she could think of, every new way this change should be wonderful, she only wanted to cry, more and more. Cry for her hands and her feet that were hooves. Cry for her face and her hair that were muzzle and mane. For her words that were neighs and whinnies. And for her private thoughts that were now the free air.

Once upon a time, the feel of a quill pinched between her fingers had been so natural, so easy, just writing and writing and writing. But now, as she tried to pinch her fingers, her hoof only pressed deeper into the dirt. Even if she did Change back into herself, would she remember how to write again? Would she have to practice? Relearn?

She'd spent so much time in the woods as a girl, but always dressed in constricting dresses. The trees had been enchanting, had called to her, and although she'd always wanted to, she'd never climbed one, never seen the world from their peaks. And now perhaps she never would.

She stepped over a puddle, catching a glimpse of her equine form.

Could she ever go back to her life as it had been?

Stop feeling sorry for yourself, she thought, splashing a hoof into her reflection.

Now, when she was so close to reaching the unicorns, was no time to stumble. The night before the full moon, she would try to retake her human form, and she would learn how to control its Change. That was only a couple days away.

And as for being a pawn, at least now she understood the dark-elves' motives. Her return to the unicorns would either be the overture to negotiations or part of the bargain. Dhuro had probably been commanded not to share the details with her. And why should he, when she might refuse to play a part in their dealings or complicate matters?

Little did he know that in pursuing the unicorns' help, they were of the same mind. She would always lend a hand—or hoof, as it were—if it meant peace instead of war. Even to someone who loathed her as much as Dhuro seemed to.

With his gaze trained on the deep woods, he led them around a stacked formation of boulders.

As she picked a path behind it, he lunged to block her way. She stopped short, nearly running into his chest.

He held up a fist, and the other dark-elves kept low to the ground. He met eyes with Kinga, the warrior who had amber beads in her innumerable long braids, then waved her forward along with Gavri.

Bows drawn, the two of them crept toward the woods.

Bella craned her neck past the boulder, but Dhuro shoved her head back behind it.

A light. Her heart beat faster.

The faintest glow of light had shone deep among the trees.

KEEPING ARABELLA BEHIND THE BOULDER, Dhuro drew one of his blades in the dark and listened. Both Kinga and Gavri had whistle-tip broadhead warning arrows, and they were his best warriors. If he needed to get Arabella out of here, he'd hear that sound. Soon.

If these were Lumia forces, his small squad would have no hope of victory. And considering their path abutted Lumia's vast territory, there was little hope of escape for them all either.

Every *kuvara* who'd come on this mission had done so knowing it might be her last in service of their queen. As much as it galled him, he could be forced to retreat with Arabella and deliver her to Gwydion himself. Mati had ordered him to trade himself with an Offering to seal the alliance. He couldn't do that if he was killed. And he wouldn't gain entry to the unicorns' grove without Arabella.

Is it—? Arabella began, but he hissed out a *shh*. Right now, Kinga and Gavri needed his full attention.

Arabella stiffened, although she didn't say anything more.

The white light glowing in the woods grew brighter, larger, closer.

His heart pounded, thudding in his chest. Had the enemy killed both Kinga and Gavri before either of them could fire off a warning arrow?

He glanced to Valka, who crouched low with her bow ready, and she gave him a grim nod. Behind her, Marysia did, too.

Darkness, he'd need to send in the rest of his squad just to cover Arabella's retreat. *His* and Arabella's retreat.

I can cast a glamour, but it won't cover us all, Noc said to him gravely. *My speed can take you to safety.*

Dhuro kept his eyes on the approaching light, clenching his jaw. Before the light-elves got to within a hundred yards, he'd have to make the decision, no matter how much he hated it.

Worse has come to worst, my friend, he thought back. Everything inside of him screamed to stay and fight, but he had his orders. Damn it all, but Mati had given him orders.

The light, maybe two hundred yards out, didn't change course. It was now or never. Clenching his jaw until it cracked, he nodded to Marysia, who mirrored the gesture and dug in.

"We're leaving," he bit out to Arabella, his voice low, and looked to Noc for permission before mounting up.

Leaving? What about Gavri and Kinga? Arabella raised her head, catching his eye as he sat on Noc's back.

They are serving their queendom, as am I, Dhuro replied soberly.

By running away? Arabella chomped down on the hem of his coat. *I can charm the light-elves. We can all survive this.*

"No," he hissed, his heart racing. She couldn't control it. Did she think he *wanted* to leave them behind? He would stay and fight a thousand light-elves and die killing these murderers if he weren't an essential piece to the alliance Mati had ordered.

There was no time for this.

He drew his blade and cut away the piece of coat she held. "You can come with us and help the queendom that saved you and spared your brother. Or you can stay here, die, and spit in Queen Zara's face for her mercy."

Arabella stared into the wood.

Valka thumped her foot on the ground, catching Arabella's attention. "Go," she whispered, and the other kuvari joined her, mouthing the word.

Her ears flicking back, her head drooping, she followed as Noc led the way, picking up the pace along the mountainside.

I'm casting the glamour, Noc said to them, and the air tingled ever so slightly around them.

Dhuro held on for dear life as the wind battered his face, as Noc's hooves tore up the ground, only glancing behind him every so often for Arabella. She charged up next to them, glistening trails falling from her weeping eyes.

If you'd just believe in me—

He shook his head vehemently. *And get us all killed?*

She forced a harsh breath through her nose.

Darkness, Gavri and Kinga could be *dead*. His squad was sacrificing their *lives* to cover this retreat. And she still pressed him on this?

All the belief in the world, he thought to her fiercely, as the woods went by in a blur, *wouldn't change the fact of your inexperience. Accept that. Respect their skills and honor.*

Wordlessly they ran, Noc and Arabella kicking up the rocky soil. If the Darkness was merciful, they'd make it far enough to find another path into the Altobelli Mountains.

Dhuro checked behind them, hoping against all odds that his squad had defeated the light-elves.

The light glowed at their position—

And sped right here. Faster and faster, picking up speed.

Mounts. They had to have mounts.

"Noc," he said breathlessly, "we need to lose them—"

I know. Both Noc and Arabella raced at a full gallop, but trees crowded the path ahead. It was dark. And even Noc wasn't always sure-footed, let alone a new unicorn.

The light gained on them, closing the distance.

Shit.

He needed to negotiate with Gwydion, but there would *be* no negotiation without Arabella's safe arrival. She needed to survive, at all costs.

Someone else could negotiate.

"Take Arabella to Gwydion, Noc. Send word to my mother when you get there," he said grimly. "I'll stay here and slow them down, give you two as much time as I can."

Wait, Arabella began, *please—*

"Don't slow down for anything," he shouted to her. Then, to Noc, "Let me off."

I'll protect her, Dhuro, Noc replied as he came to a stop.

Dhuro leaped off, drawing his blades as he faced the nearing light.

A few yards away, Arabella had stopped too, lingering and hesitating.

"Go! Now!" he roared, jerking his head to her. Noc ran to her and urged her onward, but she shuffled on her hooves.

Dhuro, it's tiny! She spoke in his mind with a rising hopeful pitch.

The size of their light-elf crystal, or—?

He was about to shout for her to run when the light closed the gap.

CHAPTER 7

*D*huro, *it's Tiny!* Bella thought to him, but he didn't waver until the pixie flew just out of range of his blades. Her name was Shrelia, but all the dark-elves and Princess Alessandra knew her as Tiny.

Dhuro's shoulders went slack, and he tilted his head, squinting past their new arrival. "A pixie?"

I told you, she said gently, approaching with Noc by her side. *It's Tiny, the pixie who helped us against the Brotherhood.* If Tiny was here, then this wasn't an attack.

Dhuro's face snapped toward her, his mouth falling open. She nearly laughed. At least no words were coming out.

Chiming angrily, Shrelia landed on the flat of one of Dhuro's blades, pointing a finger at him. *Silly dark-elf! I'm trying to help you! Which is difficult when you're running away!*

Despite being a tiny, winged, pink-haired woman the size of a butterfly, there seemed to be good odds Shrelia could verbally sting like a wasp. And Dhuro would be getting the entirety of *that* stinger.

Bella snorted, and Shrelia flitted up to her.

And you, unicorn! You should've heard my hails from far, far away! Shrelia planted her minuscule hands on her hips and glowered at Noc.

Haven't you been teaching her anything, oldster? Or is she that terrible a pupil?

Noc eyed Bella dubiously. *I am exiting this conversation.* With a toss of his tail, he trotted past a dumbfounded Dhuro and back toward the squad.

Thank you for the vote of confidence! Bella called after him with an inward sigh. She hadn't eluded being stung after all.

Shrelia zipped back to Dhuro, flying right near his nose. He staggered a step backward, waving a hand in front of his face.

Tell this silly dark-elf I'm not a bee! Shrelia demanded, flailing her arms. *And that his brother is here!*

His brother? Bella blinked. Which brother would that be? Veron, or...?

Just tell him! Shrelia flew up to her nose and prodded it with a tiny finger.

Unlike unicorns and fey horses, pixies didn't have telepathic abilities. It had to be frustrating for them to understand elves and humans, yet be unable to communicate with them.

Dhuro, Bella began, and he turned to face her, an eyebrow raised, *she says your brother is here.*

A frown tightened his features. As scary as the situation had been, it was almost worth it to see him so dumbfounded and confused.

"Veron or Zoran?" he asked.

What, does he think Prince Veron and I rode a dragon to get here first from Nozva Rozkveta? Shrelia yelled, exasperated. *Obviously Prince-Consort Zoran!*

"What did she say?" With a hand on his hip, Dhuro waited. To him, Shrelia's words probably only sounded like chimes and ringing.

Zoran, she answered, but he approached her and leaned in, again with that skeptical eyebrow quirked.

"All that to say 'Zoran'?" He huffed doubtfully. "What else did she say? Out with it."

That scent of his, fresh water and mountain stone, wrapped her up, traced a shiver down her spine with an invisible fingertip. On his breath was some delicious union of pepper, ginger, cloves, and some spice she couldn't identify, fiery, sharp, and unlike most of the dark-elf fare she'd smelled. She wanted to breathe it in, imagine what faraway places those flavors had come from, and ask him what he knew about them.

"Well?" he prompted, and she had to shake off the sensation of goosebumps prickling her hide.

I... um... She peered into the distance where Noc had departed, and huffed a half-laugh. *I... am exiting this conversation.*

As Dhuro scoffed, she trotted off on Noc's trail.

Shrelia flew next to her. *You should've just told him,* she teased, making a show of dusting off her leaf-dress.

I'm sure the myriad of messengers who've been shot don't want me among their number. She ambled, with a little bounce in her gait. *That infirmary is too crowded to add a unicorn, don't you think?*

Shrelia snickered, her cheeks rosy and her eyes glittering with glee. *He's just so grumpy to my Aless that I can't help but tease him.*

Dhuro had made no secret of his distrust of humans. It had been one of the few things she'd known about him before this trip. At least his default open hostility toward them faded to mere surliness when it came to Princess Alessandra. Despite the princess's devotion to his brother, perhaps he still didn't trust her.

And perhaps being a unicorn for the dark-elf equivalent of five minutes didn't automatically make her a non-human, or trustworthy. She sighed.

Don't let him get to you, Shrelia encouraged, gliding nearer. *Once you're with the unicorns, you'll never have to deal with his grouchy self ever again.*

True enough. Once the unicorns helped her control her powers, she'd return to Roccalano and continue her work as Renato. That would make crossing paths with dark-elf warriors like Dhuro unlikely.

And after he deals with his best friend, Shrelia added, *he can go back to brooding in his hunting blind, alone.*

Bella blinked sluggishly. *His best friend?*

The squad came into view, where a strapping dark-elf man with long, flowing hair greeted Noc with wide arms and a big smile.

Oh, yes. That's why I'm here, Shrelia replied. *Queen Zara wants me to return as soon as Dhuro kills Dakkar.*

Bella's eyes watered, and she took a step back. Queen Zara had sent

Dhuro to assassinate his best friend? The notion was so horrible it was unthinkable. Why would the queen order that?

The light-elf and griffin attack resurfaced in her mind. Had they somehow been connected to this Dakkar? Was that why Dhuro had been sent, instead of a squad of all kuvari?

Queen Zara had sent Dhuro for a reason... If he and this Dakkar were best friends, then he could get close enough to kill him, couldn't he?

She inhaled shakily.

Dhuro's mother had sent him on a mission to kill his own best friend.

All the frowns, the grimaces, the dark moods... Had this been why? Because he'd have to kill someone he loved?

This whole time, she'd been so prickly with him, so contentious. He'd fired back and held his own, but all the while, this had been simmering beneath the surface.

Whatever Dakkar had done, there had to be another way to solve this. His death wouldn't just punish him, but Dhuro. And worse, since Dhuro would have to live the rest of his life with what he'd had to do. What did *he* want to do about this?

Losing Cosimo had been excruciating. Now Dhuro would face that loss too, with the crushing anguish of striking the death blow.

She shook her head. It didn't have to be that way. It didn't. She knew it.

Tarquin had led an army of hateful bigots to murder every non-human they'd come across, innocent or not; together, they had killed and tortured. And yet, he'd been stripped of his family name, his property, his rank and position, and exiled. If someone guilty of war crimes such as Tarquin's could be punished without resorting to execution, then maybe there was hope for stopping Dakkar through other means... and hope for the executioner who'd have to live with it.

Tell me everything, Shrelia.

SHEATHING HIS BLADES, Dhuro made his way back to his squad with a shake of his head. Thank the Darkness it hadn't been a light-elf attack. Arabella—and everyone—was safe, at least for now.

But Queen Nendra *never* allowed Zoran to leave Dun Mozg, not even to visit his family in Nozva Rozkveta. If he was here now, she hadn't made that decision lightly.

Ahead, Zoran swept a graceful bow to Arabella, who bowed her head to him in turn. He said something and laughed, then patted her withers.

Dhuro grimaced. Overly familiar, as always, but that was Zoran. His brother always had an easy smile and a sincere laugh for everyone, and a heart as big as he was tall. It was difficult not to like him, even if everything always seemed to come so easily to him. In another life, had Zoran been a woman, he might've been Mati's heir. He'd certainly always given Vadiha more than a challenge.

"Brother!" Zoran rushed up to him and gave him a hug. "It's been far too long!" Zoran ruffled his hair, making him sigh. "You have the best hair, as always. Still making those hair masks?"

Dhuro groaned. Of course he still made *those hair masks*—vinegar, olive oil, egg when he could get it. Hair this healthy and voluminous didn't just happen on accident. But he didn't need Zoran telling everyone about it.

"We're just on the border with Lumia," he murmured, scanning the dark forest. "Let's get somewhere safe enough to camp before we exchange any more niceties."

Zoran huffed out a half-laugh. "We both know you ran out of niceties in the crib. But yes, let's find somewhere to rest our rears and catch up."

When he'd been little, Zoran had helped take care of him, but that hadn't come without good-natured gibing. *A lot* of good-natured gibing.

He was about to summon Kinga when Gavri stepped forward, her bearing particularly stiff. No surprise, considering her history with Zoran.

"Your Highness, allow me to scout ahead and find us a campsite." Her voice was as stiff as her bearing.

Next to him, Zoran's mouth hung open like a sack. But it would take more than that if Zoran hoped to recapture his past love. Especially when Gavri was so keen on getting away.

"Yes. Go."

With a brisk nod, she wasted no time in picking a path and disappearing into the night. Behind him, Arabella and the pixie seemed deep in conversation, with Noc hovering protectively nearby. Good— someone would keep an eye on her while he dealt with his brother.

He motioned for Kinga to take point and guide them forward, and she got into position.

Zoran cleared his throat. "How... how has she been?"

"Kinga?" he joked, raising an eyebrow. "Oh, you know, rising through the ranks per usual."

Zoran sketched a tight-lipped smile. "Gavri."

This was a dangerous game. Rumor said something had happened between Zoran and Gavri in Dun Mozg, when Veron and Alessandra had stopped there. Queen Nendra was infamous for her spite, and her memory was long.

"Work keeps her busy," he answered carefully, although he wanted to ask if Zoran knew what he was doing.

Closing his eyes, Zoran rubbed his forehead and breathed deeply. "I shouldn't ask, I know." He slowed his gait, just a bit, until everyone passed them by and the two of them brought up the rear of the group. "You have to be wondering why I'm here—"

Only a lot.

Zoran cracked his knuckles. "Look... Queen Nendra sent me to... assist against Dakkar."

Dhuro sneered. *Assist?*

Zoran was Mati's son, but married to Queen Nendra, he was no longer Mati's subject. He served a different queen.

"You're here to stop me. Mati didn't want us to take the tunnels precisely so Nendra couldn't stop us from killing her son."

Zoran grasped his shoulder. "Dhuro, he doesn't have to be killed."

"Mati wants him dead, make no mistake," he hissed. Orders were orders. Zoran knew that as well as he did. "This can't come out. The humans catch one whiff of a dark-elf leading a rebellion against them, and the entire alliance collapses. We'll starve. And that's not just Nozva Rozkveta, but Dun Mozg too."

Gnawing on his cheek, Zoran turned away and winced, running his claws along the leather of his trousers. "Look, I'm not going to hide my hand. Dun Mozg supplies Nozva Rozkveta with weapons. That'll stop if even a hair is harmed on Dakkar's head."

Ah, here was Nendra's infamous spite. She'd weaken the entire dark-elf race over Dakkar, her one traitorous son. Zoran was better than this, though. Or at least he should have been.

Dhuro narrowed his eyes. "Reduced to being Nendra's errand boy?"

This time, Zoran grabbed him by both shoulders, holding his gaze intently. "She has my daughter, Dhuro. I'm whatever she wants me to be." Zoran's voice, as strong as it was, quivered slightly. Karla, his six-year-old daughter, would likely be Nendra's heir, now that Yelena had disgraced herself when she'd helped deliver Alessandra to the Brotherhood. Although all had ended well, Yelena's treason hadn't been forgotten. "Nendra spends all her time with the rest of her consorts, and for years, I've been nothing to her but a trophy. But as long as she keeps Karla there, I'm not going anywhere."

Aside from Zoran, Nendra had at least three other consorts, as many dark-elf queens did. To be ignored by his queen, Zoran must have fallen out of favor. Far, far out of favor. But the children always belonged to the mother—Zoran had no way to leave the situation without leaving his daughter.

Zoran let out a tired breath, and they continued walking. "There has to be a way to do this bloodlessly."

There wasn't. Even when they'd been children, Dakkar had never done anything with less than his entire will. Dakkar had always fought to his last breath, beyond the point when any other novice would have conceded. In the sky realm, he'd always stayed out on the hunt until he could return with a quarry, even long after he'd run out of supplies, which risked injury or death. He'd always been a man who hadn't allowed reality to dictate what he could accomplish, as reckless as that was.

Dhuro shook his head. "I know Dakkar. He won't come quietly, and he won't stay hidden for much longer." Only long enough to gather the strength he'd need for a frontal assault.

"Surely he wouldn't want his own people to starve?"

No, Dakkar had never been cruel to his own people. "Of course he wouldn't, not the man I knew. But if he aims to conquer the humans, then revealing himself will turn the humans against us. We'll lose the alliance. Whether we like it or not, we'll end up his natural allies."

"If I get him back to Nendra, that won't happen. She'll contain him." Zoran nodded to himself.

Nendra had neglected to stop him already—Dakkar had organized this under her nose and gotten away with it all.

"Don't make me return with news that'll hurt Nozva Rozkveta. Our home. Our people," Zoran entreated, his voice wavering. "Because for Dakkar's sake, she'll do it. I won't be able to stop her."

He believed it. Every word of it. But it wasn't his choice. "This isn't up to me. You need to bring this to Mati."

Zoran leaned in. "I'm bringing it to you. Do you really want to murder your best friend? Let me take Dakkar to his mother, and maybe she can set him straight. Wouldn't that be better than having his blood on your hands?"

Dhuro combed his fingers through his hair, staring a hole through the rocky ground in front of him. The thought had been kicking around his skull the past few days. No, he didn't want to kill the Dakkar he'd once known. But Dakkar had ceased being his best friend the moment he'd betrayed the dark-elves, and now he was only a traitor who needed to be put down.

Mati had given him orders and he had to carry them out, but this was more than that. This was the right thing to do.

But he also couldn't allow Zoran to go back to his queen and set in motion sanctions against Nozva Rozkveta.

He had to walk a thin line between Mati and Nendra, at least for now. And he had to keep it that way until the moment Dakkar was in front of him. "We'll see if Dakkar can be reasoned with, and I'll tell you my decision. But not before then."

A corner of Zoran's mouth turned up infinitesimally. Perhaps this was enough to give him hope. "You'll have an extra set of hands until then. What now?"

A low whistle came from ahead—Kinga. "Gavri found us a site. Let's go."

"For now, we protect a unicorn, take her to Gwydion, and get his help in stopping Dakkar before he does any more damage," he answered.

Zoran smiled, genuinely. "Ah, I met Arabella briefly. What form does she take with the moon nights?"

The moon nights? The first of them was tomorrow, but because she couldn't control her Change, he hadn't thought about it. She had been human, of course, and had Changed into a human the night of the battle with the Brotherhood, when she'd rushed out between the human and dark-elf armies to prove to her brother she was alive.

"Human," he replied, under his breath, "but I've never seen her."

CHAPTER 8

*I*n a secluded spot among the ruins, Bella focused on Shrelia in the late-afternoon sunshine, wrinkling her nose. When they had come upon the ruins of some long-gone civilization, Dhuro had declared it a good place to rest until the early morning. In a couple of days, they'd hopefully reach the location of Gwydion's herd.

Her stomach fluttered and her neck prickled at the thought. It was finally happening. She'd find her sire among the unicorns, learn why he'd Changed her, and how to control her Change—hopefully.

But while they were here, Noc had said that it was the best opportunity they would have to resume her training.

Tonight could be the first of three days that she would Change back to her human form—or not at all. There was no telling whether she'd be able to Change, how long she would be able to hold her form, or even *whether* she'd be able to. As much as she didn't enjoy this right now, Noc was right.

There are a lot of unicorn powers, Noc began, *and although I don't know how all of them work, it's important you know about them. I would divide them into telepathic, empathic, and telekinetic abilities. The first category, you're already well—*

She nudged him gently. *Noc, I do appreciate the thought, but it's only been a few days since I nearly got people hurt with that accidental charm. I want to make sure people are safe around me, so can we please train on this part until I'm not a danger anymore?*

Besides, she'd already asked Shrelia's help, too.

All right, Noc said with a lengthy exhalation. *I can understand your concern. Let's get started, then.*

Shrelia perched on a broken pillar, fluffing her pink hair. *I can't believe I agreed to this,* she grumbled. *Just make sure you're thinking nice things—I don't want to end up with my guts splattered all over these mossy ruins.*

Bella narrowed her eyes sardonically. *The fewer interruptions there are, the nicer my thoughts will be.* She puffed a breath that billowed Shrelia's leaf dress just a bit, and Shrelia crossed her arms.

Focus, Noc said. *You need to take this seriously, Bella. At least if you plan on using these powers of yours. And you'll have to think terrible things if you want to convince yourself they're happening. So do that.*

As much as she didn't want to fill her head with ugliness, Noc was right. If her charms would ever be reliable, she had to practice.

During the battle with the light-elves and the griffins, the only thing on her mind had been saving everyone's lives. Her heart had raced, and she'd acted without thinking. That had been a much different situation than camping amid some serene ruins near a babbling brook. The crisp scent of the cedars here soothed, and just a hint of lake water mingled in the air. Wild pansies rambled across the sandy soil with cheeky blooms of yellow, white, and violet. Cosimo had given her one the third time they'd met, and she'd treasured it until her sire had Changed her unexpectedly and she'd lost it in the forest.

This paradise was a far cry from the violence of battle.

Nevertheless, she took a fortifying breath and closed her eyes, imagining Shrelia with a tiny dagger in her hands, about to do something violent... such as poking Dhuro in the nose.

Would he hiss and cover it? Would he whine and grumble? His thick eyebrows would draw together, low over his eyes, and he'd scowl in that way that was part menace and part boyish petulance.

And what if Shrelia messed up his *hair*? His precious hair? To hear Zoran tell it, fair Prince Dhuro had picked up somewhat of an obsession when he'd worked among the humans before the Sundering.

She stifled a smile. No, no, no—she would have to imagine something she'd want to stop, and harassing Dhuro was definitely not it. If anything, maybe she needed to learn a charm to *encourage* some... good-natured harassment of a certain brooding dark-elf?

Bella, Noc scolded.

All right, all right. Squeezing her eyes shut, she took a bracing deep breath. What had he said she needed to think of? Terrible things?

Attempting to chew her lip—it was not as simple in unicorn form—she pictured Shrelia charging forward with a dagger in hand, right for Noc's eye.

She tensed up, with all her might thinking, *Stop!*

Imagine the horror you want to prevent, Noc urged her. *Let it be vivid. Let it overpower you, if only for a moment, and then fight back with every bit of your willpower.*

In her mind's eye, the tiny blade plunged into Noc, unleashing a chilling otherworldly scream. She shuddered violently, her skin going cold.

Stop! she thought, with everything she had, swinging her head from side to side. *Stop right now!*

When she opened her eyes, Shrelia stood unnaturally still on the broken pillar, only her tiny sparkling pupils moving from side to side.

I did it! she thought to Shrelia, prancing.

Noc nudged her shoulder. *Well done. I knew you could do this.*

Well done, wonderful, and so on and so on, Shrelia thought, her words quivering. *Now let's undo this, all right? Yes?*

Sobering, Bella nodded. There was no sense in celebrating something only half-done, was there? Last time, she'd been able to impart her will with physical contact, but Noc had told her a thousand times how to undo her charms.

Just as she'd had to convince herself the worst had been happening and exercise her will, she now had to convince herself all was well and change it.

Her friend Shrelia stood before her among peaceful and idyllic ruins. The late-afternoon sunshine was fading to dusk, and a cool breeze was rolling in. Friends and allies surrounded them, even Dhuro as he leaned against a pillar, his arms crossed, but curious eyes surveying them through his hair.

Everything was all right.

Let my charm be undone, Bella thought to herself.

She infused it with belief, willing it to become a reality.

Shrelia fell forward, but her wings fluttered in time to catch her. She lifted her gaze to Bella's and grinned. *You did it!* she exclaimed.

Bella turned to Noc, who bobbed his head approvingly. She had done it. She had finally done it.

Thank you, she thought to Noc. *I couldn't have done this without you.*

He huffed his amusement. *You just needed guidance. That is something you would've gotten among the unicorns, but I suppose this fey horse had to do.*

She was laughing to herself when slow footsteps invaded. His hands on his hips, Dhuro canted his head, and then he gave a slow clap. "You did it."

Although he didn't say anything more, the crooked smile playing across his face spoke volumes. *You did it, but...?* she asked him.

He heaved a sigh, letting one hand fall to the side. "You did it, but it certainly wasn't very fast, was it?" He crouched to Shrelia's level. "In the time it took you to break that charm, how many times do you suppose an enemy could have killed Shrelia?" His gaze met hers.

Bella swallowed. It wasn't malice, exactly, in his gaze, nor ridicule, even. But it was more intense than idle curiosity, too. He was pushing her. That had to be it.

Shrelia stuck out her tongue and blew a raspberry at Dhuro before flying up and away. He rose, too, crossing his arms as he faced her and Noc. "Well?"

We're only training, Dhuro, Noc said, approaching Dhuro. *She'll get better.*

"She can speak for herself, Noc." Dhuro looked past him at her, his attention unrelenting. Camped as they were, he had removed his leather armor and rolled up the sleeves of a rough-spun shirt over dark slate-blue arms, and he now tapped a sharp claw on his bicep. The rhythm was slow, varied, unlike the impatient fidgeting she had seen from others, and more... Playful? Amused?

Just how bored was he? At least enough to toy with her.

She raised her head up high, facing him squarely. *As you can see, the conditions here are very different. There are no enemies. There is no danger. There is nothing to react to except that which I have imagined for myself. If anything, what I've done here is more challenging, because I have no instinct to help me.*

Dhuro's eyebrows rose, and he tilted his head. "Is that so? Out in the field, then, you would rely on your instincts, and throw all of this training away?"

Her mouth dropped open. *That's not what I meant.*

"Then what did you mean?" He took a step forward and leaned in. "Because that's what you said."

She narrowed her eyes at him. He was twisting her words, and to what end? *I meant that in the field, I wouldn't have to spend so much mental energy on imagining the danger. Instead I could focus on training.*

"You have a long way to go before it comes to that. This is only one of many powers you have yet to master. We have yet to see whether you can even Change properly." He turned away to leave.

He'd gone way past twisting and now had her in knots.

You just can't stand it, can you? she thought to him, watching his back as he froze mid stride. *Someone else having more control over a situation than you do.*

"Control?" He glanced back at her over his shoulder. "That is overstating matters, isn't it? What I can't stand is unpredictable variables carelessly prancing into combat, endangering me, my people, and my mission. Nor a unicorn manipulating me, my body or mind."

If you would just trust—

"Trust?" He spun, peering at her as though she'd said something obscene. "My people trained for decades, some of them *centuries*, not just individually, but as a unit. They possess great skill born of abundant practice."

She wanted to cover her face, but her hands weren't there. Her eyes felt hot. *No, not now.* How was she letting him get to her? Maybe she wasn't the most adept student, but one thing she had learned was how to push out invading thoughts and feelings that made her hurt. But this, now, she couldn't fathom why...

She'd only met this dark-elf a few days ago. Soon she'd be united with the unicorn herd. After she learned how to control her Change, she would go back home to her family and her work as Renato. She would never see Dhuro again, and these words wouldn't matter. None of this would matter.

So why...?

Tears welled in her eyes, and before they could fall, she gathered her composure, turned into the direction of the evening breeze, and left.

Noc called after her, but she didn't want to hear it. She didn't want to hear how she should ignore Dhuro, the excuses for his coldness, and she didn't want to see Dhuro's handsome face that hid such cruelty, such a repugnance for any idea that wasn't his own. If she were human, things would be different. At least she'd have a *voice*. A real voice. But like this?

No, what she wanted was to be alone, to close her eyes for a second, and for tomorrow to be here already when she opened them.

CHAPTER 9

*D*huro didn't need to see Noc to know that the fey horse was staring at him. He could feel it, like a polearm of disdain impaled through his chest.

He rubbed his forehead and sighed.

We meet with the unicorn herd in a couple of days, Noc said to him incredulously. *You couldn't just leave her be?*

Dhuro groaned. No, he couldn't just leave her be, and worse, he had no idea why. They had been getting under each other's skin for this entire trip, and that tension had been building and building and building, with no Ring to settle matters in, and so leaving them unsettled.

"I can't allow her to interfere, but I also can't stop her. Obviously we differ on ideology"—he grimaced—"but she's intelligent enough to discuss and understand unit cohesion."

Is it your calling to educate the world on it? Noc pushed.

Dhuro opened his mouth, but no words came out. Honestly, he didn't care how ignorant the *world* was, as long as it didn't affect his people. If Lumia hadn't attacked them yet, then they probably wouldn't in the time it took to get to Gwydion's herd. Her desire to intervene wouldn't matter if there would be no combat. "No, it isn't."

But what?

For some reason, he wanted her to understand.

She wanted so badly to do right in the way most obvious to her, so badly and so blindly that he wanted her to admit her myopia. As she looked ahead, charging toward the vision of her utopia, she was blind to everything else. She'd been relieved her charm hadn't led to their deaths, sure, but what else had she learned? Had she even considered the other ways her powers could endanger them?

If she really wanted to end all loss of life, didn't that begin by looking beyond what was directly in front of her? Looking at what could be, and not just what was?

She had shown that she had no qualms when it came to debate. And he was, maybe, ill equipped to truly take her on. But if she delivered truths so boldly, she had to be prepared to accept them herself, no matter how they differed from her philosophy. She had a sharp mind, but she quailed to accept the unconventional or consider the unknown.

He stared into the distance after her, but she had already disappeared. With assassins chasing her and Lumia nearby, she had to know being alone was out of the question. He turned to Noc. "She's coming back, isn't she?"

I'll go get her, Noc said, but Dhuro rested a palm on his withers.

He shook his head, blowing out a lengthy breath. "No. I will. I think I owe her an explanation."

You mean an apology? Noc replied, but before Dhuro could answer, Noc spun and trotted off toward the rest of the squad.

No, he wouldn't apologize for challenging her philosophy, but he wouldn't let her stay out there unprotected. He checked his blades—right where they should be—and then followed her trail.

HER EYES OVERFLOWING WITH TEARS, Bella ran among the firs and pines in the night, ignoring the prickly needles hitting her face and body. She didn't know where she was going, and she didn't care, as long as it was far away from that dark-elf.

Didn't he see that she was trying? Ever since she'd understood the risk of what she'd done to him and the rest of the squad, she had practiced, learned from Noc, trained. She had been doing all within her power to ensure she didn't accidentally repeat that danger, not because he demanded it of her but because it was the right thing to do. For years, she had condemned violence, risked her life by publishing secrets of the Sileni Condottieri, all to keep others safe. It had become her life's work, but it was also her calling, her mission in life. Did he truly believe she wasn't doing all in her power to further it? To protect those in her immediate vicinity from harm first and foremost?

She tossed her head, running faster, her speed stealing the tears from her face. Why did he have to push her so hard? Did he hate her that much?

Her mind wandered back through time, to conversations in smoky, packed nobiltà salons, where the handsome man on her arm had brought her to question the views her family had fed her. Mamma had always maintained that the Belmonte forces helped the king and signori who needed it, and that these were matters for only Papà, and eventually Tarquin and Luciano. She hadn't given it much thought, favoring her nonna's collection of myths and legends instead, poring over them with a child-like wonder long after she'd had her first moonbleed.

But Cosimo, in bringing her to those salons, had placed her face to face with the truth of her family's trade. The petty squabbling of the nobiltà was settled by rented armies, commoner soldiers who decided disputes in tallies of innocent lives. Signori didn't always risk their own lives in duels to settle disagreements, or better yet in negotiations. No, they let their vassals and citizens suffer and die to decide who was right, with paid Condottieri like the Belmontes acting as the judge.

Cosimo had pushed her to listen, to see the widows and orphans and disabled, and realize that her own family had made them so. The mirror he'd held up had shattered her, but he'd pushed her out of love, a desire for her to see the truth instead of remaining veiled in the complicit ignorance her family would've condemned her to.

She'd only loved him more for it, and would give anything and everything she had to spend a single hour more on his arm. Even a single minute.

But Dhuro, he... When he pushed her, it was because...

Was it because he wanted her to see the truth, too? Something she was missing?

Above her, bright silver glimpses of the moon peeked out from amid the coniferous forest canopy, the gentle radiance consoling, comforting, inviting.

It was one of the moon nights she'd been waiting for. Instead of excitement, her eyes and cheeks were hot, and her stomach turned. But no, as horribly as this night had gone so far, she wouldn't let it rob her of potentially Changing to her true form. She was no longer bound in arcanir, and she was strong enough.

Between the trees ahead of her shone a gleaming surface. Water.

She ran toward it, toward the Change, toward her true form as the moon kept rising. As she emerged from among the trees and onto the lake's shore, her muzzle became her face, her withers shoulders, her equine body shifting to human until her hooves became feet and hands and met the splash of the cold lake water. The chill made her shiver, but she had never been so glad to feel cold water against her bare skin as relief rippled through her, as she inhaled the lively scent of the lake.

The moon shone large and bright in the sable sky, and beneath it, the lake's surface gleamed a palette of cobalt, emerald, ruby, and amber, a dazzling rainbow of beauty edged by the reflected silhouettes of dense pines and firs. She skimmed the shining surface, and a ripple made the colors dance in a captivating kaleidoscope.

The Lago dell'Arcobaleno. She'd read a legend about it in Nonna's books, and this had to be it. The way the story went, a beautiful water-dwelling *vivèna* had called this place her home, and when a witch had glimpsed her beauty while she watched the sunrise, he tried to approach her, but she fled. Enamored, he wanted to give her the most beautiful sunrise she'd ever seen, so the next day he cast a spell to conjure a rainbow over the lake's surface of glittering jewels. When she emerged at sunrise, she was captivated by the magical rainbow, and he was captivated by her. His hands reached for her of their own volition, and when she fled in terror, he had such remorse for scaring her that he spelled the rainbow to rain down its jewels for her, so she would never be forced to surface in order to enjoy its beauty ever again. His gift of jewels to her was the reason for the lake's shining rainbow of colors beneath sunrise, sunset, and moonlight.

And now they shone just for her.

Hugging herself, she ran quivering fingers and palms over her human form. She had done it—she'd really done it. All these long months as a unicorn, she'd wondered what it would feel like to be in her own body again, and she didn't have to wonder anymore. When she wanted to move her hands, they moved; when she wanted to smile, she smiled. Her body responded to her will as it always had.

She looked over her shoulder back at the woods. It was only a matter of time before Noc—or gods help her, *Dhuro*—came searching for her. She didn't have much time, although up to her knees in the cold water, she didn't want to leave its abundance of sensation against her skin.

If Dhuro did come for her, what would he say to her now? Seeing that she'd managed the Change ably enough? Having to hear her voice instead of ignoring her? If he saw her as she was now, what would he say?

A smile stretched across her face, and surprised, she brushed her own mouth with a fingertip. The notion of him seeing her like this, not just human but naked, didn't make her feel defiant but... giddy.

She'd seen the way he'd looked at Kinga, another dark-elf in the squad, although he hadn't seemed to act on that look. The thought of it made her cheeks flush hot, her breaths come faster, coarser. Her mind had idly hinted at those desires before, but now they were possible.

He'd seemed to enjoy needling her with barbs, and she'd tried to fight back—that had been her mistake. What she needed to do, and what she very much wanted to do, was the opposite: let him in.

In the forest behind her, twigs snapped. Her smile widened.

Dhuro followed Arabella's trail. Among the ruins, her hooves had left prints on the moss and in the mud; she wasn't difficult to track. On foot, however, he'd be hard pressed to get to her soon if she'd run very far. Hopefully, she hadn't.

Her trail led beyond the ruins into a forest and toward the lake that bordered the mountains. The moon, nearly full, had eagerly risen just after sunset and lit his way. Glimpses of its reflection played between the mountain pines that descended from high, foggy peaks all the way to the water to surround it.

He emerged from among the trees, resting a hand on the rough bark. Beneath the big moon, ripples wavered the lake's gleaming glass surface, where a woman had waded in to mid-thigh.

He froze, rooted to the spot.

Her shadow-dark hair flowed in long cascades down her bare back, ending just above a slender waist and a round, full bottom.

His fingers twitched as she looked over her shoulder at him, a brilliant green eye sizing him up as a little impish smile curled her mouth. Those green eyes—

His heart pounded, a warning drum urging him to say something, anything, and look away. "Arabella?"

She slowly turned to face him, and Darkness, his meddling heart could shut up, because there was no way his eyes would do anything but devour every bit of the beauty before him as she strode toward the bank. That impish grin of hers didn't waver, but something stirred behind her sparkling eyes. Amusement. Satisfaction. He didn't know. He didn't care. He didn't care, because she stood right in front of him naked, her palm smoothing into the open collar of his shirt and coming to rest lightly over that meddling heart of his.

With a soft moan, she closed her eyes, and a little breath escaped her lips. Her luscious lips.

A sly smile. "Have I Changed properly?"

Throwing his words back at him. If she was toying with him, he'd look like a fool, but that didn't matter. Not between them. Not anymore.

He took her face in his hands, careful of his claws, and as her big eyes met his, she gave a slow nod and he kissed her.

Deep, Darkness, and Holy Ulsinael, she tasted just like she smelled, like the first hint of spring, floral and revitalizing, slightly sweet and new. She nipped his lower lip, and he exhaled a low rumble of a laugh under his breath as he deepened his kiss, claiming her mouth as her nimble fingers undressed him.

Whatever fire lay beneath her sharp tongue and her wit, he wanted to find it, unmask it, revel in its heat and challenge its need to consume, or perhaps welcome it. They didn't have the Ring, but this was how they'd work out the sparks between them.

She pulled his open shirt off his shoulders and down, and he stepped out of his clothes, out of his boots, into the cool earth, savoring the hungry eyes that took him in, the lip pinned beneath her teeth.

And when she took his hand, leading him back toward the water, it was all the invitation he needed. In the sand, she faced him, and as his gaze met hers, he tracked the shimmering trails falling from her eyes. He reached up a hand, the pad of his thumb meeting their wetness, and there was no doubt in his mind that despite standing here with her, bare as Holy Ulsinael had created his people, he had caused those tears.

"Arabella—" he began, but she raised a hand and pressed a finger to his lips.

"Shut up," she whispered back, her voice a soft rasp, her glittering emerald eyes without a hint of levity in them. He had his reasons, his explanations, and maybe even apologies, but her finger had already told him she didn't want to hear them.

A silent moment passed before a close-lipped smile slowly began to claim her mouth, and with a firm hand on his shoulder, she pressed down. As he descended to the sand, she joined him, topping his body like a she-wolf claiming her kill.

Her knees on either side of his hips locked him in, and she kissed him then, different than before, longer, each feeding into the next. Beneath her, he was ready, eager, but she'd taken the lead, and Darkness, he wanted to see where she would take him.

Her kisses traveled down his neck, where she sucked at his skin, and damn if it didn't make him moan. She must have picked up on it because she only sucked harder, and it was all he could do to not grab her by the hips and roll her over immediately, take her in the sand. He growled low in his throat, and she uttered a pleased half-laugh, raising her eyebrow as she mounted him, none too gently.

Deep, Darkness, and Holy Ulsinael—

He groaned, whether from pain or pleasure he wasn't sure, but as she moved to her liking, her head thrown back in pure joy, bare beneath the bright of the moon, nothing else in this world existed but what was happening between them here. She was a woman on a mission, working him hard, and he wasn't about to protest.

This woman—*Darkness, this woman*—she'd driven him mad for days, and although he'd felt it in every corner of his being, only now, right now, did he understand why. That madness, it hadn't been just disagreement, just clashing, but the most basic madness there was: that of a man for a woman. In her other form, he hadn't realized it, but here, now, Darkness save him, it was clear as the moon in the sky. She challenged him, she opposed him, she infuriated him, and this was the answer he would've wanted to give her, wild and mad, bare and honest, passionate and powerful. If only he'd seen the real *her*, as he did tonight.

Her entire body contracted atop him as pleasure tore free of her throat, and every sound, every shudder, every shift of her body against his brought him closer and closer to joining her, but as that full-throated pleasure faded to soft sighs, she dismounted him, replaced the irreplaceable core of her with the grip of her hand.

Every inch of his body rebelled at the change, burned to be a part of her once more, but as she finished him, everything else fell away from his care, everything but the feel of his own ecstasy cresting, waves of it over-taking him again and again and again until he was well and fully spent.

This woman. As his pleasure melted away, he wanted to both rage at her and lavish her with kisses, confusing and yet perfect and another sign of that basic madness, perhaps. But, torn, he did neither when she lay down beside him, gazing up at the sky as her breathing began to slow. She rested her head on his bicep, and when he looked over her slumbering face, anything he might've said to her in that moment didn't matter. Not one bit.

BELLA AWOKE and slowly sat up in the sand, her fingers threading among the wild pansies. It was still dark, and Dhuro lay next to her, without a scrap of clothing between them. As her eyes met his, they shared a small smile.

All this time, he'd been so cantankerous, so argumentative, but here, alongside the shimmering water and beneath the low-hanging moon, he'd given in to her every whim, had risen to the occasion, without so much as a single objection. It seemed the fair prince *did* know when not to argue. And with nary a word, she'd gotten to say to him exactly what she'd needed to. It finally felt like they were on an equal footing, and he'd revealed a side of himself that was markedly different from the grouch he'd been so far. A side she liked. A side she liked *a lot.*

She rose and waded into the cool water, an obsidian mirror reflecting the ethereal white of the moon, the shadowy peaks of the pines, and the dark high mountaintops on a surface that rippled and flowed in that dance of color.

In her unicorn form, she'd worried whether her human body would respond to her as it once had. And although the first steps after her Change tonight had been toddling, it had all returned to her... at least to the extent of this eve's activities.

The thought brought with it a smile, and she looked back at Dhuro, who had laced his fingers behind his head and watched her intently, in all his naked glory. Gods above, he was a pleasure to look at. Even the black sun tattooed over his heart was beautiful.

"Join me if you like," she said to him playfully, and he stood, dusting off his hands before approaching. "I won't bite."

A crooked grin claimed his mouth as he entered the water.

"What if I want you to?" he asked, his voice low, seductive. His palms rested on her waist, then slid down over her hips, his fingers tapping a light cascade.

"The night is still young," she whispered mischievously, eyeing his lips as he leaned in, her palms planing up his carved, muscular back.

Flush against his hard body, she met his mouth's light teasing with her own, pulling away only to catch her breath and let the throbbing of her heart slow. Gods, how long had it been since she'd surrendered to pleasure, instead of worrying about the massive changes in her life and the swath of carnage the Belmonte armies swept across the kingdom?

His tongue played against hers, and as she met his gentle coaxing with mounting urgency, he rumbled a moan of approval deep in his chest.

Far too long. It had been far too long since she'd surrendered to plea-sure—no, pursued it, as she did tonight. Since Cosimo, she'd only pursued men she couldn't become attached to, and considering Dhuro's hostility to her prior to this eve's activities, she'd found another perfectly wrong man yet again.

Bella. Noc's worried voice cut in, and whatever urgency had been mounting with Dhuro stopped short. *Are you all right? Dhuro went looking for you and hasn't returned. The kuvari are about to send a party after you both.*

"No!" she blurted out, covering her mouth, her cheeks blazing.

With a splash, Dhuro staggered backward, his mouth falling open and his eyebrows knitting together.

Exhaling a laugh, she shook her head at him. "Sorry, not you. Noc." She'd been so unused to her voice that telepathy had been natural, but now, it seemed her voice and her telepathy tangled.

Tell them... she thought to Noc, hard. Tell them what, exactly?

Dhuro's golden eyes widened, and nodding, he licked his lips before raking a hand through his hair and looking back toward the direction of their camp, an amused smile on his lips.

Bella? Noc prompted, a waver in his question.

"What should I tell him?" she asked.

Dhuro sighed, crossing his arms and slowly shuffling a leg underwater. "Tell him I found you, we're safe, and we're returning to camp."

Despite his words, his gaze meandered her body from top to bottom in a leisurely once-over.

We're safe and on our way back, she replied hurriedly.

What's happened out there? Noc answered. *There are certain unicorn abilities we haven't discussed—*

She winced. *No need to worry! Promise!*

Gods, it would be written all over her face as soon as she returned.

Dhuro's gaze lingered on her breasts before finding her face once more. "On second thought—"

She gave him a playful shove. So he wanted more, did he? She raised her eyebrow in challenge. "You'll have to realize your *second thought* in a tent at camp. Not that the mud, roots, sand, and rocks weren't a suitable bed."

"Was that what we were on? I didn't notice." Grinning, he held out a hand to her, and when she took it, they trudged through the lake water toward shore.

No, he hadn't seemed to notice, or care. If there had been anything on his mind other than the crux of need between them, she would've been surprised. That is, if she could've mustered surprise in the searing heat of desire.

There had been something very uncomplicated, pure even, about their encounter, like untying a knot. Whatever frustration had lain between them had faded away for now, at least for her part.

He cleared his throat. "You might need this."

When she glanced back at him, he had already put on his trousers and boots, and was holding out his shirt. Clothes. It had taken some time to get used to not wearing them as a unicorn, and simply being bare, but that wouldn't work at all in her human form. Not even a little.

She gratefully accepted his shirt and put it on, nearly getting lost in the massive garment.

Dhuro watched her, his eyes focused, his face hardened with intensity as he looked her over. That same intensity of his had taken her earlier, painstakingly given her pleasure, his eyebrows taut with concentration, with single-minded focus.

Gods, she wanted to fan herself. And he was still staring as she fastened the shirt, still unmoving even when she finished. He was observing this shirt-donning ritual with strange gravity. Very strange.

"So, are we married now?" she asked with a laugh, cutting the silence.

His stare shifted, widened for a moment before he blinked, and whatever hold had taken him over now broke.

"What? Married?" He swallowed, shaking his head. "Is that how your people these days—?"

She burst out laughing. "Gods, no! Of course not. I was only joking." Surely he knew that? She'd only tried to break the silence. "I didn't mean anything by it. Clearly we both know what this is."

And leading to marriage it was not. He'd practically hated her just earlier today. One tumble in the hay—er, sand—didn't change that... Not that she wanted it to.

He frowned, his arms crossed as he watched her, one eyebrow raised.

Wait... he didn't think this had been... Had he thought this had been more? More than just releasing their frustrations? Unlikely, but...

Her shoulders went slack, and she reached out to him. "Dhuro..."

He grabbed her and hefted her over his shoulder, making her yelp.

"What are you—?" she stammered, trying to tamp down her breasts as they seemed to mount an escape through the shirt's neckline.

He picked a path into the forest. "Only one of us has boots," was his gruff answer. "Unless you can Change back."

She didn't know where to begin with that. Not that she even wanted to. For so long, she'd wanted to be human again, and now that she was in her natural form, Changing back was the last thing on her mind. "I'm not sure I can make that happen."

He'd picked her up so abruptly, she hadn't gotten to ask him what he'd felt tonight. "Dhuro, about tonight—"

"It was fun," he answered, with more cheer than she'd thought him capable of. His chest puffed out as he moved aside a fir branch. "We should do it again sometime. Sometime soon. Sometime tonight."

She laughed, propping herself up on his back. Fun. That's what it had been, and his saying so meant they were of the same mind. She'd been concerned over nothing, thank the gods. "Now *that*, I can definitely make happen."

CHAPTER 10

*P*icking his way through the dark forest, Dhuro headed for the camp's distant glowing fire while Arabella wriggled over his shoulder, tugging down the hem of his shirt to cover her bottom.

With a grin, he swept it away and grabbed a firm handful.

"Dhuro!" she squeaked, incredulous and scolding, flailing about for that hem again.

"Oh, were you trying to cover that?" He laughed under his breath, adjusting his hold on her and making her squeak again. This was a whole new side of her, one he liked, one he wanted to keep looking at.

Perhaps because he'd become so accustomed to the sight of her as a unicorn, her feather weight over his shoulder came as a surprise. She was a small, slender woman, with no muscle to speak of. If she'd ever wielded anything in her life, at most it would've been a hair brush. Her form was unlike any of his dark-elf lovers, but she was all dark-elf where it counted: her attitude. Sure, she pressed for peace, but the way she did —Darkness, it would rival even the fiercest kuvari of Mati's Quorum. There were rabid wolves who let go of bones more readily than she did arguments.

He roared a call to his team as they neared, and Arabella flinched in his grasp. "Just letting them know it's us," he said quietly to her as the answering call came.

"I've heard it before, just never this... close," she replied, and he could hear the smile in her voice. Doubtless, she meant *loud*. Deep underground, among deafening waterways and thick cave walls, dark-elf calls meant always being able to find each other.

"Slightly louder than telepathy," he teased.

"Only slightly," she joked back.

Finally, just as he was about to enter the camp, he set her down on the moss-covered ruins. At least her feet wouldn't be mangled here.

She immediately set about righting his shirt over her body and smoothing her mane of thick hair into place, as if that were possible.

Beneath a broken archway, a small group met them: Noc, Tiny—or Shrelia, as Arabella had explained, Gavri, and Kinga.

Her head tilted, Gavri eyed Arabella warily. "Is that—?"

"Arabella," he answered, inviting her closer to the group with a palm at the small of her back.

"In the flesh," Arabella added with a lilt. "In the... *human* flesh."

Gavri puffed a chuckle, shaking her head, while Shrelia darted toward Arabella's face, chiming rapidly as she flitted about. Noc approached her and nudged her arm gently, with a look of—dare he think it?—pride. Arabella touched her forehead to Noc's and smiled warmly.

Did you see anything? Noc asked him, eyeing him briefly.

See anything? Darkness, he'd seen plenty. *Are you really asking me this, Noc?*

A huff. *Did you sleep? Did you see anything unusual then?*

He raised an eyebrow. *What was I supposed to have seen?* And how, while being asleep?

Noc didn't answer.

As the night wind rolled in, Arabella firmly pulled on the hem of his shirt, her face flushed.

"Get her some clothes, Gavri," he instructed, receiving a nod in reply.

"So you weren't going to give her the rest of yours?" Kinga asked him sardonically, with a hand on her hip.

"Now there's a thought," Arabella murmured mischievously, then bit her lip. Bold, maddening, irresistible woman. When he shot her a surprised look, she shrugged happily. "I'm just saying I wouldn't be opposed, is all." With that airy comment, she gave him a brisk once-over.

Kinga scoffed, tossing her innumerable braids over her shoulder.

"Why don't you come with me?" Gavri lightly grasped Arabella's arm. "Princess Alessandra sent a few things along. We'll pick out some clothes for you together."

"Yes, please," Arabella answered with a grin, tugging the hem of his shirt even lower. "It's a bit... breezy."

He couldn't help but laugh, although damn, the sight of her in his shirt did things to him. Something about it had rooted him to the spot before, at the lake. The thought of something of *his* against her naked body, wrapping her in his scent, claiming her—

He took a deep breath. For a couple more days, anyway, they'd have this... fun.

Despite Gavri inviting only Arabella to come with her, both Noc and Shrelia followed. With Kinga glaring at him, he didn't need to wonder why.

He strode past her toward the direction of his tent. If Arabella planned to stay with him tonight, he wanted to make sure she'd be comfortable.

"You couldn't resist adding a unicorn to your list of conquests, could you?" Kinga hissed as she stomped alongside him. "You really do sleep with anyone."

He huffed. "I slept with *you*, didn't I?"

She scoffed, looking away momentarily.

Yes, he and Kinga had been exchanging loaded looks since before they'd left, and although they'd been lovers once, things had gone differently this time. Perhaps with good reason. "I know there's been a tension between us since we left home. I didn't mean to mislead you. This just came out of nowhere."

Kinga tongued her teeth, then lowered her gaze to the ground and shrugged, slowing to a thoughtful gait. "There's nothing between us. I shouldn't have said anything, especially if you and the unicorn have something special." She said it like an assertion, waiting to be refuted.

Something special? He grimaced, crouching to lay out his bedroll. What did she even mean by that? Not the emotional mess, certainly. She knew him better than that.

Any dark-elf knew what it was to find a true challenger, whether a warrior or a rival or a lover, someone who could be a match in the most frustrating, exciting, difficult, satisfying way—a *sheihan*. That kind of match rarely came along, but when it did, it was something to relish. Holy Ulsinael had blessed him once before, when Dakkar had matched his martial prowess perfectly. Granted, he'd never done with Dakkar the things he'd done with Arabella tonight.

Still, he could feel it, that bond, even if he couldn't exactly name its foundation. Was she his mind's match? Or maybe the mirror to the fire that burned within him?

He clenched his jaw. Whatever it was, he could feel its heat between them like a blaze. Arabella had been quick to downplay it, but humans had rarely acknowledged the pleasure of a good challenge, at least in his experience. Anyway, her words were only raindrops to the storm they'd made together tonight. He could hardly wait for the next. Hardly. He finished smoothing out the canvas on the ground in his tent.

Kinga's gaze softened. She'd been expecting some sort of answer, but when he opened his mouth, no words would come. She looked out at the other tents, then pressed her lips together and nodded before taking her leave.

It was now well after midnight, and they'd have to continue their journey early in the morning. He looked about the camp, where only Arabella and her small group huddled at the far end, with Gavri taking watch. With a smile to himself, he plucked one of the delicate tricolor flowers spread across the campsite.

Everyone else had surrendered to some small bit of rest. Perhaps he would, too—with one eye open for light-elves and assassins, and whatever it was Noc had expected him to see.

BELLA MARVELED at the pile of clothes slung over her arm. It should've been heavy, made her arm hurt, but it didn't. Not at all. Becoming a unicorn had even made being human different. Gavri tossed on a silk scarf with a vine pattern while Shrelia tested the texture of every fabric, and held some choice selections up to her chin, assessing herself with each new look.

This pink complements my hair, don't you think? Shrelia asked, holding up part of a sleeve of a velvet dress. Before she could answer, Shrelia held it up to her skin, too. *Actually, it suits you! What would your grumpy lover think about you wearing this?* Shrelia waggled her eyebrows.

Bella fought back a grin. *I think he'd prefer something a little less... existent.* When Shrelia erupted with giggles, she added, *Although I wear clothes that I like. And I like it a lot.* Trimmed in pearlescent buttons and embroidery, the dress was fit for a princess, and one she wouldn't say no to.

Noc nudged her arm. *Did you see anything strange when you fell asleep?* he asked her, and she frowned at him while Gavri continued piling clothes and accessories onto her.

See anything? While sleeping? she replied, raising her shoulders.

Noc exhaled lengthily, what looked to be a relieved breath. *Perhaps you've avoided it.*

Avoided what?

He shook his head, and a laugh echoed in hers. *Just enjoy this time. Soon we'll be with the herd, and there will be much to discuss. But you still have a couple of days to yourself first.*

She raised an eyebrow at him while he bobbed a goodbye and headed toward the bucket of water Marysia had freshly filled. What had Noc expected her to see while sleeping? Was it another unicorn ability? She shrugged.

"Are you just having entire conversations the rest of us don't hear?" Gavri crossed her arms, and although she pursed her lips and narrowed her eyes, there was a lilt to her voice.

Bella laughed. "It looks like it's become second nature since..." Since she'd stopped being human.

Gavri elbowed her lightly. "Don't worry about it—Noc has been doing that to us for centuries." She looked away toward the outskirts of their small camp. "I have watch, but don't be a stranger, unicorn. I'm here if you want to use your outside voice."

Bella smiled warmly. That meant a lot. "I will," she replied with a nod.

Gavri returned the expression, then took her leave.

You can trust her, Shrelia said, landing on her shoulder. *At least around everything but, as you call it, "butter."*

A laugh escaped her, but she quickly hushed it. Gavri wasn't wrong —good butter was worth the effort.

She'd never had many friends growing up. Mamma and Papà had only allowed her to socialize with other nobiltà, and only "approved" ones at that. It hadn't been until she'd started running away that she'd met true friends: Cosimo and his sister, Isisa.

Cosimo had...

She swallowed thickly, her shoulders tight and curling inward.

And Isisa... Isisa hadn't spoken to her since Cosimo's funeral. Isisa had disappeared, joined some group of bounty hunters or guards.

Things are tough for her, Shrelia said gently, watching Gavri at her post across the camp. *Especially with Zoran around.*

Noc had told her all about Zoran, whom he considered a close friend, but she'd only heard inklings of this. *What happened?*

Shrelia let out a long, slow sigh. *They were together for nearly a decade before his mother, Queen Zara, arranged his marriage to Queen Nendra. He put duty above love, as they always do.*

The words wrapped her like vines, pierced her like thorns, and she clutched the pile of clothes more tightly. Nearly a decade? For nearly a decade, they'd been together, loved each other, built a relationship, only for it to be destroyed and swept aside. He'd hurt her, but nobility, royalty, they were forces of nature, too, and for the sake of thousands or millions of beating hearts in both nations, two hearts had been broken.

It wasn't the same, but she knew that loss. The cold embrace of solitude after Cosimo's death, its frigid kiss, the emptiness in her hand missing his, the emptiness in her heart missing him. The winter of that grief had passed, but the ghost of its cold lingered, whispering memories of forever-lost warmth in her ear on trying days.

A chill walked her spine; the night had cooled. She straightened.

Shrelia patted her neck with a tiny hand. *Go catch some warmth, if you can,* she added with a wink, before fluttering away.

During what had been such a curse, she'd somehow managed to make friends with kind souls, and continued to. Becoming a unicorn had brought with it unexpected blessings to counter its burdens. While once upon a time, she'd wished to ask the unicorns for a way to undo this, now she found herself wishing only for the strength and knowledge to manage her Change. A whole new world had opened before her, one she didn't want to leave. Perhaps it was selfish to want her old world, too, but she did.

The breeze chilled her legs, and hefting the bundle of borrowed clothes, she tiptoed to Dhuro's tent, finding her footing carefully so she didn't crush any of the wild pansies.

It was strange, really, being among ruins claimed by these flowers again. A place like this had been her refuge as a girl, deep in the heart of the woods near her home. She'd taken books there that her parents hadn't wanted her to read, and she'd befriended a boy there her parents hadn't wanted her to befriend. He'd plucked a wild pansy and given it to her with a smile.

Do you know what they call it? he'd asked her with a song in his voice. When she'd shaken her head shyly, he'd said, *Heart's delight. Heart's ease. Love-in-idleness...*

She'd blushed. *A lot of names for one flower.*

Tickle my fancy, he'd continued. *Come and cuddle me...*

With a laugh, she'd asked, *Are those more of its names? Or an invitation?*

A sportive grin. *Perhaps both.*

Now, she paused outside the tent, letting those whispers of memory pull back their soft breath, the ghost of Cosimo's face fading once more. She rubbed her upper arms through the rough-spun fabric of Dhuro's shirt, then ducked her head into the tent.

Wearing a fresh shirt, Dhuro sat, affixing arrowheads to shafts, with small mounds of each next to him.

"Hafting," he said, glancing up at her briefly. "It keeps me busy."

Beside him, his bedroll lay flat, with a single wild pansy laid atop it.

"Come and cuddle me," she breathed. It was uncanny.

Raising a pale eyebrow at her, Dhuro set down his work, regarding her intently.

She'd definitely said that out loud. "Oh. It's what people sometimes call this flower. Wild pansy." She entered the tent and sat down on the bedroll before gently plucking the flower from its resting place.

"Is that what they are? Veron was always better with the sky realm botany than I am." He pushed aside the arrow parts and sat close to her. "Earlier, at the lake, you seemed to like them."

He'd noticed that? Her breath caught as she looked away. What else had he noticed?

"I... I do." With a quick smile, she kissed his cheek, and his eyes widened. *I just didn't expect you to get one for me*, she thought to herself. *It brings back memories.*

"What kind of memories?" he asked softly.

With a gasp, she started, falling away from him and landing on her palms. Gods above! "You heard that?"

He stared at her blankly. "Yes, just like I have been this entire trip."

She covered her face with her hands. Merciful gods and empyreal Veil threads! She could just *scream*. Why, why was this all so difficult?

"Was I not supposed to hear that?" he asked, watching her carefully. "Is this about controlling your unicorn abilities again?"

This time she really did scream. Inwardly.

When she wanted to be heard, sometimes she couldn't be. When she *didn't* want to be heard, sometimes she was. Privacy, her voice, her thoughts, things she had taken for granted, very *important* things, were out of her control. And now, in her human form, somehow it seemed even worse.

She couldn't control her form.

She couldn't control her voice.

She couldn't control her thoughts.

Dhuro canted his head, watching her with a soft, cautious gaze as he set aside the arrows. "Arabella?"

"Bella," she said, and climbed into his lap, where he made room for her.

Something deeper stirred in his gaze as his eyes searched hers. Whatever it was, she wouldn't give it time to surface. She stroked her fingers through his hair, and he closed his eyes, exhaling a long, slow breath.

"Bella," he repeated back quietly, and she covered his mouth with hers. Privacy, her voice, her thoughts... so much of what she needed felt beyond her grasp, but Dhuro—his passion, his pleasure, he was right here, solid and warm and *real* in her hands.

CHAPTER 11

*W*hen Bella opened her eyes, the sunny world around her wasn't one she recognized. Nestled in the middle of a crowd, she lost herself among the people in long, sleeveless wool dresses and robes, secured at the shoulder by a brooch in a prism of colors—yellow, bright blue, pale green, bold red. Some men wore short-sleeved tunics of white linen, belted at the waist, with bare legs and the same simple sandals with cross-straps.

Past the people was a great structure with rows of stone pillars beneath a deep portico. Adorned with figures and sculptures, it had to be a temple of some kind, like the historical Sileni buildings she'd seen in books. She was about to step forward to get a closer look, but instead her body turned right, of its own will, into a line of people heading down the wide thoroughfare.

She tried to look back, but couldn't. Her body wasn't her own as she walked with the crowd's current, only pausing to glance at a spice stall. More than a glance, actually. Her heart beat faster, and her legs diverged from the line of walkers to push through shoulders and approach the stall.

A young woman shouting her wares quieted, locking eyes with her and grinning broadly. The woman's long brown hair tumbled down her back, some styled over her bare shoulder, where a moon-shaped silver brooch secured her bright blue dress. Thick, shining locks fell over her face, where she swept them from her brown eyes.

"Dhuro!" the woman greeted cheerily, a hand anchored on her hip. "Great to see you again. You just couldn't resist the Thelesa family's spices, could you?"

Bella tried to glance around her, but her gaze remained locked on the woman. Was Dhuro here, too? If he was, why was this woman staring directly at her?

"Janessa," Dhuro's deep voice rumbled pleasantly. In *her* chest.

Gods above, what was this? But as she involuntarily closed the distance to the woman, the reflection in her eyes had golden irises, pale eyebrows, slate-blue skin, and perfect white hair.

I'm in Dhuro's body!

She wanted to pull back, to run, anything, but instead, her body— no, *Dhuro's body*—leisurely shopped, choosing spices from the array of piles that the woman... Janessa... bagged for him.

"What about this? What is it?" He pointed to a bag of black pepper.

He didn't know what pepper was?

Leaning in, he smelled it, then as its scent tickled into his nose—she could feel its tingle as if it were *her own* nose—quickly pulled away and sneezed.

"Pepper," Janessa said, laughing heartily. As the sound faded, her eyes meandered to his and held his gaze for a moment before glancing away.

She... she was flirting? And as warmth spread in Dhuro's chest, the feeling was clearly reciprocated.

"It might seem awful right now." She puckered her lips, bobbing her head this way and that in what appeared to be a grand display of thought. "Why don't you join me down by the river tonight? The fishing spot at dusk?" Janessa offered, twirling a lock of hair around her finger. "I'll cook up something special for you, and you'll see pepper is not what it seems."

He chuckled low in his throat. "I'd love to see its charms. But are you sure it's all right...?"

All right to what? Have dinner? To court? To...?

Janessa waved a hand dismissively. "You've been shopping here for months! It's the least I can do to addict you to another one of my wares," she said loftily. "I'd also like to get to know you better."

She needn't have said that. It was completely obvious. Bella wanted to roll her eyes—or Dhuro's, she supposed—but couldn't.

As he paid Janessa for the spices he'd bought, he grinned. "Wouldn't miss it," he said, accepting his spoils with one muscular arm extended. "I'll see you tonight, Janessa."

She replied with a little smile, but when he turned to leave, she added, "Bring wine!"

He looked back at Janessa and nodded, waving a goodbye before he rejoined the crowd, his purchases in hand.

How strange. And not even just this experience, which was strange enough, but *him*. This was not a Dhuro she knew or recognized. It had been his voice, his face reflected in Janessa's eyes, but there was a joy to him, a zest for life, and—did she dare think it?—optimism.

He headed toward a forest with a spring in his step, grinning to himself.

What was this? Was it a dream? Or could it possibly be *Dhuro's* dream, or his memory, that she'd somehow tapped into? But if so, how was this possible?

She wanted to shake her head, but again, not *her* head she had here but his.

If this was somehow a memory, then was Janessa truly the type of woman he liked? Bright, bubbly, and eager to cook for him?

As he approached a small hunting cabin in the woods, two dark-elves emerged, a tall lean man with long hair, who bore a striking resemblance to Prince Veron, and a brawnier dark-elf with broad shoulders and a hard-set jaw.

As Dhuro raised the sack of spices, the two strangers ahead exchanged knowing looks.

"It's not fair at all. Why is it *you* always get to do the spice shopping?" the brawny dark-elf called out good-naturedly, rubbing his chin as if he were seriously pondering it.

"Because I always win when you challenge me to shooting?" Dhuro remarked with a snort. When the other man narrowed his eyes sheepishly, Dhuro added, "At least you still get to enjoy the spices, Dakkar."

Dakkar?

The Dakkar?

❧

W HEN D HURO OPENED HIS EYES, he found himself sitting in a ruin, beneath a stone archway wrapped in creepers. Light filtered in through a dense tree canopy swaying in the wind, dappling the forest floor in a dance of sunshine and blessed shade. Those same flowers were here, the ones Arabella had called wild pansies, covering the sandy soil like a tricolor carpet of yellow, white, and violet.

He breathed in, slow and deep, closing his eyes. There was a calm to this place, a solace, and it seeped into him, embraced him with comfort, and he let it.

When his eyes opened, he was peering down into his lap at an open tome. His hand reached down to turn a page, only—

His hand was small, delicate, and... *human.*

He tried to pull it back, but nothing happened. He tried to look around and rise, but his body wouldn't move at all.

His... No, not *his* body.

What was happening? He needed to be able to *move*, to see, to assess the situation, to fight if need be.

But this—this was familiar. Infuriatingly familiar.

Darkness help him, had Arabella used some kind of unicorn magic on him *again*? After he'd explicitly told her not to?

This woman. She'd come into his tent, acting odd, but the type of odd that didn't matter at all the moment she'd started to take his clothes off. And he'd forgotten all about it as she'd let him take her how he wanted to, right then and there. Maybe he should've spared a second to ask a question or two or ten, but when she was naked, it was hard for questions to compete. And she'd seemed to know that, with her little mischievous smiles, as all his arguments melted. Besides, he'd thought, there was always time *afterwards* to talk, if it was necessary.

It wouldn't be the first time his *thoughts* had let him down. He sighed inwardly.

Last he could remember, she'd fallen asleep on his arm, and he'd been drifting off, too. Was this some sort of dream?

But as the human hand turned another page in his lap, no—this was unlike any dream he'd ever had before.

Did you see anything? Noc had asked him earlier.

Was this it? The thing he was supposed to have seen?

Leaves crunched behind him. He tried to turn around, look over his shoulder, but nothing happened. His eyes remained focused on the page, on words, words he did *not* care about as a threat closed in.

Louder crunching, twigs breaking, distant voices—two, a man and a woman.

Everything in him raged to rise, to *move*, but this body, this Darkness-damned body, did nothing but stare at the page.

Move, damn it! he seethed at himself, to no avail.

"Greetings, signorina," a melodious, masculine voice called out, and at last Dhuro's eyes looked away from the tome and over his shoulder. "Please, do not be disturbed. We mean you no harm and are but passing through."

A man and a woman stood, far enough away to indeed pose no immediate harm. Both wore modern Sileni attire, although not the luxurious finery Alessandra tended to wear. Their cloth was plain wool and linen, and the woman wore dark, loose breeches tucked into laced boots. They both carried rapiers, and despite the man's peaceful greeting, the woman hovered a hand near her waistband, where no doubt a dagger was sheathed.

The two resembled one another, both young, in their late teens maybe, and dark skinned, with dark hair to match. The woman kept hers loosely bound at the nape of her neck, and the man's looked tousled, carefree, matching his coy smile. Trim, close-cropped facial hair framed his mouth. Relaxed, the man leaned on his back leg, openly looking him over.

Who are you? Dhuro wanted to say, but his mouth wouldn't cooperate. Instead, his hands shut the tome, held it close to his chest, and regarded the two strangers thoughtfully.

"I have supplies," Arabella's voice offered kindly. She was here? He wanted to look around, but his gaze remained fixed on the strangers... and the closeness of her voice, the vibrations of his chest...

Deep, Darkness, and Holy Ulsinael—I am in Arabella's body.

He wanted to laugh, he wanted to cry, to yell, to roar at the top of his lungs. But just as everything else he'd wanted to do since awaking in this place, all of those attempts would end in failure. Whatever this was, spell or dream or memory or who-knew-what, he seemed to be a passenger with no options.

"Are you hungry or thirsty?" Arabella asked.

Don't invite them to stay! You don't know who they are, what they want, or what they're doing here.

The man's coy smile widened to a grin. "That is most kind, signorina."

"No," the woman with him hissed, grabbing his arm, but he rotated it casually, breaking her hold.

"May we?" the man asked, nodding to the distance between them.

No! Dhuro grunted. *You may not!*

"Of course," Arabella said, sitting up, pulling her shoulders back. She licked her lips.

How transparent. He sighed inwardly. *Darkness, at first glance? Really, Arabella?*

She gestured to a small camp she must've made, where a couple of bags and books lay spread over a blanket on the forest floor, ringed by the ruins.

"I am Cosimo," the man offered with an abundance of charm, extending a hand to help her up.

Don't let him touch you. He's a stranger.

Arabella took his offered hand and let Cosimo help her rise. "Arabella."

Cosimo tipped his head toward the woman he'd arrived with. "This is my sister, Isisa. Don't mind her—she trusts no one, and assumes everyone is a bad sort. You're not a bad sort, are you, Arabella?"

A girlish laugh. "Are *you*?"

Holy Ulsinael, spare me.

Gracefully, Cosimo lowered to a seat on the blanket and shrugged a languid shoulder. "Only the good kind of bad."

It was some kind of torture to endure Arabella's flirtations with another man. Not just because it wasn't *him*—which was bad enough—but because this Cosimo was so incredibly obvious. Not a hint of subtlety. Not to mention, Arabella had been instantly receptive to Cosimo's advances, so there was no challenge in it at all. What fun was that?

Beside him, Isisa rolled her eyes as she knelt, sitting back on her feet. "Your jokes are still the bad kind of bad, *fratellone*."

Dhuro laughed along inwardly. Isisa—now here was a woman who saw the truth in a situation and didn't bother hiding it.

Cosimo grimaced and shrugged again. "Isisa, if you can acquire a better big brother, you are welcome to try. Until then, I fear you are stuck with me and my lackluster wit."

Arabella sat, and her hands were immediately busy laying out and assembling a lunch of bread, cheeses, olives, and various cured meats, but Dhuro could feel the small smile curving her mouth. "I like your wit," she said softly, under her breath.

"Ah, if I have even a single admirer, then I can die happy," Cosimo joked. Arabella met his dark eyes as they danced, as that mirth faded to something deeper, firmer.

Arabella's heart beat heavier, and Dhuro felt its enamored beating as if it were his own.

This—all of this—it was far too real to be just a dream. Arabella herself was different, however. Still bold, but like a breeze, not a gust. She was still reckless, careless with her own safety especially, but it came from somewhere else. Not a desire to protect others, but a... a sort of kind naivety, perhaps something she'd been raised with? Something she'd later learned from?

She wasn't yet the Arabella he knew, but her surroundings, this event, felt real enough. Could this, then, be a memory? Was he somehow reliving something that had truly happened to her?

Did you see anything? Noc had asked him.

This had to be what he'd meant. If Noc knew this would happen, then perhaps it was normal to experience this with unicorns. But why? Was it just because he'd tumbled her?

If he'd known *this* would happen, then...

No, he *still* would've done it. The woman knew a thing or two about stoking a man's desire.

Another inward sigh. All right, fine. If this was something that had to happen, then he was here and part of it.

What is it you need me to see, specifically? And why?

Holding Arabella's gaze, Cosimo smiled playfully and slowly

reached a hand toward her lap. "I'll accept this crostino as a sign of your affection."

He swiped the bread, piled with cheese, cured meat, and an olive, from her hand and popped the entire thing into his mouth, barely containing it as he chewed.

"Gods above," Arabella gasped, covering her mouth with a hand as a laugh exploded from her lips. Crumbs flew from Cosimo's mouth as he chortled with her, and—if Dhuro's, or rather *Arabella's*, eyes didn't deceive him—even Isisa cracked a grin and glanced away, shaking her head.

Darkness, he didn't need to see this. He didn't need more proof that she was generous, loving, and selfless. Regardless of how clearly they'd approached a physical relationship, closeness still risked becoming intimacy, especially when sharing thoughts and now dreams, seeing into someone's heart. He wanted none of that, least of all imposed on him without his consent.

She'd said she wouldn't do that anymore, manipulate him or use her powers on him. Regardless of how innocuous this dream was, he didn't need, want, or agree to any more. When he came to, she would understand that once and for all, and comply. He'd make sure of it.

CHAPTER 12

*S*haken awake, Bella cracked open her eyelids to see Dhuro's frowning face over her in the dark.

"Arabella," he hissed, still holding her by the shoulders and shaking her. "Arabella," he hissed again, a bit louder.

It was still dark, with not a single sound coming from outside the tent. Blinking, she pushed him away.

"Stop," she murmured. "I'm awake, all right?"

He leaned back, then sat up on the bedroll, blanketed to the waist. She held on to her side of the scratchy thing—at least it was warm— keeping it up to her neck. With a grunt, he handed her more of the blanket's slack.

"What in the name of the Darkness was *that*?" he snarled at her, and even in the dark, she caught the flash of stark-white fangs.

Rubbing her eyes, she yawned. "What was what?"

Had she spoken in her sleep? Snored? Elbowed him in the face? Broken wind? Not all men seemed to expect that from women.

He huffed and crossed his arms. "You know what," he bit out. "Your magic. Your unicorn magic thing."

"My... unicorn magic... thing," she repeated, propping herself up on an elbow. What was he talking about?

It was warm under the blanket, and quiet outside, and her eyes burned for more sleep.

She'd had a dream, but... It had been strange. She rubbed her forehead, trying to recall it, and fought back another yawn. The dream had been in Dhuro's body, in some city she couldn't identify. Had he somehow been in the dream, too?

"Oh," she said with a gasp, sitting up higher. "The dream."

Another huff as Dhuro rolled his eyes. "So you *do* remember."

The crowd, the temple, the spice market stall. *Janessa.*

"What did you just say?" His gaze snapped to hers, and he sprang to his knees.

Her heart raced and her mouth fell open. Gods above, it had happened *again*. He'd heard her thoughts!

But... it had been what he was referring to, right? "The dream. It was about Janessa, and—"

His eyes squeezed shut, and a growl rumbled low in his throat. "*Never* speak that name to me ever again."

"You're the one who brought it up," she shot back, sitting ramrod straight, clutching the blanket in a tight fist. "Why mention the dream if you didn't want to discuss it?"

"The dream *you* forced me into was about *you*," he snarled, "throwing yourself at some rake, with his sister *right there*, letting him put his hands all over you and—"

"Don't. You. Dare." She glared at him, every bit of her feeling as stony as her own voice sounded. The shock of him seeing Cosimo didn't matter, not when Dhuro presumed to disparage him. This liaison of theirs would be cut very short if he continued on this subject. "He is the only man I have ever loved. You don't know the first thing about him, or me."

Dhuro's eyebrows shot up at that, and a moment passed in silence. There were some lines, perhaps, that he wouldn't cross.

At last, he let out a sharp, harsh breath. "Here's what I do know. I already told you not to use any more of your unicorn powers on me or my people. You did that last night anyway."

She jerked in her chin, shaking her head. Did he honestly think—? "I didn't mean to."

He shrugged, mumbling angrily in words she didn't recognize, appealing to some invisible advocate in the dark. Finally, he turned back to her. "What was all that talk about controlling your powers? Was that all it was? *Talk*? How am I supposed to keep my people, or even *you*, safe, when you can't control what you do?"

She stared at him, unblinking, and swallowed hard. Somehow his words had slipped past this stupid blanket, her skin, her sternum, and had gone straight for the heart, because hot tears welled in her eyes. Did he think she didn't care about control? Did he think she didn't care about his safety, that of everyone here, and her own? Did he really think that?

Lately the thought had been sitting on her chest like a demon, and more and more, she couldn't breathe. Not being able to control her powers. Not being able to control her form. Not being able to control her speech. Her thoughts. The list of things she could control waned by the second, as even her tears seemed to have made that list now.

"Dhuro, I am trying." Her voice was hoarse, and she sniffed, then dragged a bare arm across her eyes. Hopefully he hadn't noticed her tears.

His arms slowly fell into his lap, where he rubbed his palms over the blanket on his thighs. "I know this is hard for you, I do. You're not the first person I've met who's had to deal with a major change like this. But tell me, Arabella, are you looking past what's immediately in front of you? You say you're trying, but tell me, and be specific, what are you doing aside from what's right before you?"

"I'm training with Noc," she blurted out immediately. He was making it sound like she was ignoring the problem, when she'd been working hard on fixing it.

"Training to learn *one* thing. What about all the rest? Other risks, like what happened tonight?" he asked quietly.

He... he wasn't wrong. They'd primarily focused on her ability to freeze others. They'd practiced for several hours, but it had seemed so important that she hadn't asked Noc about all the other risks yet. When she encountered a problem right in front of her, it was easy to become single-minded and focus on it to the exclusion of all else.

"Do you even know what *all* of your abilities are? Have you ever asked?" His voice was quiet, barely audible, void of any anger now. And yet these questions hurt, perhaps most of all.

The abilities she *was* aware of, she couldn't control. Knowing that made simple existence hard, made her want to scream and cry and grieve for all she'd lost and all the chaos she'd been given. Any more, even a single thing, felt like it would be the last straw. The one that would finally break her.

A whole host of *additional* abilities she couldn't control? When the ones she already knew about made this new life of hers miserable?

It was too much. She already gave everything she had to the problem at hand, whatever it happened to be at the time, and did her best to focus on the most important thing. But... it was hard to be sure what was most important when she ignored all else around her, shut out other risks and possibilities.

She shivered, but for the first time in months, she was being completely honest with herself.

In the past, it had been harmless to shut out everything but what she needed to focus on. Shut out Mamma, Papa, Tarquin, Luciano. Shut out the family business. Shut out the rules and the household and their family's subjects watching. Shut out even her own life, and all of its burdens and restraints, and be *Renato*. Be only her immediate goal, her ideal, her ambition. Cast away everything that dragged her down and be only that which lifted her *up*.

Those moments when she was Renato, when she wrote as Renato, she had worked toward a peaceful Silen and a peaceful world, but they had also been blissful relief. She'd chosen all the parts that had formed her pseudonym, and she'd been in control of all of them. Nothing had felt so comforting, so *right*. She'd thrown herself into it and ignored all else around her.

Leaving Arabella Belmonte behind hadn't harmed anyone, because Arabella Belmonte had never been capable of anything, really, much less true harm.

And now, that small life as incapable, harmless Arabella Belmonte called to her like a siren song. She'd finally received—in her new unicorn abilities—the tools she'd always claimed to have wanted as Renato, and the irony of it all was that she just wanted Arabella Belmonte back. The fruit of ideals and ambition had landed in her lap, and she had but to take possession... but all she wanted was her fruitless old life. *Coward.*

The truth was, her new unicorn self wasn't incapable. Or harmless. And shutting this new self out to pine after the old *could* harm others. It nearly had. Focusing on one thing at a time, the most important thing in front of her, had been comfortable, had been easy. It was opening her eyes to the possibilities beyond that was difficult. Difficult, but critical to avoid making mistakes. Big ones.

Dhuro remained silent, his arms at his sides, and as her gaze traveled down to his hand, the comfort it promised made her reach out. Being with Dhuro was pleasure, sure enough, but it was also the embrace that sheltered her from these truths, both within herself and on his lips.

He pulled away and took a slow, deep breath. "Arabella, I'm a man, but I'm not an idiot," he said quietly. "You can stop me from confronting you, but you shouldn't stop yourself."

A soft laugh escaped her, although a part of her wanted to cry. "You knew?"

He laughed in reply, too. "Of course I knew. But I wasn't about to turn down"—he looked her up and down—"all of that."

"How kind of you," she joked.

"Never claimed to be." He shrugged contentedly. "Besides, you were in desperate need," he joked. "It would have been cruel to turn you away."

"And you would never be cruel, Dhuro," she said, fighting back a smile. All this time, whenever she'd wanted to avoid arguing with him, he'd just obliged her preference for pleasure, even realizing what she'd been doing: changing the subject.

He shook his head. "Someday, you'll have to tell me the secret to being so distracting, Arabella. It could come in handy."

"You'd make a poor student." She pulled her shoulders back and winked. "It's all in the breasts."

A laugh exploded from his mouth, but he quickly covered it, rubbing his jaw.

Despite his sharp questions, it had been kind of him to give her a way out if she wasn't ready to face them. Still, he was right. She shouldn't shy away from confronting herself.

It wasn't true that during the entire time she'd been a unicorn, her powers had been out of control. There had been a time, a long and painful one, when she'd been unable to use her powers at all, a time when someone else had been in control.

A time she didn't like to remember.

Her own brother Tarquin had tortured her for four long months with an arcanir net, sealing her magic and burning her constantly, not knowing the unicorn he'd imprisoned was his own sister.

Months of incessant pain and fear... Four. Long. Months.

Her skin afire with the memory, she looked around the tent, where the predawn dimness had begun fading the darkness. Dhuro's set of blades lay sheathed beside him, one of the finest steel and the other, his vjernost blade, of sage-tinted arcanir.

Just like the net that Tarquin and his men had used. To capture her, to imprison her, to torture her.

A tremor shook her chest, but she didn't look away from the blade. Yes, arcanir had hurt. Yes, it scared her. But it had also bound her powers.

Letting go of the blanket, she scrambled across Dhuro and grabbed the sheathed vjernost sword. She sat back down, holding it close, and began pulling it free.

Dhuro grasped her arm, wide eyes locked with hers. "Arabella, what are you—?"

"It's all right," she told him, with a thin smile, the best she could muster. "This is the answer."

If she could face this right now, willingly, then she could do whatever it took to control her powers and reduce the risk to others.

She took hold of his wrist where he secured her arm and pulled his hand away, her strength easily the equal of his. For a moment, his eyebrows drew together, and right then, she pressed the flat of the blade to her bare chest.

It burned, searing hot and painful, echoing screams in her mind from when she'd called for her brothers, for her mother, for mercy all those months ago. When she'd begged, wept even for her departed Cosimo to somehow set her free.

The burn of tears matched the burn of the arcanir, and she let them both come.

Last time, she'd had no power over this tool, this weapon, and it had taken away all hope for anything she could have done.

But this time would be different. She had chosen this, and she could choose to stop it at any time. With the binding of arcanir keeping her—and everyone around her—safe, she could learn about all her new abilities without fear of their consequences. Once she could control them all, she wouldn't need the arcanir.

He reached for the sword. "You don't have to—"

"I do." She took his reaching hand, and this time he let her. "You're right. And deep down, I know it, too. For now, this is the answer. The only answer."

Despite the constant pain of it, she held the sword across her chest. She had borne this pain before for months on end; it was an old acquaintance of hers.

"Arabella—"

"Bella," she corrected. "Call me Bella. And don't try to change my mind on this."

He nodded. "Bella, then. Don't worry, I won't. Just, maybe we find you something smaller than an entire sword?"

That... would probably be more convenient. She wrinkled her nose. And also, he could have his sword back, which... he probably wanted. That was likely for the best. "If you could."

But she was ready. Arcanir had been used against her before, against her will, and it had led to horrible consequences that still haunted her. But that didn't mean she had to let it control her. She still had the power to decide what she wanted to do, and as much as arcanir had hurt her in the past, she was ready to try again for the sake of others, and for herself. She was strong enough. Brave enough.

"We can, and we will. Just not this second." He held out his hand for the blade, and she gave it to him. Once he sheathed it, he laid it at his side once more.

She shivered, lacking for warmth, or maybe the familiar pain of arcanir. She was about to reach for the blanket when instead, Dhuro picked it up and wrapped her in it, his arms around her from behind. He rested his chin on her head, rubbing her upper arms through the blanket, warming her up.

"You're very brave, Bella," he whispered, his voice a comforting caress. "And dedicated, and selfless."

No, she wasn't any of those things. She was *afraid*, both of hurting others and being powerless. It was just that her fear of the former had overwhelmed her fear of the latter. It didn't count.

But she accepted Dhuro's embrace nonetheless. "I didn't mean for the dreams to happen," she whispered back.

"I know you didn't." A heavy silence lingered a moment too long. "I shouldn't have said what I said, about *him*."

She paused, her breath, her heart, everything. Those words were the last ones she'd expected.

At least Janessa would never come up again. "With the arcanir, at least the dreams won't happen again."

His hold loosened, and he turned her face up toward his, holding her chin there. Whether it was his hand or his intent gaze doing the holding, though, she couldn't tell. His golden eyes locked on hers, glowing but soft like an embrace in the fledgling morning light.

"I don't expect you to sleep wearing arcanir. It's agonizing enough during the day. You need to be able to rest." Although he released his hold, she didn't look away.

"What if the dreams happen again? I understand if you... If you..."

If he didn't want to continue this with her. She'd understand, even if she wouldn't prefer it. This wasn't anything serious, but it was better than the cold nights alone.

"If they happen, then they happen. Now that we know what they are, we don't need to talk about them anymore." He said it with confidence, so much so that it sounded like he was reassuring himself more than he was her.

Maybe he was.

She swallowed, with a nod.

If Dhuro had seen her first time meeting Cosimo, what else would he see? She looked away for a moment. It was obvious, wasn't it? If he'd seen their first meeting, he'd see more of them together, wouldn't he? He had to know that. Judging by his reaction, he hadn't been pleased, not just with the dream-seeing, but with *what* he'd seen. Perhaps even a little jealous, as she had been, seeing him with Janessa.

These nights together were worth that frustration to him.

They were worth it to her.

She turned in his embrace, then took his face in her hands, soaking in the intensity of his gaze, the firmness of his stance. She could throw herself at him, and it wouldn't push him an inch unless he desired it. They'd agreed this was only desire, but when he looked at her—only at her—and when he moved for her—only for her—desire was beyond precious. Invaluable.

He didn't move right away, but when she leaned in to kiss him, his eyes slowly closed, shuttering their golden radiance, and his lips gave in to hers.

Letting the blanket fall, she took his mouth with slow, coaxing kisses and slid her fingers into his long hair, fitting her body flush to his as he held her closer. His hold was deliberate, wanting, his hands firm and bold on her body. He knew what he wanted, and he took it. And every part of her enjoyed knowing what he wanted was her.

Outside the tent, a throat cleared.

Bella froze, even if Dhuro didn't. She hissed at him, chiding.

"Look, um," Gavri's voice began, and then she cleared her throat again. "We didn't want to interrupt, but everyone here is ready to head out."

And just like that, Dhuro paused, heaved a sigh, and grimaced. "Be right out," he grumbled back to Gavri. "Tell Zoran I need to talk to him."

Something like a gurgle sounded outside the tent. "Yes, Your Highness," came Gavri's nauseous-sounding reply, before stomping footsteps faded away. Considering what Shrelia had told her, any interaction between Gavri and Zoran had to be difficult.

When she thought of them, of everyone here, she shivered. Until she had arcanir, there was no telling what she might do unintentionally. "Before we leave, you'll help me find some arcanir?"

Dhuro kissed her again, and then regarded her with a glimmer in his eye. What could *almost* resemble a smile.

"What?" She reached for her face, hoping she hadn't drooled in her sleep or something.

"I will. Zoran will help me." A corner of his mouth curled up. "You are brave, sheihan, and I'm fortunate to bed you."

She didn't know that dark-elf word, but more importantly... If he thought he'd be bedding her now, while their entire party awaited them outside, he was dreaming. Ducking her head, she slipped out of his grasp with a half-laugh. "Pray to the Darkness your good fortune holds out 'til tonight."

He let out an exasperated groan, but she only winked back, dressed, then flounced out of the tent.

CHAPTER 13

*D*huro kept a close eye on Bella as they made their way from the campsite in the late-morning drizzle. Raindrops softly pattered on the leafy canopy above them, greening the view of the cloudy gray sky. The air was thick with musty, earthy petrichor, but what he smelled was that first hint of spring, a flowery meadow, slightly sweet and revitalizing. Her. What he smelled was *her*.

Hooded in an emerald-green cloak clasped with an opal brooch, she sat atop Noc, who'd graciously offered to carry her, and chatted with him, Shrelia, and Gavri. She smiled and laughed so freely, her face alight, ringlets of her dark hair escaping her hood.

As they approached a fallen pine, Noc took a small detour around it rather than jumping it. Amused, Dhuro shook his head, stifling a scoff in his throat. There was no question Noc was protective of her; he was her mentor to the life of an Immortal, of a unicorn, but more than that, he seemed to have a genuine fatherly fondness for her.

Dhuro jumped over the tree, and several booted steps followed in succession behind him.

"I'd ask what you're so happy about, but I already know the answer." Grinning, Zoran jogged up next to him and pulled his hood further over his head, stuffing his long hair into it. "Gavri said you wanted to talk? Come now, tell your big brother all about your blossoming love."

"It's not—" he snarled, his face hot, but as heads turned toward him, even Bella's, he rolled his eyes and sighed, rubbing his face. Darkness, Zoran could be annoying. "Would you stop?" he hissed.

"There's nothing to be embarrassed about. True love is a beautiful thing." Zoran elbowed him, but he ignored it, shrugging him off.

Dhuro scrubbed a hand over his forehead as he grimaced. There was a price for asking Zoran's help. There was always a price. "Since we're close to Dun Mozg, you know this area better than I do. Tell me where we can find arcanir, something small, wearable."

Raising a thick eyebrow, Zoran canted his head before a sly grin claimed his mouth. "There's plenty of arcanir in Dun Mozg."

Dhuro sighed what felt like a thousand exhalations at once. "You know I'm not going anywhere near Dun Mozg until Dakkar has been dealt with, one way or another." The last thing he needed was for Queen Nendra to take him prisoner or worse, so that Dakkar could roam free and kill humans, endangering the fate of all dark-elves in Silen.

"I had to try," Zoran said, lazily shrugging a shoulder.

"This is important." Dhuro tipped his chin toward Bella, who listened intently to something Shrelia was saying. Following his line of sight, Zoran too watched her, the levity fading from his facial expression until at last, he frowned.

"She wants to bind her powers with arcanir?" There was no trace of teasing now in Zoran's deep, deadly serious voice. "But for a unicorn, that has to be—"

"Torture. I know." Something ached in his chest, and he kneaded away at it.

When it came to her abilities, he'd been hard on Bella. And when she'd suggested arcanir, it had clearly pained her. He could've fought her on it, spared her, and it would've no doubt been a comfort. But she was someone who prized the lives of others, and she was growing to see beyond the immediate. The safety of his squad, of everyone, was reason enough, but now knowing how devastated she'd be by any loss of life, ignoring the risk her abilities presented would be not only reckless but cold.

Even without the pain of arcanir at night, it still wouldn't be easy to bear. But it would be up to her now to weigh the importance of others over herself. He'd gotten to know her well enough to be certain which she'd choose.

"It's important to her."

Taking a deep breath, Zoran nodded, wiping rain off his brow. "Say no more." He eyed their surroundings, squinting into the distance. "Normally I'd say the market at Dun Mozg, or maybe happening by a human traveling merchant on the main roads. But if you need something now, and near here, I'd say the *janas*."

The janas... He'd heard of them but had never seen them himself. Only about a foot in height, the janas lived in small caves, fairy houses, near a lake of rainbows. They collected treasures of gold, silver, and jewels, stored in chests guarded by monstrous insect-like *maceddas*, which attacked anyone who stole from them. "They're nearby?"

Zoran nodded. "You know the lake in the shadow of the Altobelli Mountains?"

The lake where he'd seen Bella in her human form for the first time? There was no way he could ever forget it. "I do."

Zoran leaned in. "It's also known as Lago dell'Arcobaleno, the rainbow lake. On full moon nights, the janas go there to pray."

"But not the maceddas?" He didn't enjoy the thought of endangering everyone for this, but if they prepared, they could handle it.

"I've heard that they punish greed," Zoran answered pensively, ducking under a low-hanging pine bough. "So, in theory, if you take only what you need and nothing else, they should remain dormant."

What Zoran had *heard* and *in theory*. Dhuro's gut didn't like staking a mission or those under his command on hearsay and theories. But he liked staking them on Bella's fledgling control even less. If this would help keep them all safe from her unpredictable powers, and help her stay in control, then they would devise a plan.

"Their sting is poisonous, Brother. It can affect even us. And the janas have a power of incredible luminance, so if we're caught, they could give away our position easily. Keep that in mind."

Then he'd take the risk himself, and act with an abundance of caution. "I will. Now show me the route. And let's come up with a strategy."

❦

SHAKING OFF THE SLIGHT CHILL, Bella placed her bare foot on a sturdy gnarl of the towering white pine, one arm wrapped around the trunk while she reached up for the lowest branch with the other. She gave it a tug, testing to see whether it would hold her weight, and it felt solid. The bark was rough and sticky, but that wouldn't stand in her way.

Ever since she'd started running away to the woods and the ruins as a girl, she'd wanted to do this. She'd always loved the woods, their quiet serenity and vibrant life, how the trees gave her respite and comfortable solitude, and yet kept her silent company. It had been a sanctuary when home had shaken with arguments about politics and battles. She'd spent days with her back rested against trunks, and days stretched out on the forest floor, gazing up at the leaf-and-sky patchwork of the canopy. But she'd never seen the entire woods from a tall peak, the vast sea of trees and where it ended. She'd imagined it, of course, but her eyes had never feasted upon the sight, upon the new perspective she'd longed for.

Holding the large branch from underneath, she pulled herself up until her arms rested on it, then tried to swing one leg up and over. It took a couple tries, but she caught it at last, and swung herself up onto the branch. Once there, she wedged a foot perpendicular to where the branch met the trunk, and she reached for the next hold.

This wasn't so bad. Silly things had held her back—not wanting to rip her dresses or get them dirty, the notion that she could always do it tomorrow. But she'd had her tomorrows as a human taken away from her once, and there was no telling how long she'd have them now. She had today, however, and she was grateful for it. There was no telling how long she'd have control of her form, so when Dhuro had stopped to confer with Zoran, the perfect chance had presented itself. Of course, the riding habit Gavri had given her, a thing of Princess Alessandra's, made this a bit easier than a dress would have.

Pulling herself up, she ascended, one branch after another, while the trunk narrowed and narrowed.

The wood crunched.

Her heart racing, she reached for another hold and swung herself up quickly.

Beneath where she'd stood, a crack split the bark. The wood there had been damaged. As the wind rustled through the trees, she held on, clinging close to the trunk. Above, the canopy cleared, as if the blue sky hung low enough to touch. She was close, very close, and she wouldn't let one damaged branch and some wind stop her.

Gathering her courage, she looked for the next sturdy branch, and carefully made her way up. Strangely, the top forked, but she was almost there, and the trunk was still about the width of her foot. She'd never climbed a tree before, but that had to be safe, right?

With a nod to herself, she pushed herself the rest of the way, gaze fixed on that nearer and nearer expanse of vivid blue. Almost there, almost there, almost there...

At last, her head poked above the canopy. She held on to the trunk and her handhold, and looked out above the woods.

A verdant ocean of green peaks sprawled as far as she could see, a line that met the bright golds and blues of the sky and stretched to infinity. Puffs of white clouds floated in the dizzying expanse, lined with hints of gray and bright with warm sunlight. With this sublime beauty came awe, but also a peace in her heart she'd never before felt.

She'd known the woods, at least those surrounding Roccalano; she'd known them so well she could've walked them blindfolded. She'd known their solitude and their comfort.

She'd *thought* she'd known the woods.

What she had loved so deeply and so well looked very different from here; she'd had no idea what the woods had actually been. Something that had seemed simple to her, straightforward and familiar, had in truth possessed a vastness and a depth she'd never thought possible.

"Bella," Dhuro's voice called loudly.

With a start, she held on and peered down through the pine branches and their needles to where Dhuro stood next to her discarded boots, his eyes wide.

Her head spun. She wrapped her arms and legs tight around the tree.

Wood crunched. The forked top. Weak after all, despite its thickness.

"Bella," he called again, hoarse. "What are you doing up there?"

Clearly, she was holding on for dear life.

"Climb down. It's not safe."

She tried to look down, but the wood crunched again. Merciful gods and empyreal Veil threads. Her body, arms and legs both, clutched the trunk tightly with no prompting from her. With a swallow, she shook her head. "I... I don't think I can."

All her life, she'd never climbed a tree, and so excited by the prospect, she hadn't thought about the critical part—descending it.

"I'm coming up," he shouted.

Gods above, wouldn't that make the tree *less* stable? She chanced a look down.

Dhuro backed up, then ran toward the trunk. He planted the ball of his foot on it and pushed himself upward. His arms caught the first branch, and in a movement that looked like a dance or a swim, he flowed up the tree. It shook as he ascended, and she squeezed her eyes shut, ignoring the speeding pulse pounding in her ears.

At last the movement stopped.

"Bella," his voice came from below, grave but soft. "That forked top won't support us both. You're going to have to drop down to me."

Drop down? Are you insane? Her arms gripped the trunk closely.

"It's either that or stay up here."

She winced. He could hear her thoughts. Of course he could.

At least if she did stay up here, no one would have to risk their lives to help her acquire arcanir. And she wouldn't endanger anyone with her powers.

"The view *is* breathtaking."

She glanced down at him again. His gaze rested on her backside. "Dhuro," she chided.

He opened his arms wide for her. "Trust me. I won't let you fall to the ground."

He wouldn't—she knew that much.

With a deep breath, she pulled away a little, and the trunk cracked. Gods above, would it give way completely?

"Let go."

Nodding to herself, she squeezed her eyes shut again. Trust Dhuro. She could trust Dhuro.

She let go.

Her body slipped along the pine's coarse bark, and pure terror rushed through her veins like ice. Only a second later, she landed in a strong embrace, held against a firm chest. Dhuro's.

"I've got you," he whispered, that firm chest rising and falling quickly.

Her eyes fluttered open, enough for his intense golden gaze to pierce her, boring into hers. His racing heart beat against her body, slowing a little now, and his grip was tight—a little *too* tight. Although she tried to move her arm, it didn't budge at all in his hold.

That golden intensity in his eyes didn't fade, holding her in place as strongly as his arms. Warmth swelled in her chest, spreading pleasantly. He hadn't wanted her to fall. He *really* hadn't wanted her to fall.

"You've got me," she whispered back, her face feeling stretched from smiling. As she held that intense look of his, his eyes widened and he blinked it away.

She fought another smile. He was relieved she was safe. He was *really* relieved. It seemed she'd made something of an impression on him. At least a little.

Before she could tease him about it, he quickly moved her to his back, wrapping her arms around his neck. She locked her legs around his waist instinctively, and he shifted them slightly.

"I'm taking us down."

No better words had ever been spoken. Closing her eyes, she held on tight as he began the descent.

"What were you doing up here?"

She fought back a scoff at herself. "I'm sure you'll think it's foolish, but I've always wanted to climb a tree and I never have. I wanted to see the woods from above and experience them in a new way for the first time."

A laugh rumbled beneath her.

"I knew you'd think that." She sighed, hiding her face in his hair. Not that he could see it.

"No, it's not that." He paused in his descent. "It's just... When I first visited the sky realm, I loved it. But among my people, I'm a volodar, a hunter. I ended up spending much of my days up in a tree, and it became... common."

"I'd love to do this every day," she blurted. "If I could climb down, I mean."

He laughed again. "That is an important part."

Was he laughing at her?

"How was it? At the top?" He moved beneath her again, resuming the descent.

"It was..." There had been so many feelings, she wasn't sure how to describe it. "It was peaceful, unlike anything I've ever felt. And I saw a side of the forest I've never imagined, like seeing a color I didn't know existed. I've lived in Silen all my life, but it's as though I've just seen it for the first time."

"You thought you knew the woods," he agreed, "but you realized they were different, yet not unsettling. Beautiful."

What she'd thought she'd understood had changed before her very eyes, but it hadn't scared her. It had dazzled her.

He stopped moving. "You can let go. We're at the bottom."

She cracked her eyes open, and the forest was again what she'd always known. The view at the top had been beautiful, but the ground felt safe. It would be some time before she found the courage to climb up again. Some time, and probably a lesson or two in climbing back down.

She let her feet find the cool dirt and slipped her arms free of Dhuro's neck. As he turned to face her, she wobbled a little, and his hands on her waist steadied her.

"Thank you," she said softly, avoiding his gaze.

He gently raised her chin, holding it up until she met his eyes. They weren't giving her the scolding glare she might have expected, but gleaming half-moons. He stroked a slow caress along her jaw. "You see the world in a way I don't, sheihan."

If she'd seen it the way he had, she might have thought ahead to knowing how to climb down. And what did "sheihan" mean? He'd called her that before, when he'd very optimistically tried to charm her into bed. She had been tempted then, and as she looked him over—gods above—she was tempted now.

There was a spark in his eyes, and the slightest mischievous upturn of his lips. Had he heard that thought, too?

He nodded, giving her a pleased once-over. "Don't worry. Zoran and I have a plan for helping you control your abilities," he said, but his gaze lowered to her lips. "I was just coming to get you."

"Then let's go," she breathed. Being this close to him was dizzying.

"You might want to put on your boots first." His mouth twitched in an almost-smile as he leaned in and kissed her, his lips meeting hers gently. As he pulled her in close, deepening the kiss, her hand slipped up his chest toward his face. He caught her wrist in a loose grip.

She blinked up at him as he raised an eyebrow. "What is it?"

A soft huff, and he tipped his head toward her hand. Her dirty, sticky hand. "I like where this is going, sheihan, but tell me, have you ever tried to get sap out of hair?"

❦

BELLA SAT ON THE GROUND, turned away from the fading-ember light of the sunset. All around her were the other dark-elves, Noc, and Shrelia, and none of them seemed disturbed by the plan Dhuro and Zoran had shared.

She shook her head, burying her fingers in the leafy deadfall. "We should try asking the janas for arcanir."

A few heads turned to her, and Kinga scoffed under her breath, rolling her eyes.

"We can't," Dhuro said, crossing his arms, and all eyes turned to him. "They have claws that can hew stone, and they'd attack us on sight, and sic all the maceddas on us. The janas are very insular, they don't trade, and they trust only children."

"Does having the worldview of a child count?" Kinga asked, with an amused pout, glancing back at her.

Gods above, this woman—

"I'm sure you'd be convincing, but no." There was a conspiratorial gleam in Dhuro's eye as he caught Bella's gaze. Although Kinga opened her mouth, he continued, "The only thing janas hate more than flying creatures is us, both elves and humans. We're wicked in their eyes, and they'd attack us on sight. So stay hidden. Remember, if we're separated, we'll meet on the southern shore of the lake."

While the dark-elf squad prepared, Bella tossed a handful of leaves with a sigh and rose to her feet.

Don't let the silly dark-elf get to you, Shrelia chimed, flitting to her shoulder, where she sat on the cloak's grass-green wool and held on. *He sounds grouchy as always, but did you notice the plan doesn't involve fighting anyone?*

That was true. Was that just for the sake of the mission, or was it for her, too? *I just don't want anyone hurt on my account. Not because of my powers, and not to help bind them, either.*

It's a solid plan, Noc added, nudging her with his nose. *Granted, it would be better if you were going with us to the lake instead of to the domus, the fairy houses where the janas live.*

Noc and Shrelia would await them at the meeting point, lest his size and her light give them away. But Zoran had insisted, despite Dhuro's protests to the contrary, that Bella be present, since the treasure's guardians would only allow taking for true need, and she was the one who needed the arcanir.

The last thing she'd ever want would be for Dhuro to risk his life doing something she needed to do.

It's my responsibility to be there, she said to both Noc and Shrelia, giving him a hug while Shrelia held on to her shoulder. *I wouldn't expect others to take risks for me while I wait in safety.*

You'll be safe with Dhuro and Zoran. Noc huffed into her hair, making her laugh. *Because if not, they know to expect a set of hooves kicking in unfortunate places.*

The silly dark-elf makes a good shield, at least! Shrelia added, fluttering over to nestle between Noc's ears, her hair a shock of pink against his midnight-black mane.

Beside her, a shadow loomed—Dhuro, his arms still crossed, his face hard. He rubbed his jaw with one clawed hand, regarding her ruminatively.

"Go with them," he said quietly.

She frowned. "But Zoran said—"

"I know what Zoran said," he hissed under his breath, then leaned in as his pale eyebrows drew together. "Go anyway."

She looked back over her shoulder at the dark-elf squad and Zoran, who looked right back at her and held her gaze. If she was needed, she wasn't about to run, not even if Dhuro asked her to. She rose on her tiptoes and kissed his cheek softly, and although he stared at her with full golden intensity, she slipped away toward Zoran and the rest of the squad.

"Are you ready, Arabella?" Zoran asked her, approaching one side of her just as Dhuro moved to the other, scowling.

"Yes." She faced the squad. "I want to thank all of you for doing this. You didn't have to, but I appreciate that you are."

While some of them nodded in reply, Kinga leaned back, rolling her eyes. "I don't think you understand what 'orders' are."

Gavri elbowed her, receiving a snarl in reply. Dhuro turned his scowl on Kinga, who shrugged a shoulder and lowered her gaze. Despite her biting words, Kinga had been nothing but a dedicated warrior this entire journey so far, with her own reasons for serving, even if they didn't include the sake of an incompetent new unicorn.

"Let's get into position," Dhuro ordered. With a nod, Zoran headed among the pines, and the squad followed.

Looking her over with a creased brow, Dhuro held out his hand to her. She pulled up her hood—hopefully the green wool would conceal her well enough—and joined her hand with his.

Through the underbrush and among the darkness of towering trees in the night, he led her carefully, holding back branches and taking her around stones and fallen deadwood. All the while, his large hand held hers, warm and secure, and an old familiar sensation feathered over her skin, one she had never again expected to feel, a frisson not unlike a soft breath over bare flesh.

She swallowed, but her throat was tight, like her chest. Something had spread its wings there, and the emptiness she had become so accustomed to was quickly disappearing.

The faint silhouettes ahead of her lowered, and Dhuro nudged her to follow suit. As they all crept closer—just beyond the pines—the foothills came into view, low and sprawling at the base of the mountain.

He swept her slowly behind him as he took a position behind a tree and a large shrub, and all the dark-elves followed suit. Nothing sounded, not a twig breaking, not leather creaking, not even a breath. In the dead silence, her own breath and the rise and fall of her chest was clumsy and oafish, but she did her best.

As she stared into the distance, the view was clearer than expected; earlier today, Noc had told her that unicorns had enhanced senses, in addition to the ability to hear thoughts and speak them to other minds. He'd said they could influence emotions, move or control objects with their minds, create visions, heal others, and for the strongest, oldest, and most skilled, even cross great spans of time and space in an instant. And that was just what he knew—he'd said there was more that only the unicorns themselves could tell her.

It had been hard to believe all of that was possible, but as she waited here, looking hundreds of yards ahead at a clear sight, more than she'd ever believed was truly possible.

Beyond the sloping low foothills, tucked into the rough granite higher up, were small holes, entrances to what Zoran had called the domus.

A faint luminance glowed from within the caves, but slowly its radiance intensified, brighter and brighter, like darkness giving life to stars. To a soothing, melodious song, tiny pale blue-haired forms emerged, their skin so light it was translucent, clad in the finest linen and brocade garb accented with golden buttons, fit for a royal, fit for a deity. With silvery eyes, they surveyed the foothills, in their small arms bearing loaves of wafer-thin bread, hoards of jewels, bolts of fine cloth, and treasures of silver and gold.

Zoran had said that on nights like this, the janas brought offerings to the tower-temple of their mother goddess, Jana Mariedda, whom men had turned savage, but whom the generosity of a child had restored.

Beneath the full moon, at least a hundred janas gathered, maybe more, weaving into a line that threaded into the hills, to the steep, perilous, thorny paths. They moved in a slow, shining procession, with the occasional flutter of delicate iridescent wings that caught the moonlight like resplendent gossamer.

It was the most beautiful thing she'd ever seen. An awed sigh quivered off her lips, and Dhuro wrapped her closer, folded her into the circle of his arms and against his large frame. She hadn't meant to make a sound—had the janas heard? But when she glanced up at him, as the lambent light faded away, his eyes were soft, their gold warm, inviting her to melt into him, into his embrace.

She'd been held like this before, had felt safe, at peace, as though the distinct body she inhabited didn't confine her at all, because some part of her was greater, an aura beyond, and it existed in the union of a loving embrace. It was tempting to give in to, alluring, like a warm bed on a cold morning. But it wasn't safe at all. At any moment, it could be taken away, lost, forever. It was an illusion, and as unreal as illusion was, the pain of its truth was excruciatingly keen, and very real.

A shiver trembled up her spine, and Dhuro rubbed her back with a gentle hand. He thought she'd caught a chill, maybe. And it was a kind of chill, she supposed, but not one that could be soothed away with a caress... no matter how alluring.

At last, the radiance of the janas vanished, leaving only the night behind. Stillness and silence claimed the space of a breath, and then carefully, Dhuro released her from his embrace. His hands on her shoulders, he steadied her, urged her not to move, until another figure approached with gentle, barely audible footfalls. Gavri.

With a nod, Gavri moved next to her, palm hovering over the hilt of her vjernost blade. Dhuro dipped his head in response to them both, and with a final, lingering look at her—gods, she didn't want him to do this—he forged ahead with the rest of the squad.

Her foot took a step forward of its own volition, as eager to stop him as she was, but Gavri grasped her arm, turning to her with a vehement shake of her head.

For a moment, the question of how strong Gavri's hold truly was flashed into her head. For a brief moment.

This was about his life, his safety, his protection. And as badly as she wanted to race after him to stop him, to protect him, the way to do it was complete antithesis to what she felt.

No, to truly protect him, she had to refrain from interfering. Any wayward move now only served to endanger him, and his plan was sound.

Once this was done, it *would* protect him from the unpredictability of her powers.

Just have faith, she told herself. *Try to have faith.*

Gavri's gaze flickered to hers, eyebrows knitting together, but then she bobbed her head.

In reply. To her thought.

Bella's heart sank, but while Dhuro and the rest of the squad were out there, she wouldn't feel sorry for herself. She wouldn't *dare* feel sorry for herself.

She squinted across the distance, where they crept toward the domus, and the shadows inked in around them.

CHAPTER 14

The janas' soothing song was faint but still present as Dhuro shoved his hand into the first cave entrance, feeling around for chests of treasure, just as the rest of his squad did. He didn't like this position, out and exposed on the foothills, but Valka kept a lookout and gave no sign of danger. Still, despite the moon above them in the clear night sky, the hills cast a shadow over a swaying field of tall grasses, and that darkness closed in like a pack of hungry wolves.

At last, his fingers closed around the cold smoothness of a metallic box, and he tried to pull it out. Clutched in his grip, it was too big to take through the domu's entrance. *Shit.* He gritted his teeth and readjusted his grip until finally it fit through, a golden cask big enough to contain a dagger, heavy enough to be full with coin. Engravings wrapped the exterior, depicting winged demons with long, sharp teeth, rubies inlaid for eyes, and extended from their mouths—large stingers, nearly as big and tall as their bodies. The maceddas.

In his decades as a hunter and his travels with Ata and Dakkar, he'd seen many things, but none so grotesque, so chilling, as this. A warning, clear as spring water, deadly as Deep-spider venom.

Pushing past the dread, he cracked open the box. A bounty of jewels, gold, and silver, among trinkets and baubles, shimmered inside. None of it shone the telltale sage of arcanir they sought, but with a deep breath, he sifted his bare fingers through it, hoping to feel the same mild sting his vjernost blade gave him.

Nothing.

The janas' distant song continued—he and his squad remained undetected, for now. But the janas would return, and considering their steel claws and the lethal maceddas at their call, he didn't want to still be here when they did.

With a grunt, he slammed the cask shut, shoved it back into the domu, and crept to the next entrance in the faint silvery moon glow. All around him, his squad did the same, rifling through casks of various treasures and coming up empty-handed.

He shoved his arm into the next domu and removed a silver box, casting a quick glance at Valka to check for any changes. Unmoving, she peered out into the darkness with squinted eyes, while the rest of the squad advanced to the remaining domus. He opened the box in his hand, shifting pearls and coins, until—

A tingle, on his fingertip.

His chest tightening, he sifted the other treasure away to reveal a tiny stud earring—a pearl, at first glance. But he touched it again, and sure as the Stone, it had the feel of arcanir.

Darkness, they'd done it.

Zoran looked up from the box he was searching, and Dhuro caught his gaze, then glanced at the one he held and nodded. Zoran dipped his chin, grinning broadly. He had been right after all. Now they just needed Bella to take the earring from this box, return the rest, and leave no trace behind.

With a slow exhalation, he began to look back to the tree line toward Bella, but Valka crouched and signaled.

One hand holding her bow, she pointed the other into the shadowed grasses, her thumb down and all other fingers curled.

Enemy in sight.

Shit.

The enemy.

But no, the janas' song still carried on the air—this wasn't them. This had to be *another* enemy.

Shit, shit, shit.

A quick glance to the tree line—Bella was safe.

Holding the box behind a pillar of granite, he raised his arm over-head, palm front, and waved in large circles as eyes turned to him, then pointed to where Gavri and Bella remained hidden among the trees. Everyone needed to move into their concealment.

His squad set down the boxes and crept toward the rally point, with careful eyes on the shadows Valka had indicated. With any luck, they'd fall back before the enemy caught sight of them.

The box in his hand weighed heavily. There was a chance that taking it away to Bella would unleash the wrath of the maceddas. But there was no telling what threats awaited in the shadows. He wasn't about to leave what she needed here.

Tucking it into his jerkin, he stalked toward the trees, with Valka bringing up the rear.

Grasses rustled. Moonlight refracted off steel as swift knives cut the air.

Drawing his vjernost blade in an instant, he parried one. Valka took another in the shoulder. She kept retreating, casting him a look with a nod to indicate she remained able.

Out here in the open, they were easy targets. And unless he brought this arcanir to Bella, there was no telling what her powers might do.

Dhuro, watch out! Bella's voice screamed frantically in his head.

He hurried backward, batting away another throwing knife. A second knife caught him in the side, sharpness searing under his rib.

A cry lanced through his mind, shrill, tremulous, agonized. *Ulsinael,* he prayed, *keep her safe, keep her hidden.*

He yanked the blade out, clenching his teeth, as a team of black-clad combatants emerged from the shadows. Humans.

Valka loosed an arrow, hitting an enemy in the thigh, and didn't stop, loosing shot after shot as she secured their exit. As an enemy lunged at her, she drew her blade and met a strike with a metallic clang and a parry. Zoran, Kinga, and Marysia defended against their attackers.

The janas' song stopped.

His legs already closed the distance when another slash came down on Valka. He met the blade with his own, instinct taking over. With her shoulder injury, she wouldn't last long in battle, even against this human.

A flurry of thoughts raced through his head in an instant: The janas were coming. They'd unleash the maceddas. And these human attackers were here for Bella's head.

He dodged a pommel strike and kicked the human right in the chest. Dhuro shoved the silver box against Valka. "Go," he gritted out.

A quick nod and she was gone.

The human swept his blade low. Dhuro moved to defend when a punch thudded against his wounded side. Bright white seared his vision. His body contracted, but he resisted, defending. Another enemy. They would be overrun.

As he fought, his foot landed on something hard—a box.

A radiant light shone from the steep path up the foothills. The janas were coming.

He grabbed the box, yanked it open, and threw it toward the humans, scattering all its shimmering contents at them. A few sets of eyes widened, and another spread of jewels and precious metals sparkled in the moonlight as they flew at the humans.

Heart pounding, he ran as Kinga and Zoran tossed the contents of two more boxes and followed suit.

A cacophony of shrieks ripped through the air, ear-splitting and eerie, echoing from the domus. From the bleak darkness of their holes, shadows spilled out, and slowly, slowly, two points that elongated, extended into thin antennae.

From the paths, the shining janas charged downward, their sharp claws glinting in the moonlight, their cry high-pitched and legion. They sped at the humans, some of whom bore armfuls of treasure.

Dhuro and his squad nearly reached the trees when silhouettes blotted out the moonlight. Massive wings catching the air, griffins descended—at least a dozen of them with riders.

He hissed, keeping pressure on his wound, retreating into the woods as large insect-like heads emerged from the domus, with blood-red eyes glowing in faces of pure darkness.

"There!" one of the griffin riders shouted, urging her beastly mount faster, pointing directly at him.

BELLA YANKED at her arm in Gavri's firm grasp as Dhuro and the others ran for the trees, but to no avail. He was hurt!

"Let me go," she demanded, digging her heels in as she pulled.

Gavri didn't answer and didn't let go, her stance solid, stony. Dhuro and the other dark-elves were in danger! Didn't she care?

A shadow squad of assassins chased them.

A glowing army closed in from the foothills.

A fleet of winged beasts and their riders descended from the night sky.

And from the entrances of the domus, monsters emerged, demonic and deadly, wings buzzing and eyes gleaming red. The maceddas.

Dhuro clutched at his side, where glistening blood seeped down his jerkin, and her heart twisted in her chest, pounding harder for every second he wasn't in her arms. War, the legacy of her family, followed her everywhere. Even here, after Dhuro.

Trembling uncontrollably, she swept a shaky hand across her forehead. Every part of her screamed to do something, *anything*, but gods above, if she immobilized Dhuro as she had the first time, there was no telling what could happen. She couldn't risk it.

Couldn't risk *him*.

As soon as he reached the woods, he took a silvery box from Valka—who had been injured too—and he tucked it into his jerkin. Only then did Gavri let her go.

She fell onto the ferns, into the dirt and roots, but scrambled up and ran to him. "Dhuro, are you—"

Before she could finish her question, he picked her up and threw her over his shoulder, then ran among the pines, deeper into the woods. Carrying her, his wounded side would only bleed more heavily.

"Dhuro," she cried. "Put me down—I can run on my own!"

"Hush," he hissed, so sharply that she heeded him. He picked up the pace, and she jostled atop him, catching only glimpses of what unfolded behind them.

The other dark-elves fled with them in teams of two. Past their swiftly running forms, the radiance of the janas crashed against the shadow of the human assassins at the base of the foothills. The insect-like monsters from the domus clashed with the griffins and their riders, silhouetted against the moon.

A loud buzz trailed them, but she could only catch four glowing red pinpricks in the dark as she bobbed on Dhuro's shoulder like a sack of stolen silver.

An eagle-like cry resounded above them, beyond the coniferous canopy.

For a moment, the jostling stopped as they soared over a fallen pine. Dhuro raised a hand and gestured something. He landed hard, and she braced on his back as best as she could.

The teams of dark-elves broke off in different directions, roaring calls booming from each except Dhuro. He remained silent.

They were leading the enemies away. Decoys, for her sake.

Dhuro and Valka injured. Zoran, Gavri, Marysia, Danika, Halina, and even Kinga risked their lives for her.

But the red pinpricks behind them, two sets of two, only grew bigger. *Dhuro,* she thought, as loudly as she could, *the maceddas are still following us. They're gaining.* She listened hard, straining; this was much more difficult in her human body.

If you can hear me, Bella, his voice rumbled into her mind, *stay quiet. If they catch us, hide. I will deal with them.*

Perhaps her powers, if she could summon them, would help, but the last thing they needed was another risk. If Dhuro said he would deal with them, then she trusted him.

The two monsters stayed on their trail. *Why are the maceddas only chasing us?*

His body went rigid beneath her, and a bough of pine needles raked across her back as he changed direction. He leaped over the massive exposed roots of an ancient pine, then set her down.

Breathing hard, he tossed the silver box at her, drew his vjernost blade and his dagger, and stood ready. "You'll feel the arcanir earring when you touch it. Take only that, then throw the box as far as you can."

Bewildered, she had a dozen questions, but her fingers did as he instructed. She opened the box to reveal a dense pile of jewelry and valuables—she was to find a single earring in this?

Dhuro's blade sliced through the air, striking a hard exoskeleton with a clank. Her heart racing, she sifted her fingers frantically through the smooth metals and jewels.

He ducked a stinger the size of his head, then plunged his vjernost blade into the mouth of the other macedda. Its deafening shriek pierced the woods as he rolled, yanking at his blade stuck in the monster's body.

Another buzz closed in from the distance.

Her fingertip brushed something that sent a lightning bolt up her hand. Arcanir. Had to be. Her grasp closed around it, a small bead or pearl. She plucked it out and shut the box.

"Run, Bella!" Dhuro shouted.

A stinger charged toward her face, a gaping maw full of razor teeth, big enough to close on her head.

Screaming, she held up the silver box as her eyes shut of their own volition. Teeth grated against metal. It pushed against her, pressing her into hard roots and pebbled dirt, its buzz vibrating her ears, its screech rattling her bones, and gods, it was going to—it would—

Teeth squealed along silver as it scraped down—

Hot tears fled her eyes as innumerable knives plunged into her shoulder. An unbearable heat seared her flesh like acid.

Her body wanted to break out of her skin; she cried out, her voice tearing from her throat like life from the dead. *Help! Please, anyone... Please—*

CHAPTER 15

*H*er scream shook him to his core, a strike splitting his heart. She struggled beneath the macedda with nowhere to go.

His blood roaring in his ears, Dhuro dodged a sting from the macedda above him and buried his dagger into its eye. It shrieked, clawing his hand and pulling back. No sword. No dagger.

Bella—

He leaped to his feet and over the pine's massive exposed roots, tackling the macedda pinning her. With his bare hands, he grabbed its stinger with one and plunged his claws into the macedda's head with the other, spearing them in again and again, ignoring the painful impact of the exoskeleton as some points found vulnerable, wet targets.

An unbearable screech pierced his ears, its limbs clawed at his body, and sticky ichor spattered his face, but he didn't stop until it no longer moved.

At last, its remains lay in a sprawling, gore-strewn mess, and he caught a breath, his gaze snapping to Bella, who—

Who didn't move either. She lay curled up, her form small.

The macedda's sting was lethal, Zoran had said.

Deep, Darkness, and Holy Ulsinael—

Dragging a wet sleeve across his face, he scrambled over to her and carefully rolled her into his hold. "Bella?" he asked, low, his voice breaking.

With her eyes closed, her body limp, something inside of him clenched and broke. A shudder tore through him, but he leaned in close to her nose.

Breath. Faint, but present.

A relieved exhalation left his lips. She was alive. *Praise the Dark.*

The sting was large, the size of a wolf's bite, and although he knew how to treat the bites of at least four dozen native species, all of that was useless to her. The best he could do was ensure the wound stayed clean.

In her grasp, she held the silver box, but two of her fingers curled tight. He opened them, revealing the arcanir earring, then stashed it in his pocket for her.

A buzz sounded in the woods. He went rigid as the Stone. More maceddas. And beyond them, the din of battle.

Rushing, he took the silver box from her grasp and threw it, as hard and as far as he could. They needed to get away from here as fast as possible; there was no telling who or what had heard them.

He scooped her up, minding her wound, then retraced his steps to his stuck vjernost blade. Bracing his foot on the dead macedda, he dragged out his blade, swiped it on his trousers and sheathed it, then took off for the rendezvous point.

Racing through the dark woods, he left the buzz of the maceddas behind, but shadows still blotted out the night sky above them—griffin riders seeking them.

He'd been a hunter nearly all his life and knew how to go unseen, especially from flying beasts. Keeping in the shadows and beneath the tree canopy's concealment, he made his way around the base of the mountain, casting glances to check on Bella from time to time. Her condition hadn't changed, but the sooner he reached the unicorns, the better. Without the wisdom of Nozva Rozkveta's oldest dark-elf and elder mystic, Xira, the unicorn herd was their best chance.

If this had been Vadiha, or Veron, or any of his other siblings, this would've never even happened. Mati had kept expectations for him low, and Darkness, did he meet them. Although others of his family chose to remain volodari and hunt for the queendom, if they had chosen battle,

Mati would have granted them distinguished positions in their military. Because *they* were capable.

For him, remaining a volodar wasn't a choice. It was a consequence.

Not capable enough to lead. Not smart enough. Not good enough.

This mission had been his chance to prove himself to her, to earn his place and stand tall beside his siblings. Laughable. Like him, it had been a failure from the start. And not only would he fall miserably short of proving himself to Mati, but Bella—whom he should've kept safe, protected—was paying the price. He wasn't good enough for her either. Not even good enough to be her shield.

Two griffins flew overhead. He paused in the shadow of a white pine, deathly still. In his arms, Bella breathed irregularly, her brow furrowed.

He wasn't good enough, but until she was with the unicorn herd, he was all she had, and he would try his best for her. He wasn't the man she deserved, but right now, he was the one she had. *Whatever you need.*

Not far from here was a river that would lead directly to their rendezvous point by the lake. He just had to cross the sparser woods before him to get there, edge around a small glade ahead.

With a deep breath, he picked a careful path in the shadows, pausing when anything crossed overhead. A branch snapped in the trees behind them, and he ducked behind a trunk, then froze. He listened, but no more sound came.

An animal?

Scenting the air, he clenched his teeth. Not only was the odor of macedda ichor overpowering—his arms were coated to the elbow—but he was upwind.

Shit.

An animal or an enemy, and considering the maceddas and the janas weren't stealthy, that meant human or elf.

He glanced down at Bella, poisoned with macedda venom. There would be no waiting this out and hiding. He'd either have to set her down and engage, or take his chances and run. Already injured, missing his dagger, and with Bella incapacitated, combat posed too many risks.

His face tight, he took in the silence for a moment longer, then bolted.

Branches cracked behind him. Pine needles swished.

Like a stygian wind, a form leaped to the ground before him, rolling to a stop with a dark, smooth laugh. He knew that voice.

"Dakkar," he hissed.

Brushing off his leathers, Dakkar straightened, arms wide, a rictus grin splitting his mouth. He nodded toward Bella and rubbed his square jaw. "My, my, what strange company you keep, Dhuro."

He held Bella closer, although his fingers ached for his vjernost blade. This was *Dakkar*, his best friend since they were children, and the man Mati had sent him to kill.

Dakkar rested his hands on the hilts of his twin blades, then strolled confidently before him, as if he hadn't a care in the world. "When my warriors said they'd fought you, I couldn't believe it. I didn't believe it was really you. I had to see for myself, my brother casting off the mantle of the volodar for the kuvar, just as he'd always wanted? Congratulations are in order, my brother."

Long ago, he'd shared those dreams with Dakkar, who'd been his closest ally, who'd supported him with all he had. They'd been true brothers in all but blood.

But Dakkar endangered all dark-elves. He endangered Nozva Rozkveta. He endangered Bella, right now.

"Do you need an army to congratulate me?" Dhuro asked, forcing a casual tone. He'd had a chance of escape, maybe, when it had been a nameless, faceless nobody pursuing him through the forest here. But injured, with Bella at risk, he had no chance at all of beating Dakkar at his best. This was now a game of negotiation, evasion, and survival.

"Oh, they would all congratulate you, I'm sure," Dakkar said with a lilt, slowly approaching. With every step, Dhuro matched with a retreating step until Dakkar paused and beamed a close-mouthed grin. "I know she only *looks* human, Brother. Although I wonder if they can truly shed their treacherous nature, even when gifted an immortal life."

Treacherous? He could've laughed. Dakkar had turned on the interests of all his people, and he spoke of treachery? "It is those treacherous humans that help us survive this new world."

Dakkar puffed, eyeing him peripherally as he paced lackadaisically. "Help? We are dark-elves, Brother. Looking for *help* has never been our way. We take what we need"—he grasped a fistful of air and tightened—

"but some of our leaders have fallen short of their foremothers. And it falls to me and my army to strengthen them."

He dared call Mati and his own mother weak? "Then challenge them. Any of them. You speak of 'our way.' The Ring, too, is our way."

"There are no dark-elf kings, Brother," Dakkar bit out, his light-hearted mask slipping for a moment. "I use the paths open to me."

It was true that their people did not have kings; yet if a man could not take the rulership, that didn't make treason just. Legitimate means were attempting to win the minds of their queens and their people, not forcing their hands by committing atrocities. "When your queen and your people don't agree with you, that doesn't mean you're justified in forcing your way."

"They seem to believe I am." Dakkar held up his hands at his sides, looking up at the sky, where griffins soared with their riders. "And you, my brother, you really don't agree? You'd rather go to the humans and kiss the ring than take what's rightfully ours?"

Dhuro shook his head. What could have possibly taken Dakkar to this extreme? A man who'd loved nature, who'd mingled with humans and Immortals of all kinds?

"The first woman I ever truly loved was a human," Dakkar said pensively, letting his gaze rest on Bella's face. "What she'd really been after was the lifebond, and when she got it, she was gone. Immortal life. It had always been about what she could take."

Human—after a lifebond—but it couldn't be. His mouth went dry, and he swallowed. "Janessa?" he croaked.

Dakkar caught his eye and nodded. "The deceitful bitch."

His youth came rushing back to him, dizzying and storming. Nights with Janessa, when she'd made him feel like he was everything to her, and the thrill of keeping their relationship a secret, as she'd suggested. Nights he hadn't seen her—had Dakkar been gone, too? Had she played them both, gambling on the odds of winning immortality from one or the other?

And Dakkar—she'd managed to trick him into a lifebond.

"You don't understand the disloyalty of humans," Dakkar bit out to him. "They can't help themselves."

"I do know the disloyalty of humans," he hissed back to Dakkar. Ignoring the roar of blood pounding in his ears, he pushed on. "While neither of us knew, Janessa attempted the same thing with both you and me."

Dakkar's eyes bulged, and he blinked over them rapidly. "She... You... what?"

"I found out she had another lover, and I left her. I never imagined it had been you." Before the Sundering, humans and Immortals had mingled, and dark-elves hadn't been uncommon in the sky realm, but Janessa had been beyond bold to target the two of them, as close as they were. And both of them had been as oblivious as she had been bold.

Although he'd felt betrayed then and might have clawed out her *lover's* heart in the moment, now there was nothing left in him for her. No feeling toward her. No burning desire to fight over her.

All that remained was a hollow ache, for the way she'd broken his best friend.

"Then you were smart enough to do what I couldn't. You're well rid of her." Dakkar strolled right in front of him, faced him squarely, and tightened the grip on each sword's hilt.

He was well rid of her. Dakkar, however, lifebonded as he was, never would be.

"Now, Dhuro, you choose. I know where you're going and whose aid you plan to beg. Will you really cast aside your loyal brother and your people's values to side with these duplicitous weaklings? Or will you join me, and fight beside your people to take what's rightfully ours?"

Even if he and Bella went with Dakkar as a pretense, there was no telling what would happen to Bella; if Dakkar wanted to stop him from getting to the unicorns, then Bella wouldn't receive their aid. And they were her strongest chance of surviving the venom.

The picture of health, Dakkar stood tall, his light armor unblemished, with both blades at hand. Between them lay leafy ferns and root-laden dirt, with the watchful pines edging the glade, their silent spectators.

Bleeding, down a weapon, and winded, Dhuro faced him.

He had no chance at all of beating Dakkar at his best.

But he looked down at Bella and her still slumbering face. *Whatever you need, Bella.* He had no chance, but he would give everything he had.

One last try. "You won't allow even your so-called brother to pass?"

Dakkar drew in a lengthy breath, then shook his head. "You know I can't. You'll go straight to *them*." Dakkar stared at Bella. "Join me, or defeat me."

Long, long before now, Janessa had set them at odds, and neither of them had even realized it. But here they were, at long last to cross swords. Yes, Janessa had set it in motion, Mati had ordered it, but his reason—his true reason—graced his arms, and to get her even a second more of life, he'd fight Dakkar. He'd fight Dakkar a thousand times.

He laid Bella down against a tree trunk and placed the arcanir earring in her palm, closing it tight, then stood. His hand on his vjernost blade's hilt, he stared down Dakkar, shifting the dry dirt with his boot. "Come, then. Come test the sword-arm I honed training with you."

His mouth a grim line, Dakkar pulled his twin blades from their scabbards, flourishing them both, but then tossed one aside.

So he had his pride, at least—he could afford it.

Narrowing his eyes, Dhuro drew his blade and leveled it at Dakkar.

For a moment, silence claimed the small glade. Dakkar's gaze bored into him, but he only watched Dakkar's form for any sign of movement.

A sharp cry rang out above them, a griffin's call.

Dakkar sprang at him, whirling his sword. Parrying down and to the outside, Dhuro struck back with a riposte that Dakkar ducked. In the same instant, Dhuro kicked up dirt into Dakkar's face, and set upon him with strike after strike, hit after hit, unrelenting on the offensive, his best strategy.

Meeting his strikes with blocks, Dakkar moved to slash right—but no, a feint—Dakkar hit him with a pommel strike right in his wound.

Pure, bright agony seized his body, and he hissed as it curled of its own volition, backing up to stay out of Dakkar's range.

Dakkar swept the dirt off his face, his eyes watering. "Where's your honor, Brother?"

"Where's yours?" he snarled back.

Dakkar re-engaged with a flurry of quick strikes that he tried to block, but Dakkar cut him once, again, again. Dakkar was toying with him, and no more, like a cat with a wounded bird. On the defensive, Dhuro angled toward a dead tree. A cut at his arm, a slice to his side, to his thigh—

Dakkar thrust his sword forward—

With a bloom of pain to his palms, Dhuro caught it and then Dakkar's arm, redirecting the thrust into the tree trunk behind him. He followed with a closed-fist hammer strike to Dakkar's temple, but it hit his jaw.

Dakkar leaped back, and Dhuro lunged for him, but not in time.

Shit.

"Not bad, Brother." He spat blood on the forest floor. Huffing a half-laugh, Dakkar kicked up his other sword and caught it, then drew a dagger from his belt. "But I think this ends now."

Dhuro retreated toward the tree, holding back a wince, and yanked out Dakkar's second vjernost blade, then flourished both as Dakkar had, pushing the bravado. Holding one ready for parrying, he leveled the other at Dakkar. "I think so, too."

Dakkar's eyebrows shot up for a brief moment before he engaged.

Twigs snapped overhead, closer and closer, and as Dhuro pulled back, a dark blur tackled Dakkar to the ground. Dakkar roared a deafening dark-elf call to his army, but it was cut short with a punch.

"Disappear!" Zoran bellowed, rolling in the dirt fighting with Dakkar.

Shoving his vjernost blade into its sheath and Dakkar's into his belt, Dhuro rushed to Bella and scooped her up, running for the woods, for the river, as fast and as far as he could.

CHAPTER 16

*E*verything inside of her burned as Bella cracked open her eyes, blinking through the blur at Dhuro's face above her. His eyebrows sloped down low over his eyes, tight, determined, and his hands holding her so securely were stained black, reeked of blood and musty ichor, and seeped red against her skin and clothes. He gently rearranged her to close her fist, where she grasped something small and delicate.

"You're... bleeding..." she tried to say, but the words came out slurred.

"Rest," he said softly, peering down at her with perturbed eyes, flashes of shimmer caught in the moon's scattered light. "Don't overexert yourself."

Overexert...? The last thing she remembered was...the air vibrating around her, red eyes, and teeth, sharp teeth. She shuddered violently. Her entire shoulder burned, and as she shifted, it stung sharply.

"You're safe," Dhuro whispered, holding her closer, although his mouth pressed into a thin line. "We are far from there now. I'm taking you to the unicorns. They'll know how to handle the venom."

The venom. Gods above, the maceddas' *lethal* venom. *Am I going to die?*

"No, you're not," he said, his voice firm, unwavering. "I make you this promise, Bella: whatever you need, I will give you."

She believed him.

When the macedda had set upon her, it felt like the end. But she was in Dhuro's arms. He'd saved her.

She must have passed out, and he'd taken her away. That's right—they'd planned on meeting across the lake with Noc, Shrelia, and the others. And in her hand was the arcanir earring. Sluggishly, she blinked again as water splashed below her. *Are we in a river?* she wondered.

"No tracks."

There was no point in guessing whether he'd heard her thoughts or not. Of course he had. But rather than the usual disappointment and panic that brought, this time she felt relief. She didn't have to stumble over her words, and he knew what she meant.

The river's fresh coursing water did nothing to dull the coppery smell of blood. How badly was he hurt? *Dhuro, you're injured. You need to rest, too.*

His face slackened, just a little. "I'll be fine. I can rest when we get to the others."

One of his hands held her just beneath her thighs, and she reached her fingers out, searching for it until she touched his skin, sticky and tacky with blood and ichor. It didn't matter. *Please.*

He heaved a long-suffering sigh, but nodded, rolling his eyes.

If he wanted to be grumpy, he could be grumpy, as long as he agreed to take care of himself. If she weren't so exhausted, she could've laughed, but instead it only emerged as a breath.

The splashing quieted as his movement slowed, only the coursing of the river claiming the air. His chest expanded, tense. He leaned in and grazed her forehead with his nose.

"This isn't going to be pleasant for you, but I need you to get on my back, Bella."

She nodded, or thought she did.

Slowly, very slowly, he lowered her feet to the water. As she moved to stand on her own, boots sinking into the shallows, searing heat pulled at her shoulder, a fire burning deeper into her body that flashed stark white at the edges of her vision. A whimper left her lips, but she choked down on it, and fought not to double over. Things were already difficult enough without her collapsing and crying all the way.

"Let it out if you need to. We're far enough away," he said, carefully moving in front of her while bracing her. He descended, gently securing her injured side's arm around his neck while the pain burst tears from her eyes. She tamped down on it, trapping her tongue between her molars—something, *anything*, to distract from the torture in her shoulder.

They stood on the edge of a cliff, a river delta flowing into a spread of waterfalls, she realized. At any other time, she'd take this place in, its beauty, long and serene. But today, she could barely see through the shroud of pain.

A few breaths later, he brought her other arm around, then hefted her thighs up around his waist. She buried her face in his hair, breathing him in, his spring water and mountain stone scent, resting her face against his head as the tears flowed freely. "Hold on tight, Bella."

She did her best as he rose, digging her fingers into the flesh of her other arm, focusing like a needle on that contact and it alone, trying desperately to ignore the screaming of her own body.

Cautiously, he approached the cliff's edge, then began to climb down, navigating the handholds with care. The waterfall's spray misted onto them both, and even as it refreshed her, the slightest contact with her wound made it burn anew. She held on as best she could, keeping her mind on that bite of her fingernails into her arm.

At last, they reached the bottom, where the wide falls met the lake's surface. Dhuro took her to the rocky shore and crouched to let her down delicately, but every movement aggravated her burning shoulder. When her bottom hit the pebbles, she didn't care about the uneven ground, as long as it stopped spinning; she reclined to lay down, letting the rocks dig into her back, neck, and head. It wasn't perfect, but it was rest.

His brow furrowed, he crouched beside her shoulder and raised his eyebrows. "May I? I'll be gentle."

She nodded.

With a lengthy breath, he shifted aside her cloak, unfastened her shirt and pulled it away. That furrow on his brow furrowed deeper, and his gaze flickered to hers. "We need to get you to camp, now."

His hands were still steeped in ichor and blood. His jerkin was slashed in multiple places, revealing his bloodied shirt beneath. She shook her head. *Take care of yourself first. Then we'll go.*

With a sigh, he raised his hand to his forehead but stopped just short of smearing the gore all over his face. He worried his lower lip with a fang, shook his head, and shrugged. "Fine. But be ready to move again in a couple minutes."

If she never moved again, it would be too soon, but she nodded.

Careful to stay in her line of sight, he approached the water, then knelt to scrub at his hands and arms. He removed his jerkin, revealing a torn, bloodied shirt, and removed that, too.

Beneath was a chaos of cuts, bruises, and wounds around his black sun tattoo. His limbs had long, superficial cuts that had seeped down in long trails. An enormous bruise darkened his side, and its center, a stab wound, had bled profusely. How had he moved? How had he fought? How had he carried her so far and for so long? It had to have been excruciating.

The longer she watched him, the more her eyes stared into that wound.

When she'd seen it, that thrown knife finding its mark in his side, it had felt like her heart crushed in her chest. The wind had been knocked out of her, and her legs had begun running to him of their own volition. Only Gavri's hold had stopped her.

He'd risked his life to help control her power. He'd been out there for her sake, and it had been the human assassins hunting *her* who had nearly taken his life.

Not only had she been unable to stop it; she'd actually been the cause. As a Belmonte, war would always dog her steps. And every moment she spent with Dhuro, she risked his life.

Her dalliances since Cosimo had been short, and that had kept her lovers alive, and safe. This, with Dhuro, was already longer than she should allow, than he could bear—if the assassins kept coming, and sure as death, they wouldn't stop.

Dhuro had his own orders to see her to the unicorns and to do business with them, but the sooner they parted, the sooner he'd be safe again. Once she was with the unicorns, once he left her and was far away, the assassins would leave him be. He'd be safe, and live a long, happy life without her. *I'm so sorry you got hurt, Dhuro.*

He threw on his shirt and his jerkin but left them unfastened and open. "I'm already healing, Bella." Taking a knee, he dipped his head down until he met her gaze where she lay, then glanced at her wound again. "It's you I'm worried about."

His wounds hurt her heart in a way nothing had since losing Cosimo, but it was his life she worried about. Maybe he didn't see it yet, that the noose tightening around his throat since he'd met her was made of Belmonte blood and fibre. But whether he saw it or not, she'd cut him loose of it the soonest she could.

Let's hurry to the unicorns, then, she thought, and his eyes softened as he nodded and helped her up.

IN THE DISTANCE among the dark woods lining the shore, Dhuro could only just make out the shimmering glow of a pixie—Shrelia, flitting about Noc's head, with the squad. They'd made it.

He looked over his shoulder, where Bella rested her head, but she didn't stir. If she was resting, she needed it, and he wouldn't rouse her.

Gavri ran out to them, her face lined. "You made it! We were beginning to worry." She glanced at Bella, her gaze roving to the wound, then her eyebrows shot up. "Is that a—?"

"It is," he bit out, and she fell into step alongside him.

Noc picked a careful path on the rocky shore, but Shrelia shot from her vantage point beneath his ears straight for Bella, hovering over the wound, her tiny hands on her face. Chiming furiously, she grasped his shirt collar and thrashed it, then shot up to his nose and smacked it.

He didn't react. He didn't deserve to. Frankly, with things as they were, he should rightly accept any castigation or punishment they had. He'd agreed and promised to protect Bella. The weight of that promise now measured heavy upon him, injured, pained, poisoned. And if he didn't get her help in time, much worse.

Gavri looked past him, squinting into the distance. "Where's Zoran?"

He paused, frowning. "He's not with you?"

He'd assumed Zoran would take another route to the rendezvous point, and be there faster since he'd seemed uninjured and wasn't carrying anyone. Perhaps the fight had lasted longer than expected?

Gavri's face betrayed a much bleaker worry, but that wasn't possible.

Zoran had stayed behind to fight Dakkar, but he was Dakkar's step-father and Nendra's prince-consort. Zoran *belonged* to Nendra. Dakkar, even feeling the height of hubris right now, wouldn't dare harm a queen's consort, least of all Nendra's—not even considering that she was Dakkar's mother.

At best, Zoran had captured Dakkar and was taking him back to Dun Mozg. At worst, he was simply behind. "He'll catch up, Gavri."

Her eyebrows creased together, but she nodded, twirling one of her braids nervously.

Zoran was alive, of that much he was certain. If Dakkar had taken him prisoner, he would come for Dakkar and see to Zoran's freedom personally. If—Darkness help him—if Dakkar had killed his brother, then not only would he see Dakkar's head roll to the floor personally, but both Dun Mozg and Nozva Rozkveta would be out for blood.

Noc approached, raising his head to eye Bella's wound. *You were supposed to keep her safe. Instead you let her get stung by one of the few things that can kill her.*

I know. He looked back at Noc, taking full responsibility. *Please tell me how to help her.*

Noc turned and flicked him in the face with his tail.

I deserve that. Please just tell me.

I'm not about to let her suffer. Looking back at him, Noc tossed his head and then moved toward the rest of the squad. *Follow me.*

Dhuro did as he was told, and Noc led him deeper into the woods, where they had made a small camp. Danika and Marysia kept watch, nodding in acknowledgement as he passed. Halina laid out a bedroll near the campfire, presumably on Noc's instruction, and their treat-ment kit. It contained the barest essentials, but that was the most dark-elves tended to need; something to staunch the bleeding of a major wound, a splint, but little else.

He counted Noc, Shrelia, Gavri, Danika, Marysia, and Halina. Zoran wasn't here, but neither was Kinga. "Halina," he called, and she looked up from preparing rations. "Where's Kinga?"

"Last I saw her, she ran north, Your Highness."

North? Back the way they'd come? Why?

He gave Halina a nod, and she returned to her work. Perhaps Kinga had been caught, or delayed by the same reason as Zoran.

Bella cringed, her entire body slowly tensing. Darkness, he couldn't stand to see her like this.

We need to get her to Gwydion as soon as possible, Noc said as Dhuro gently lowered Bella to the bedroll. *They have specific magic that will help her. For now, the best we can do is clean and dress the sting.*

Dhuro shook his head as Bella winced, her eyes fluttering open, her face twisting. This was his fault, and he wouldn't rest until he got her to Gwydion. Gavri brought a pot of boiled water; he touched it, and it had cooled enough to use. The last thing he wanted was to cause Bella further pain.

She'll need to stay in this form, so if you did find arcanir, make sure she stays in contact with it, Noc added.

He nodded, then retrieved his hair's olive-oil soap from his pack and lathered up the water. He knelt next to Bella, meeting her heavy-lidded eyes, and took her hand, giving it a light squeeze. "I'm going to clean your wound, sheihan. It'll hurt."

Her head slowly rolled toward him, and she mustered a thin smile. *I can take it.*

With a bracing inhalation, he gently cleaned her shoulder with the soapy water, mindful of her winces, slowing to avoid causing her unnecessary distress. When he finished, he applied a clean dressing. At last, he retrieved the arcanir earring from her belt pouch, but hesitated.

Her eyelashes fluttered as she regarded him, that slight smile in place again. *Go ahead. This will be fun.*

You need help, he thought back sternly. *This isn't funny.*

Still smiling, she closed her eyes and made a show of exposing her ear to him.

Shaking his head, he fought back a laugh. This was no time for her to be making jokes. But he relented, leaning in to put it on her already pierced earlobe, the motion strangely complicated but intimate.

When he finished, she opened one eye. "Well," she rasped, "how does it look?"

He huffed an amused breath. "Like you're wearing one earring."

A weak half-laugh escaped her lips before she closed her eye once more, her face slackening.

Noc nosed his shoulder with a slight push. *Now change into something that makes you look less like a corpse. I'm taking you both to Gwydion, as fast I can and as she can handle, before the venom takes her life.*

With Noc's speed and stamina, they'd be there within a few hours. And the sooner Bella had the unicorns' help, the better.

He rushed to his pack and ripped off his ruined clothes, then quickly threw on whatever he could find, hastily fastening closures. Gavri jogged up to him.

"Noc said you're leaving?"

"We're taking Bella to the unicorns," he said, pulling on his boots. "See what you can find of Kinga and Zoran, and then track us to the unicorns."

She straightened. "Yes, Your Highness."

He yanked on a fur-and-leather jerkin, the only other overcoat he'd brought, then leaned in. "Don't let Dakkar find you."

As she inclined her head, he passed her, but she grasped his arm. When he turned back to her, she said, "Don't lose her, Your Highness."

He would do everything in his power not to.

CHAPTER 17

Strong arms steadied Bella as she began to slip; she was moving. An unyielding throb beat from her shoulder. The sting.

From her earlobe, something else tingled, like a minor burn—the arcanir earring. The tingle was distinct, but nothing compared to the macedda sting, and nothing at all like when she'd been kept under the net by the Brotherhood. It would still bind her powers, just with so much less pain.

As she blinked her eyes open, light assaulted them, the sunshine dappling through a leafy canopy. They were still in a forest, then. Beneath her was Noc, his sable mane catching the air as he moved at a steady clip. Shrelia had nestled between his ears, dozing, her limbs entwined with his mane. And around her were Dhuro's strong arms, one clawed hand lightly grasping a fistful of Noc's mane.

"Shh, sleep," Dhuro whispered into her ear, gentler than she'd ever heard him, and he nuzzled her head, his nose grazing her hair. With the firm warmth of his embrace around her, his low voice in her ear, she wanted to do as he said, she truly did, if only it weren't for the pain, the persistent sunlight, and the jostle of riding a fey horse.

Ahead, a grotesque face came into view, as if rising from the ground, made of stone. Against her, Dhuro straightened. As they neared, it revealed a cave carved into the shape of an anguished countenance. She knew this thing—the Griever—and had been here once before.

"The Parco dei Mostri," she said, her voice hoarse.

"The what?" Dhuro asked, handing her a waterskin that she eagerly drank from.

She'd learned about this place as a girl, but she'd only come here when she'd lost Cosimo. "A few centuries ago, there was a wealthy signore who lived in these parts, very happily married. When his wife fell ill and died, he was so bereft that he could find no way to relieve his grief. In the lowest, deepest pit of it, he commissioned an artist to sculpt his grounds to reflect his heart."

They passed figures of roaring beasts, screaming mouths, a titan fading into nature, even the Great Wolf Himself and god of death, Nox, howling. The castle had fallen into ruin, and the grounds were rarely tended, but somehow it was right that nature welcomed this garden of grief into her waiting embrace.

"His loss must have been unfathomable," Dhuro said softly. His arms held her a little closer.

When she'd come here, she'd felt in this place an instant kinship; these savage beasts and ugly faces had been a mirror held up to her own heart. Those deep voids within the gaping mouths were places she'd felt inside herself, places that Cosimo had filled when he was alive, that she had filled with love for him... Places that had been ripped out, root and branch, when her family had killed him. Cosimo had been a sculptor himself, and when she'd visited, it was the closest she'd come to feeling his presence again since before his death.

Even now, she could picture him shrugging, attempting to act nonchalant while he explained the techniques used to create these pieces. He'd always been able to talk about art for hours on end, and she'd spent those hours soaking it all in, his enthusiasm, his melodious voice, the way his face lit up when he hit on a particular subject he liked. They'd been together for four years, and it had been nearly six years since he'd died.

Noc took them farther in, past a sculpted elephant dragging a mortally wounded gladiator away, and then Forza himself defeated, carved lying supine in death throes. The crisp scent of autumn shrubs took her back. She shivered, retracing her steps all those years ago. Past the horrors and the penitents were Immortali beasts among trees and shrubs, peering, haunting. A unicorn with oversized eyes. Sirens sitting on a rock, extending their hands, mouths open in song. A small Fata in a cone-shaped hat, beautiful and fey, half-transformed into a water snake.

Near the end was a fountain featuring a great phoenix, its wings spread wide but its beak open in a silent cry.

"He overcame his grief," Dhuro said smoothly.

"The phoenix might be taking flight," she answered, eyeing some of its broken stone feathers sadly. "Or it might be releasing an anguished cry. Or... perhaps both."

When she looked at the phoenix, she still saw herself in her nightgown, out in the forest surrounding Roccalano. Her arms outstretched in the rain and screaming at the sky, she'd demanded to know why Cosimo had been taken, and why she had been left behind in pieces without him. They'd given her no answer, nothing but purpose to fill the void, and a cause to throw herself into so there would never be another Cosimo taken from another Bella, not if she could help it. She'd worked tirelessly as Renato for years, only for her work to lead her here, where assassins hunted her and those she cared about.

Maybe she'd offended the gods that night, and they'd shown her that fate would have its due regardless of what she did.

Or maybe being a Belmonte was fatal. Thousands, if not more, had died due to the Belmontes already, and Cosimo had just been another tally mark on that grim ledger. And if she didn't part with Dhuro soon, he'd become one more.

She shifted in his hold, her dressing rubbing painfully against her sting, and winced. The ache had spread through her left side and her upper body, like flames singeing her veins, burning constantly, and all the more when she moved. "Are we near?"

Dhuro went still for a moment. "Noc says he can hear them."

She looked ahead into the dense woods, where deep, deep, deep past the autumn trees and a veil of falling leaves was a light, pale and white, far into the living wilds like a distant star. As they drew closer, it cast a glow, brighter and brighter, but gentle, like moonlight.

His form came into focus, immaculate on four legs, with a pearlescent horn and eyes the darkest black of the night sky. The warm autumn woods around him greened, grew lush, bloomed like some dream of spring reclaiming the slumbering land, and as Noc's hoof landed on a patch of impossibly emerald ferns, her vision blurred, and everything faded to white.

$$\text{\&}$$

BELLA WOKE to a sea of stars glittering above her in the black velvet night sky. Gods above, it was beautiful, serene, with the soft babble of river water nearby, and a few quiet bird calls. A breeze lightly teased the bare skin of her chest, just cool enough to be comfortable.

A weight lay on her lap—someone. Someone with a very girlish giggle.

When she peered down, it was Janessa lying sprawled, her head on Dhuro's naked—very naked—dark-blue lap and gazing up at him with gleaming brown eyes. Not what she wanted to see, him with another woman, *any* woman.

Another dream? She'd awoken in Dhuro's body again, in his memories. He lay on a woven blanket in a lush glade, over thick green summer grass.

His clawed hand reached out to Janessa, delicately stroking her soft, brown tresses as if she were a rare treasure. His mouth curved into a smile, something it never did with *her*, and such a calmness claimed his body, as if he had no fears, no secrets, no shadows in this evening entangled with Janessa. The long, comfortable silence between them ached.

"Do you think it's time, my love?" he asked with a lilt, an unabashed joy in his voice that she'd rarely heard.

With another giggle, Janessa walked playful fingers up his abdomen, biting her lip. "There are still many promising hours left before dawn."

A laugh rumbled in his throat, and he reached down for Janessa, drawing her up to his chest, where she rested her head and held him close. "Don't worry—I intend to fulfill every promise before the sun rises," he said mischievously as Janessa draped a leg across him, "but it's been months. I know you wanted to keep this secret, but I'd like to tell my father about us."

Janessa stiffened against him, curling. "I... Dhuro, you know we can't. Anything less than marriage, and my father will send me away to the monastery."

Something tightened in Dhuro's chest, and he rubbed Janessa's upper arm reassuringly. He opened his mouth, then closed it again.

Don't say it. Bella willed him to keep his words in, begged him with every ounce of her strength, but he opened his mouth again.

"Why not marriage?" he ventured, his voice calm but his heart racing, hammering in his chest.

Janessa rose on one arm, her thick dark locks pooling over her bare shoulder, and she met Dhuro's eyes, her own wide over a slowly broadening smile. "Dhuro... you... Are you asking what I think you're asking?"

With a grin of his own, he nodded, and to his credit, did not lower his gaze to Janessa's naked breasts.

Bella wanted to shake her head. Just like that, after a few months, he'd decided to wed a woman who'd wanted to keep him a secret? And if Janessa's father was so cruel, why didn't she just leave? She certainly seemed capable of taking care of herself.

Or maybe I'm just jealous, Bella thought with an inward grimace. Dhuro's face, however, couldn't be further from grimacing.

Janessa leaned in, her breath balmy on his mouth before her lips brushed his. "We'll be together for the rest of our lives," she said between kisses, then frowned, her smooth face lined. "Or... at least for the rest of mine." Her smile had turned wistful.

Slowly, pensively, Dhuro ran his fingers through her hair. "My mother owns my life. It is hers to bargain away as she pleases, my love."

Janessa sat back and turned away, hugging herself. Dhuro sat up too, reaching for her. "So what is a marriage to a human, then? A blink of your eye, and then your mother would marry you off to royalty."

"My love—" He reached out for her, but she pulled away, flinching.

"Am I? Truly?" Janessa looked over her shoulder with tears welling in her eyes. "To me, you're my everything," she said with a sad, tearful smile that soon faded. "To you, I'm just a moment in your immortal life, until I die... and you eventually join your true soulmate."

Merciful gods and empyreal Veil threads, this woman was audacious. He was offering Janessa his love, his commitment, only to have it rejected for not being enough. What more did she want from him?

Bella wanted to shake some sense into him, tell him that he mattered, he was worthy, that he deserved better than this, but... There was nothing she could do. This had already happened long ago. All that remained was to learn what decision he had made, although the sinking feeling she had already whispered the answer to her.

He shook his head vehemently. "Janessa, it's not like that at all. If you would please—"

Grabbing for her dress on the grass, Janessa rose. "No, it's fine."

Please. He'd said *please.* This wasn't the Dhuro she knew; he was vulnerable. And this woman wouldn't even hear him out.

Janessa stepped into her dress. "I think I need to be alone. It's a feeling it seems I'll need to get used to."

His throat tight, he stood and took her hand. "Just listen for a second, please. I want to—"

Janessa pulled her hand away, abruptly slipping it from his hold, and shook her head, looking away. "Think about what this means to you. What this *really* means to you. And unless you tell anyone about us, you'll know where to find me." With that, she gathered up her things and left.

Swallowing past the lump in his throat, he stood there, staring after her.

Bella's heart broke for him, and she wished she could put her arms around him, even here, in this dream, this memory that had already happened. For all that it twinged to see him with another woman at all, it cut deeply to see him remove the armor around his soul, share it with someone, leave it exposed... only for it to be rejected as not enough.

His vision blurred, and he rubbed a hand over his face. And with that darkness, he was gone.

WHEN DHURO WOKE, he was in a familiar ruin, beneath a stone archway wrapped in creepers. The fading sunlight reached through a leafy deciduous canopy, green and thriving in spring. Birds chirped and called above, while the wind whished through the trees.

An arm pulled him closer, where he rested his cheek against a warm, firm chest, and gazed down at a book held open by a dark-skinned masculine hand.

"You're not falling asleep on me, are you, darling?" Cosimo teased softly, his hold squeezing for a moment.

Darkness, not *again*. It was just like last time, taken into Bella's memories by her unicorn magic. He sighed inwardly. There was nothing for it but to get through it and wake up.

"It's only because you're so comfortable," Bella replied, fighting back a yawn.

Cosimo sat up, and she moaned in jest.

"Does the latest volume of *Court Duelist* bore you?" he asked incredulously, a smile in his voice.

They'd read books together in the forest on trysts? Dhuro wanted to grimace, but Bella's face didn't respond to his wants; it would do nothing but smile. Was this what her relationship had been like with Cosimo? At what point did one betray the other? Because that was what always happened. For all her talk of loving only Cosimo, nothing was ever perfect. Not relationships. And certainly not relationships between humans.

Bella shook her head. "No, not at all. I loved the... court... and the... duel in it." She sheepishly picked her words.

"Mm-hmm," Cosimo crooned in play. He shut the book and set it down, then looked to the west. "Let's get you home, darling. It'll be dark soon."

At least Cosimo cared for her safety. Dhuro could respect that. After all, it seemed that at least while alive, Cosimo had done a better job of it than *he* was doing now. The unicorn sentinel had allowed them entry to the Eternal Grove, where Gwydion and his herd made their home, a realm tucked seamlessly into the Sileni forest beyond the Parco dei Mostri. The herd's mystic had used her healing magic on Bella, but she hadn't awoken. Not for days. The mystic had said only time would tell when she'd recover, and how well.

He'd removed Bella's arcanir earring, and had kept vigil at her side, waiting for any change. He had yet to speak with Gwydion about business, but that could wait. There was no way he'd leave Bella behind— that is, not until she recovered.

"Do we have to?" Bella asked with a little moan. Her arms closed around Cosimo, and her palm pressed into the firm muscle of Cosimo's abdomen, slipping lower past his navel, and lower, and lower—

Darkness, no. That was the very last thing he wanted to touch, let alone in Bella's body. He tried to pull away to no avail. *Please, please, please no—*

With a wicked rumble in his throat, Cosimo caught her hand and brought it to his lips, brushing her fingers with a tender kiss.

Dhuro could've exhaled his relief. Praise the Dark, at least *one* of them had mercy.

"Persuasive. Very persuasive," Cosimo remarked with a low laugh, "but the last thing we need is your brothers hunting you down."

She pouted. "You mean hunting *you* down."

A half-laugh. "Yes, that." Cosimo rose and helped her to her feet, then pulled her in, meeting her gaze with adoring, soft eyes. The wind tousled his dark hair, and as much as Dhuro was in no way interested in men, the warmth spreading in Bella's chest and her weak knees made an irrefutable argument.

She raised her hand and retrieved something from inside her bodice, a delicately embroidered handkerchief. With cautious fingers, she unfolded it, revealing a flat, dried, lacquered flower. It was a deep, vivid purple with a sunny yellow center, just like the blooms at the campsite near the river. Just like the one he'd left on her bedroll. Wild pansy. She'd looked at it with such shock.

"You kept it." Cosimo's chest expanded, and he raised his eyebrows. "I gave that to you."

"The third time we met." She smiled faintly. "Whenever I miss you, I look at it. I've looked at it a lot, Cosimo." She swallowed, and her chest tightened. Vaguely, he realized she was trying not to cry. "I wish we could just run away together."

She'd looked at that flower with such shock, and this was why. He'd meant it as a small token to cheer her up, no more than an apple or a sweet. But to her, it had meant so much more, and her reaction hadn't been to him, but to this. To Cosimo.

Cosimo nodded, drawing her into his embrace. He just held her close, and she breathed him in, a scent like vetiver, citrus, and cedar, and with every breath, she clung to him more tightly.

"Do you want to leave your family behind?" Cosimo asked, and Bella rubbed her cheek against his linen shirt but didn't answer. "I don't ask any more of you than you wish to give, darling. If days spent in these ruins are all we have, then I'll cherish them, because they're with you."

Dhuro scoffed inwardly. This man couldn't be serious? Surely he expected more, wanted more, or had some other goal in mind. Everyone wanted something, after all, whether it was power, status, coin, or even something so basic as pleasure. Either this man was using her, or she was using him—the sum of all connections like this.

Bella looked up as Cosimo gazed down at her and stroked her cheek affectionately. He dipped down to kiss her, his lips sending a shiver through her from her mouth to her furthest reaches. She deepened the kiss, and her eyes welled with tears that rolled down her cheeks. "It's harder to say goodbye every time."

Cosimo caressed them away, mustering a smile for her although his eyes were over-bright, too. "Then promise to meet again."

"I promise," she breathed.

"I promise," Cosimo replied.

These were familiar words, practiced words, tailor made for each other. These were steps of an old habit that came so naturally they required no thought, like stringing a bow for the thousandth time.

These dreams of memories had let him into her mind, into her heart, but seeing this felt wrong, too intimate, not just witnessing a moment but thieving it somehow by taking it from just the two of them, where it belonged.

She had said Cosimo was the only man she'd ever loved. He hadn't disbelieved her, exactly, but the passion with which she'd said it, the fire, it had felt much too intense to him. And it hadn't been because she'd overstated things; no, it had been because he'd never felt this before himself.

Something broke inside of him, like a bowstring that had been held taut for too long, for far too long, and what it had held together came undone.

Bella did love Cosimo, and he was the only man she'd ever loved.

The only man she ever would love.

CHAPTER 18

The sweet scent of spring grass graced her nose as Bella opened her eyes. A bright radiance shone overhead, but not blinding, like early summer sunshine behind a sheer veil of clouds. She glanced down and raised a hand to examine, just to make sure this wasn't another dream.

It was her hand all right, and it responded to her will, thankfully. All around her was something out of a daydream—a forest of birch trees with dense crowns, nestled among the liveliest green undergrowth and tapestries of colorful windflowers. Songbirds warbled their pleasant calls among the trees, their feathers brilliant pops of yellow, blue, red, and orange among the verdant leaves, and butterflies fluttered in the clear air like variegated jewels. It took her breath away.

On her stomach, Dhuro rested his face, his cheek against the blush-pink velvet of the gown she wore, doubtless another of Princess Alessandra's. He'd shed the fur-lined jerkin and wore just his shirt tucked into his trousers, and no weapons—he must have been at ease here. She seemed to be on a bedroll placed over a bed of supple grasses, and he sat next to her, holding one hand as he curled over her in slumber. His pale hair pooled over her belly, and when she stroked its softness, his eyes slowly blinked open.

The corner of his mouth turned up in the slightest smile, one of the rare few she could ever recall seeing on his face. He brought her hand to his lips, kissing her fingers lightly in what was a very familiar way, and some brightness faded in his eyes. How long had he been here, by her side?

The last thing she remembered was his memory of Janessa, and when she saw him now, it was with new eyes. When she'd first met him, he'd been no more than a bitter prince, brutally handsome and strong but full of bile. That had been his sum. But now... he had softened to her some, yes—that came with sharing a bed. But more than that, his facade had a lining now, a fragile gray silk of memory. Love wasn't always required, and rejection happened, but she'd caught only glimpses of a pain that went deep, that underlaid his facade. Just how deep that pain truly went, she didn't know, but it was visible now, and spoke.

"Dhuro," she whispered, her voice a hoarse rasp. She wanted to ask how long she'd been asleep.

"Wait." He rose, then passed behind her, where water splashed quietly.

When he returned, he bore a wooden cup and slipped a hand under her back, helping her up. He raised the cup to her lips, and she sipped from it, carefully taking hold of it herself. If he was being this tender, he must have really been concerned.

"Thank you," she said, her voice a little clearer.

He nodded, dropping into a crouch beside her and looking away. "You didn't wake for four days." It was a crestfallen murmur, heavy, as if he'd stung her himself. He swallowed. "Their healer wasn't certain you'd recover, even with their magic. The"—he took a deep breath—"arcanir inhibited your natural unicorn healing. Because of that, you were closer to..." He swallowed again and shook his head. "I should've thought of that."

"It's not your fault." With a groan of effort, she sat up and reached for him, but he pulled away. "I decided I needed the arcanir. And I still do, to control my powers when I need to."

He dropped his head in his hand, rubbing his brow. "It's only by grace of the Darkness that we got you here alive. I've failed this mission and you and in every way possible but one."

He was being too hard on himself. There had been nothing simple about this journey, from her uncontrollable powers to their unexpected connection, and he couldn't take responsibility for all of that. It was too much. "But we made it. I can learn whatever I need to do to control my Change and go back to my normal life. And you can talk to Gwydion about allying with Nightbloom. Isn't that what matters?"

For a moment, he studied her, evaluative, then looked away again. "Dakkar is still out there."

She shrugged a shoulder. "Maybe the unicorns could help with that, too."

"Help me kill him?" He puffed. "I won't hold my breath."

"He doesn't have to be killed." She wriggled closer and rested her hand on his forearm, beneath his rolled shirt sleeve.

"My mother has ordered it." He covered her hand with his, peering down at their joined touch. Although he protested still, it was much softer than his usual.

"Is that what you want?"

Letting her hand slip out of his grasp, he rose to his full height and anchored his hands on his hips. "You say that as if a prince of the blood can disobey his queen."

That loyalty seemed to be at the crux of his unhappiness. Even in that memory, he'd told Janessa that his mother controlled his future. Duty came with positions of privilege, but mere orders weren't always duty. Some orders were, and others were unconscionable, and simply because they came from power did not make them just, or right, or something one could live with. "But how would you feel if not for your mother's orders?"

His gaze flashed to hers, but his brow furrowed. "What?"

"What would you feel is the right thing to do about Dakkar if you had no orders?"

Scoffing, he gave her an incredulous look, shaking his head slightly. He raked a hand through his hair, eyeing the grass contemplatively.

"Setting aside what you think everyone else wants of you... what is it that you want, Dhuro? What is most important to you?"

He didn't answer right away, but she didn't expect him to; figuring out what he truly wanted could take a lot of soul searching, especially for a man who'd spent most of his life submitting to what others wanted and expected of him. She didn't know everything about the dark-elves, but she did know they were a utilitarian society, and the needs of the many outweighed those of the few. It was a stark contrast to the Sileni people, whose individualism no doubt shocked most dark-elves.

Humans could be incredibly selfish, yes, and self-serving—she'd seen it—but they could also be merciful. Forgiving. Kind. And one single-minded individual, if ambitious enough, could change the fates of many for the better with one choice.

Dhuro didn't have to subscribe to her worldview, but if he suffered with what he'd been ordered to do, if he felt it was wrong, he did have a decision to make about what he believed in, and what he couldn't live with.

Soft hoofbeats neared in a gentle staccato, and a young unicorn approached them, his white mane and tail swaying in the breeze.

Elder Gwydion is ready to see you now, Your Highness, a child's voice spoke into her mind, and the unicorn blinked over sky-blue eyes.

Surely he meant Dhuro? Did he think she was his wife? But it was all she could do to nod her understanding, and try not to make embarrassing noises at how adorable his little horn was, and his short little legs, and tiny hooves.

With a swish of his tail and a bob of his head, the small messenger departed. She was beaming, she realized, but couldn't help herself.

Dhuro tipped his chin up to her inquisitively.

"He said Gwydion wants to see us," she relayed to him.

He reached out a hand to help her up onto unsteady, bare feet. "Yes, he said he would meet with us both when you awoke."

This Gwydion had delayed discussion of an alliance and let it rely on her waking? Not only was that unnecessary, but it revealed priorities she couldn't begin to understand.

But had that been why Dhuro had kept such a close eye on her? Because he was eager to finally treat with the unicorns' elder?

He did care for her, she was sure of it, but today it had seemed like more than just as a bedmate or his charge. Had this been why?

Dhuro linked his arm with hers and led her slowly through groves of birches and flower-studded shrubs, across a comfortable carpet of supple grass. Colorful birds and butterflies passed overhead, and fat, fuzzy bees lazily meandered around them. A clear route wound among the trees, and its end framed a gateway to a sprawling meadow.

At its center was a gathering of at least thirty snow-white unicorns of varying sizes, from the youngling who'd delivered the message, to larger ones long in the tooth, along with Noc and Shrelia among them. They both bowed as she and Dhuro passed, a confusing act. They hadn't seemed affected by Dhuro's royalty before.

In the middle of the gathering stood a man, tall and lean, in voluminous white robes. His angular face and pointed ears almost made him seem elven, beautiful with thick waves of snowy hair. But he had a shimmering sun-shaped rune on his forehead, and... and the most intense violet eyes she'd ever seen.

A gasp escaped her parted lips. Could it be?

"It is good to see you again, Arabella," he said in a deep, soothing voice, his immaculate face serene. "You are most welcome here."

He... *he* was her sire?

Casting his intense gaze downward a moment, Gwydion smiled, and something like a wave of small laughs crested in her mind. Could she hear *all* the unicorns?

"Yes," Gwydion answered with a slow nod. "All of us hear each other's thoughts. There are no secrets between us. But for the benefit of our guests, I have taken this form to speak with you."

All of them knew her thoughts? Did Dhuro?

"Unfortunately only we can hear them," Gwydion answered, strolling toward her.

"Why do I feel as though I'm only getting half of a conversation?" Dhuro murmured to her, raising an eyebrow.

"I hope you will bear with us, Prince," Gwydion said with an airy half-smile.

Would they discuss control over her Change first, or matters with the dark-elves?

Gwydion's eyes met hers, and she felt instantly reassured, safe, supported. "Do not worry, Arabella. As long as you stay with the herd, you will have control over your Change. You can choose whichever of your forms you prefer at any time, and you may learn to take still others." When her mouth fell open, he continued, "I still had much to teach you, my heir, but you fled before I could."

That first day came rushing back to her in flashes of surprise and horror. She'd wished to be like the unicorns, yes, but it had never crossed her mind that such a thing would be possible. In all her shock, she'd run.

Gwydion extended a hand and rested it lightly on her shoulder. Comfort radiated from that touch, although Dhuro flinched next to her, his narrow gaze flickering from her face to Gwydion and back again.

Also, heir? Heir to what?

With a slow smile, Gwydion faced her. "To the herd, of course. I am immortal, but not invincible. In these modern times, our people need a bridge between our philosophy of peace and the hegemony of humankind. That bridge is you."

Her legs weakened. That was a lot—*a lot*—and he hadn't breathed a word of it to her.

"You fled before I could, and I could not abandon my duties to the herd. I had faith you would find me, and here you are. Those pure of heart who wish for us reach out and pull in their fated sire like a thread of destiny. When I felt your wish, I did not imagine that knowledge of us had become lost among your people, that you had not meant to reach for your destiny."

Destiny? Then—

"You were meant to be among us."

What if she wanted to go home? All this time, she'd wanted to return to her family, to Mamma, Luciano, and Tarquin. To her old life, so she could continue to work toward changing the brutality of the world that had taken Cosimo and countless others like him.

Gwydion let his hand slip away and paced pensively near her, his snowy eyebrows drawn together beneath that shimmering sun rune. At last, he took a restful breath and leaned in, locking his eyes with hers. "I am very much alive and in no immediate need of replacing. If you wish to leave, you are free to do so, and there is another way for me to help you retain your control. I believe your people," he said, looking at Dhuro, "call it a lifebond."

CHAPTER 19

*L*ifebond? A hard lump settled in the pit of Dhuro's stomach. The less he heard of lifebonds, the better. But Gwydion looked at him expectantly.

"Some amongst my people do form lifebonds, yes." Raising his chin, he looked down at Gwydion, willing his face to give away no expression, no openness to further questioning. With any luck, that would be the last he had to hear of lifebonds.

His bearing slack, Gwydion gave no indication of being dissuaded, but he did turn his placid gaze on the circle of unicorns around them. With just that look, they all slowly left the meadow.

"Forgive me," Gwydion said lightly to Bella, who admired him with wide eyes, "but I thought you might be more comfortable if we spoke privately."

She replied with a slow, bewildered nod. They'd barely arrived here, she'd just laid eyes on the man, and she already adored him? Did she trust him that easily, or was she just besotted?

With a lofty laugh, Gwydion eyed him dubiously.

If all the unicorns here heard thoughts, then his were probably no exception. But at least Gwydion seemed to do him the respect of not acknowledging them with a response. At least a verbal one.

Averting his gaze, Gwydion took Bella's hand gently in his own, an overly familiar gesture, but one she didn't seem to mind. "Arabella, I had heard your wish to become like us, and I had heard your thoughts of peace. It was my decision to Change you," he said to her, and she only tilted her head in reply. "And it is my responsibility that you struggle with the Change. If you do not want to stay here, you do not have to. There is another solution." Gwydion's gaze turned to him, giving him an evaluative once-over.

Dhuro stiffened. Deep, Darkness, and Holy Ulsinael, the very *last* thing he needed to hear was that Bella would require a lifebond with him. He'd sooner let a woman mount his back and ride him around like a pony, tugging him by the ears. He'd sooner slam his face into the Stone a thousand times and call it still more merciful than those words.

"A lifebond would grant you strength, enough to master your Change," Gwydion continued, and she nodded along happily.

Dhuro shook his head. No. The answer was no. He'd had enough of being manipulated and used, twisted into a tool and a resource. And this —this was why they could only ever be trusted to pursue their own ends. Women. Not just one, but every woman he'd ever tumbled had only wanted one thing—his ties to the queen, or his so-called riches, his body, or even a claim on his immortal life.

Eventually, as long as they'd been honest, it became convenient, and it became sufficient. If he knew what they wanted, at least expectations were clear. And he'd *thought* Bella had been honest—their joining was just for pleasure.

But she'd been talking about needing to go to the unicorns and controlling her Change ever since they'd met. Had she known what it would take? Why else bother tangling with a dark-elf? With him? What resources he had to offer her were the sum of his worth.

Gwydion took her other hand in his as well, their eyes locked, and then Dhuro's chest tightened, his heart knocking hesitantly in his chest like a guest with bad news.

"Although it is akin to marriage for humankind, I would have no such expectations. None, actually, unless something more arose naturally between us." Gwydion lifted her hands to his face and, closing his eyes, brushed her knuckles with his lips while she gaped.

That guest with bad news inside of him knocked harder, faster.

With *himself*. Gwydion had been offering Bella a lifebond with *himself*. He wanted her—for *himself*.

Gwydion's gaze flickered to his, for just a moment, and then he released Bella's hands. "You don't have to decide now."

She blinked rapidly over those wide eyes while Gwydion, smiling, took a step back, clasped his hands behind him, then inclined his head and left.

Even after the man had left, she stood there, dumbfounded, staring at the ground wordlessly. Dhuro waited, watched her, and with every passing second something hardened within him, harder and harder and harder until his limbs weighed him down like a mountain, and nothing in this world, tangible or not, could penetrate him. Nothing.

When her face finally turned to his, she flinched.

His hand grabbed her wrist, and he dragged her away, impervious to her words as he strode deeper and deeper into the trees.

BELLA TWISTED in Dhuro's grip as he dragged her into the forest, but his hold was uncompromising. "Dhuro, will you please stop for one second?"

Although she dug her heels into the grass, it didn't matter. He was stronger, and unless she wanted to fight him, she would go wherever he was going. The deeper he stalked into the woods, the denser the trees became, the more the shade defeated the light, and the more distant the bright meadow became.

After Gwydion had left, that look on Dhuro's face—it had been unlike anything she'd ever seen. Those brutal lines had become hard, inscrutable, and his entire body had gone so taut he'd looked ready to break out of his own skin. A tempest had churned in his eyes, a storm— one that could claim her, claim everything, and rage over it for a thousand years. And although she twisted in his merciless grasp, a part of her, the most reckless part, longed to take that audacious step forward... and lose herself to what primal forces stirred within him.

He pulled her past a thick tree, then turned on her, eyebrows drawn together, and pushed her step by step until her back met the trunk. A breath whooshed out of her, but he took her face in his hands and suffocated it with his crushing kiss. Her palms planed up his firm chest and over his shoulders, gliding up his corded neck and into his hair; one unyielding hand held the back of her head, while the other veered down to her breast. He took hold of her, kneading her to his liking, as his tongue invaded her mouth.

His rhythm awoke something within her, something that rose against his storm, built and built to meet it, and gods above, whatever had brought this tempest on, she didn't care as long as he didn't stop. And he didn't, parting her ankles with his boot, thrusting his thigh to settle between her legs. That touch stoked the rising need within her, and a wanting sound escaped her throat.

He gathered her skirts, raising them to her hips, then freed himself. His fierce eyes met hers as he broke their kiss, as his hardness met her core, and gazes locked, he entered her, quaking out a breath as she shivered.

Merciful gods and empyreal Veil threads, nothing felt so good, so right—*nothing*—as this did right now, being one with Dhuro.

He lifted her, leaving her back to brace against the tree trunk, and she wrapped her legs around him, trapped him between her thighs as the fullness of that raging storm within him crashed into her.

Holding her gaze intensely, he took her, pleasured her, but he didn't close his eyes, bury his face in her neck, or look away, not like they'd become accustomed to; something she saw there drew her in, held her in a grasp as uncompromising and as merciless as when he'd brought her here. As her need built and built and built, that look intensified, pinned her as surely as his body pressed into her, and the promise of pleasure seized her body in a tight grip; her head leaned back of its own volition, but he grabbed her face in one hand as she peered into his ruthless eyes.

He trapped her gaze with his as she shattered, peaking against his relentless rhythm, quivering between the ecstasy at her core and the challenge in his eyes, breathless and gasping, whimpering and crying, tears rolling down her cheeks as he spent every last bit of her pleasure.

Abruptly, he pulled away and finished as he usually did, his face creasing in that way she loved to savor in small, stolen glimpses. These things they had done with the distance of looking away had become intimate now, allowing nothing to hide in the clarity between them. But even as she watched it all, devoured every moment spent in his lambent gaze, what stirred in those golden eyes was no clearer than the storm that had taken her.

It had been the most intense lovemaking she'd ever experienced.

Something had happened in that meadow, something that had driven him to a consuming madness. Gwydion had offered to lifebond with her, a union greater than but not unlike marriage among the dark-elves. She wasn't in love with Gwydion, but she and Dhuro had also been very clear with one another about the confines of their relationship; he'd planned to complete his mission and return to Nightbloom, and she'd planned to take control of her Change and return to her own life. At no point had he asked for more, and even today, he'd only waited with her until he could speak with Gwydion. When Gwydion had mentioned the lifebond, Dhuro's face had been unequivocal in expressing his loathing for the very notion.

It was clear Janessa had betrayed him in some way; maybe she hadn't been the only one. Maybe he always kept things simple with women, as she did with men.

Maybe this was his way of saying goodbye.

The thought of it—goodbye—made her shiver. It was what he wanted, wasn't it? And with war always shadowing her steps, he'd be safer away from her. It was best for everyone.

He helped her down, then righted his clothes as she did her own, shaking her head. She opened her mouth to ask him what this had been, but he spoke first.

"Will you lifebond with Gwydion?" He tightened his belt, finding the right notch.

"I don't know," she said, shifting the hem of her dress. And she really didn't know. Continuing to have no control over her Change wasn't an option, and her other choices were few. "I don't want to rush into anything, but I miss my family, and someone needs to speak out against our warmongering nobiltà. I want to go home to Roccalano. I also don't want to be caged again, even in this beautiful place." The arcanir net that had tortured her for months was never far from her thoughts.

"A lifebond will be another kind of cage," he bit out under his breath.

Of her few choices, it would present her with the most freedom. She could leave here, for one, and take her human form whenever she chose while still retaining her unicorn abilities. She could use them to do more for the cause of peace than just her treatises had done. "I need it for control, Dhuro."

He hissed a breath. "Why *him*?"

When she simply stared at him, he didn't offer anything else. Not a word, not a hint in his expression, nothing. It wasn't as though anyone else was offering, and Gwydion *was* her sire. "Why *not* him?"

Dhuro sneered, narrowing his eyes. "But I'm good enough for this, aren't I?"

Those words knocked the wind out of her.

He could've slapped her, and it would've hurt less.

She pulled away, wrapping her arms around herself. "I... I thought this was what you wanted."

"It was." Clenching his jaw, he refused to meet her gaze. That was for the best, because if he did, she probably wouldn't be able to hold the tears back any longer. If this was what he truly thought of her, then she would have to live with that when he left. But what she couldn't live with was him thinking so little of himself.

She turned away from him, then glanced back over her shoulder. "Dhuro... you have more to offer than your body. You tell yourself this is all you want when really, you've convinced yourself it's all others want of you."

CHAPTER 20

*A*s soon as she walked away, Dhuro punched his fist into the birch's trunk, shaking leaves off its boughs to rain down on him. What he *really* wanted to do was ram it with his forehead. Possibly twice. Or a hundred times.

Darkness, what was he doing? What stroke of stupidity had led him to open his fool mouth and allow words to come out? Much less *those*?

He'd been jealous enough times in his life to recognize the feeling like an old enemy. What he didn't recognize was the reason.

He was having fun, mind-blowing sex with a beautiful woman, and she didn't ask anything more of him than that. What did it matter that she was considering a lifebond with another man? It changed nothing.

With a sharp exhalation, he tried to compose himself, checking to make sure his clothes were fastened, then slowly made his way back toward the meadow.

If he really had to pin down what infuriated him about all of this, it was that lifebonds were supposed to *mean* something. Veron and Alessandra had claimed to love each other, at least, before forging one. He'd never want one, but they were for people who loved one another deeply, and more than that, *trusted* each other more than he'd ever believe possible. It was a sacred ideal, not something to be entered into lightly.

Janessa had wanted to corrupt it, for the mean purpose of stealing immortal life, and worse, she *had*. She'd succeeded with Dakkar. She'd been selfish, false, and manipulative, and considering Dakkar was still alive, that meant she still was, too, out in the world somewhere.

Bella had seemed so different from her. From the moment he'd met Bella, she'd hated him, and that had been perfect, hadn't it? A woman who hated him could be trusted—she didn't pretend to love him for the purpose of *taking* something. Things were supposed to have been easy with her. Simple. Because she was so different from Janessa.

But she wasn't, was she?

The moment she had been presented with a lifebond for her personal gain—with no love or trust involved whatsoever, let alone deep —her eyes had shone. She'd been tempted, had seen no issue with taking what she needed, even when there was no genuine love behind it.

Even if it wasn't him that she was planning to use, it grated. Because Janessa had proved herself morally bankrupt. And Bella, for all her talk of peace, appeared to be no different.

Holding out his hand, he let the lush forest's undergrowth pass through his fingers.

Things were supposed to have been easy with her. Simple. So when that realization had dawned on him, it shouldn't have mattered. He was going to leave this place and return home anyway, wasn't he?

If only he hadn't fallen in love with her.

But he had. And that was the entirety of the problem. He'd kept his barriers in place, had been harsh enough to push her away emotionally but not physically. And still, somewhere along the way, between their arguments and their kisses and hearing her thoughts, both intentionally and not, her touch had roved from where he liked it to where he didn't. Right into his chest.

When she'd seemed so agreeable to Gwydion's offer, his image of her —and his world—had been falling apart in that moment, and yet the notion of some other man laying claim to her had made him want to possess her in every way possible, greedily and fully, and never let her go.

That clash had resulted in the fiercest sex he'd ever had, and some of the stupidest things he'd ever said.

But the worst part about it was that he'd been right to keep things simple with her. Because when it came to more, even sacred ideals he'd never want, she couldn't be trusted not to exploit it for personal gain.

All women wanted to take something. Arabella Belmonte, for all that he did love her, was no different.

Despite his feelings for her, he was no fool. If she wanted to take a lifebond from someone, it wouldn't be him. He'd nearly fallen for that once, and he would never let it happen again.

When he reached the meadow, it was empty but for the rare roving unicorn, and Gwydion at the far end, staring into a bowl of water intently.

Mati had sent him here to negotiate an alliance, and to bargain himself away if necessary, and he wouldn't fail her, Nozva Rozkveta, or his people. The Immortal beasts were still a threat over their territory, and now, with Dakkar's army wreaking havoc, Nozva Rozkveta would need all the help it could get.

He approached Gwydion from behind, clearing his throat to announce his presence.

"No need for that, Prince, as I can hear your thoughts from across this meadow. The courtesy, however, is appreciated." Gwydion continued staring into the bowl of water, which—despite the conversation he was here for—was fascinating.

"May I ask what it is you're doing?"

"Scrying," Gwydion answered thoughtfully. "We are about to have a visitor, and I am weighing whether I shall grant her entry."

He tried to peek over Gwydion's shoulder at the water's surface. "Anyone I know?"

"From a memory, perhaps. She has not come for you, however." With that, Gwydion straightened and turned to him. The scrying bowl vanished behind him in a flash of light.

Unicorns were powerful magical beings, but it was still a rare sight to see feats performed with no visible effort. The fact that it appeared to be nothing to Gwydion, less than nothing, spoke to the immense power he must possess. It was humbling, in a way he imagined was similar to meeting a titan, or a god. Chilling.

"It was not meant to be disconcerting," Gwydion said with a kind smile. "To our kind, it is merely natural."

Dhuro managed a nod, although having his mind read didn't exactly lessen the unsettling feeling. "I've come to discuss—"

"Prince Dakkar and his rogue army, yes," Gwydion offered, strolling past him with his hands clasped behind his back. "And the Immortal creatures that threaten your people and the humans near you."

Darkness. He resisted the urge to hiss. This did, after all, make this negotiation much more efficient.

"It will also help you save your breath, Prince." Gwydion rested his gaze on two unicorn younglings playing together. "We do not fight wars."

"Not even to save lives?"

Gwydion eyed him, canting his head. "Taking some lives to save other lives? Even more lives than are taken? No."

It had never been a secret that unicorns favored peace. But peace didn't happen on its own; too many beings lusted for blood, for wealth, for land, for power. The innocents who suffered at their hands needed to be protected.

"Not a war, then. What about bringing peace? No killing, but rather ending violence." To anyone else, it might've sounded like a difference of semantics, but if Gwydion truly could read his mind, then he would know it was an entirely different offer. Not to fight together, but to *stop* fights together. Bella had stopped a fight with her abilities, but she'd been untrained and unskilled. Gwydion, however, if vanishing scrying bowls could be believed, possessed an entirely different skill level.

A hearty laugh. "Do not be so harsh on my heir. It is not her fault she was so unprepared." Gwydion paused, looking up at the sky pensively, crossing his arms in a swish of long white robes. "As I said, we do not fight wars. Nor do we often involve ourselves in the affairs of humans or elves."

Dhuro puffed an amused breath. "Not often. So you do, on rare occasions, involve yourselves?"

Gwydion looked him over and gave a nod of approval. "We keep to ourselves, but we are always moving this Eternal Grove due to violence. The affairs of humans and elves spill over into our territory, and although we keep sentinel over the bridge between realms, we are not infallible. We have children here, and innocents, and we would happily reduce the risk to them."

Mati wanted to protect the territory above Nozva Rozkveta, and the unicorns needed territory that could be capably protected from violence. With both the dark-elves and the unicorns keeping watch, the land would be clear. "What if we were to offer you the sky realm land above Nozva Rozkveta?"

"I believe we can come to terms."

His lungs expanded to their fullest with deep breaths. Perhaps it wasn't exactly how Mati had envisioned it, but he had completed the second of the three tasks she'd given him, in his own way. It would benefit all involved. Mati would be pleased.

With a grin, Gwydion continued his walk, this time toward the waterfall and forest pool close to where Bella had been recovering.

Now, however, a unicorn and two light-elf women splashed in its iridescent waters, casting prisms that danced in the air. Other than himself, Noc, and Shrelia, he'd only seen unicorns here, so the women must have taken their other forms.

"Such alliances are typically sealed with bonds," Gwydion said, and Dhuro stiffened. "Would you make the Offering, as your people say, to one of my line, have your children carry the blood of the herd?"

This was why Mati had sent him, to bargain himself away if a deal was reached. To some woman of Gwydion's line.

When he and Bella had met with him earlier, Gwydion had called her *my heir*. Bella was one of Gwydion's line. He swallowed over the lump in his throat. "Would it require a lifebond?"

Gwydion exhaled lengthily, watching his people in the forest pool. "You may choose an agreeable partner. Only one of my line requires a lifebond."

He'd set out from Nozva Rozkveta with the goal of proving himself to Mati, and he'd had three tasks—to safely deliver Bella here, to forge the alliance, and to execute Dakkar. Once he completed them, he could return and claim a place of worth as a kuvar. As a dark-elf, what mattered most was martial prowess, and that place of worth was within his grasp. He'd already completed one task, was close to completing the second, and would have only the third left.

Yes, his goal was within his grasp, but more than that—Bella. For all that he'd learned about her today, he did still love her. She was of Gwydion's line. And he had to make the Offering to someone of that line. An Offering, so similar to human marriage, was one thing, but combining their life spans into one shared unbreakable bond, across which they'd sense each other, feel the other's hurt, even die if the other died? That was different. Vastly different.

If she was set on a lifebond, she was not even an option. Even if she did love him and accept his Offering, which judging by the events today, he was reasonably certain she wouldn't.

Perhaps Gwydion knew all of this, knew that he loved Bella, that she needed the lifebond, that he needed to make the Offering to seal this alliance—and that it would all resolve itself together.

Gwydion just wanted to use him instead, didn't he? It'd be easier to sacrifice a stranger to a lifebond for Bella's control than to sacrifice himself.

Dhuro grimaced, chancing a look at Gwydion, who beamed back at him knowingly. Because of course he knew. He knew everything.

"I must leave you now—I believe our guest has arrived, but do not trouble yourself, Prince." With a laugh, Gwydion patted his back heartily. "You don't have to decide anything now. Think on it, and return tomorrow."

CHAPTER 21

*B*ella paced the small glade one of the unicorns had led her to. By some magic, there was a sprawling bed here, canopied with gossamer sheer silk. Lavender wisteria twined the four posts, studded with climbing vines of flowers in pink, white, and yellow. A brook whispered nearby. It looked like something out of her dreams, but after the day she'd just had, even this beauty couldn't reach her.

Although his touch still ghosted on her skin, although his phantom embrace still held her, Dhuro's harsh words cut as deep as her affection for him had taken root. He truly believed he had no value beyond his body? That his pleasure was all she wanted?

He'd made it clear he hadn't been interested in her heart. That had been perfect for her, because she hadn't been interested in losing hers. Her family's legacy of war had followed her everywhere, and it still did. Assassins shadowed her steps, and anyone near her could be caught in the crossfire. Cosimo hadn't even been a warrior, and she'd lost him to one. But Dhuro... Blades spun endlessly in his path.

He thrust himself into battle, into war, without a second thought. He didn't seem interested in attempting peace, diplomacy, negotiation instead—anything but battle. Unless that changed, there was no way she could live a life beside him, not when he could be taken from her at any moment. And although she had worked tirelessly to end wars in Silen—and she still would—she had no illusions that she would be able to stop all violence on her own. Cosimo died because of her, but she'd be damned before she'd lose Dhuro to her family's legacy.

If he truly thought so lowly of her, then although it hurt, she wouldn't protest. If he didn't want to be with her, then it would only make things easier to ensure his survival and to protect her heart from losing someone so dear to her again. She wouldn't throw herself at him anymore. It would be easier this way, easier because...

Although she'd decided not to give her heart to him, he had taken it anyway.

She loved him.

She'd seen one man she loved die, and she would never be able to bear seeing another. It wasn't worth the pain, the heartbreak, the years of grief and inconsolable sorrow.

He hated the notion of her lifebond to Gwydion? Good. That would help him hate *her*, and walk away before it became a tragedy.

As for her own sake, if she didn't love Gwydion, she would be in no danger of having her heart broken and being hurt. Perfect.

A shadow darkened the path into her small glade. She paused in her pacing, fidgeting, and followed the stretch of its darkness to black boots, crossed arms, broad shoulders, and Dhuro's downcast face.

"Bella," he began softly, taking a step forward.

She took a step back, eyeing the space between them.

He stilled and nodded to himself, chewing his lip. "That's fair." A moment passed in silence between them, only the breeze, the birds, and the brook gracing the air with their sound. "About earlier, I shouldn't have said that to you."

Shouldn't have said it, but not *didn't mean* it. Maybe he regretted voicing those words, but that wasn't the same as regretting them altogether. Or being sorry.

But she couldn't let him underestimate his self-worth, not if she could help it, even if he did think so poorly of her. "Even if we never lay together again, I'd still... I'd still want you in my life, Dhuro."

"Never again? Let's not tempt the Darkness with ill-spoken words." He cracked a smile, a hollow sketch of one. Although he rarely smiled, seeing a forced one like this was worse than none at all, and it seemed impossible to address his mean self-image when he obscured it with a veil of overconfidence.

"I should tell you that I spoke with Gwydion about an alliance," he said, promptly changing the subject, "and we've come to an agreement."

Even as hurt as she was by what he'd said to her earlier today, she could be nothing but happy about this news. "That's wonderful. I hope it will benefit you both."

He cleared his throat, covering his mouth with a fist. "When my mother sent me on this mission, she told me to seal the alliance with an Offering to one of Gwydion's line." His eyes cautiously met hers then, but she quickly looked away.

An Offering? That was the dark-elf equivalent of a wedding. He'd be getting married?

He'd said nothing of the sort throughout their entire affair, but then, it wouldn't have affected something purely physical, would it? Perhaps, in his mind, it still didn't.

But he'd also said *to one of Gwydion's line.*

She was one of Gwydion's line. Did he mean—? A thrill fluttered through her chest, but she tamped down on it. "Dhuro, I..."

"A lifebond isn't required," he swiftly added. "But I will be making the Offering to one of his heirs, if she'll have me."

A lifebond wasn't required. Making the Offering to one of Gwydion's heirs.

Bella's heart sank, and with it her voice. He'd wed a complete stranger happily, but wouldn't even consider her because she was weak and required a lifebond.

She didn't want to wed anyone she loved. Not after Cosimo.

But a lifebond meant sharing a life. If she could've lifebonded with Cosimo, she would have; sharing a life would've meant that when one of them died, so would the other. Dying together was easy. Surviving and living on alone was hard, and she never wanted to do that again.

But a lifebond...

It would help her gain control over her Change and retain her freedom, and it was an answer to the sorrow that had trapped her heart for years. She didn't fear love; she feared loss. A lifebond meant never having to face the loss of someone she loved ever again.

And she loved Dhuro.

Did he really not feel the same? Could she really know if he didn't tell her?

Her instincts told her to focus on what was right in front of her, to not delve too deeply, and what had been right in front of her had been a simple, uncomplicated physical relationship. But this was what Dhuro had talked to her about before, wasn't it? That she rarely looked beyond the immediate to consider what could be, whether that was a threat like her unknown powers, or something entirely different like now.

She and Dhuro had agreed on something simple, and she hadn't questioned it, but he was right; she needed to consider more than the immediate. And she'd never considered that Dhuro might want something more from her than uncomplicated pleasure.

Could he want her for his wife? Could he become more than a lover, but a spouse to her? A partner?

Although their agreement had laid boundaries, she evaluated them differently now. It was possible. More than possible, given his care and sweetness over the past few days, even amid the turbulence of raw emotions. And the idea didn't displease her. No, it... She liked it. Very much. More than she'd ever thought possible after losing Cosimo.

She eyed that space between them again, fidgeting, but this time she bridged the gap and threw her arms around him.

He stiffened, but then he closed his arms around her, too, wrapped her in his embrace. His hold was solid, warm, and comforting, and his soft strokes down her back weren't the lust of a purely physical relationship. They were more, weren't they? They had been for some time, if it wasn't all in her own head.

She had to ask him. She had to.

Gods above, it wasn't easy, but she would never know if she didn't ask. And when he was about to walk out of her life, the time was now, or it would be never.

"Do you love me, Dhuro?" she murmured into his chest.

He went rigid and pulled her away by the shoulders, peering down at her with an imperious gaze. "What is this, Bella?"

His voice was cold, so cold it was as though she were a stranger to him. Where was this coming from? As difficult as it was to ask, it was a simple question. He either did or he didn't. She searched his eyes, but they gave nothing away.

Then it hit her: she hadn't told him first. Asking him how he felt about her without telling him her own feelings first—did that hurt? Had it been too much to ask?

She had to try. "Dhuro, I love you."

"I will *never* lifebond." The venom with which he said it bit, plunged its fangs in deep. And it was as if she hadn't said anything of substance. As if she hadn't said anything at all.

She shook her head; she didn't understand at all. "But—"

"Never," he repeated coldly. "And I may love you, Bella—"

He loved her? He *did* love her?

"—but I don't trust you. And now I never will."

His hold on her shoulders began to hurt, and something like a whimper escaped her throat. When she glanced at her shoulder in his grip, a small red stain darkened her blush-pink dress where his claw dug into her flesh.

With a horrified gasp, he released her instantly, staring with wide-eyed disbelief. "I'm sorry. I didn't—"

Before he could finish whatever painful thing he would say next, she pulled away from him, turned on her heel, and ran.

BELLA DIDN'T LOOK where she was going; it didn't matter.

Her bare feet crashed through the underbrush, gathering cuts and scratches. Small twigs reached from branches and grabbed at her hair, her dress, pulling, tearing. Leaves slapped her skin, and it did hurt, but at least she knew she was still alive, and those words of his hadn't killed her, even if it had felt like it.

He didn't trust her.

All she had done was be open with him. She'd told him everything, been forthcoming with it all, so much so that much of it had been without her volition. Her thoughts had opened to him. Her memories had opened to him. He'd had complete reign over every intimate part of her.

With all of her open to him, what he'd seen had been someone untrustworthy. A woman he'd never hand his heart to, much less his life.

She'd never been a cruel or malicious person, and for the past decade of her life, she had worked tirelessly to help others, and had denied herself love or commitment in order to protect those unlucky enough to enter her life. She had subsisted on crumbs of affection, mere physical relationships, for so long. Too long.

He'd looked at all of her and found her deficient.

Was he right? She'd told him she loved him, and he'd recoiled. If it hurt this much for him to reject her, then she couldn't take anything more.

Tears welled in her eyes, and she ran faster among the birches, not toward anything, but away, from him, from it all, and hopefully through.

She passed a copse of vibrant green, and then a shroud of muted colors claimed the woods around her. No, it was as if the brightness of life had abandoned the forest. Or maybe only her.

She spun, searching for that vibrant copse, but it was gone. All around her was only that muted shroud.

Had she somehow unknowingly crossed the bridge between realms? Left the Eternal Grove?

When she turned again, a black mask faced her, and a gloved fist collided with her face.

৯

DHURO STALKED THE SMALL GLADE, raking his claws through his hair, seething.

It was happening again, all over again, just as it had with Janessa. If all Bella needed was a safeguard, she was just using him.

She could say whatever she wanted, but he'd felt Bella's love for Cosimo. When she'd told him she would never love anyone like that again, he believed her—least of all him. They'd agreed to have fun together, had arrived at the end of the mission, and like an idiot, he'd lost his heart in the bargain. Not only to a woman who could never truly love him, but to one who grasped for a lifebond to help herself.

All the more reason why giving in would be so dangerous. And he didn't plan to even consider that.

Hoofbeats thudded nearby, and Noc's head poked into the entryway. *Is it a good time?*

Dhuro puffed. "Define 'good.'"

Noc ventured in, glancing around.

"She's not here. She threw a fit and stomped out of here."

And just like that, Noc hit him with a face full of tail. *I'm sure your sunny disposition had nothing to do with that.*

Shaking his head, Dhuro strode out of the grove toward the large meadow. "I was right about her. About all of them."

Them? Humans? Noc trotted alongside him, staying close.

"Women."

Oh, Lord of Horses... Noc said with a neigh. *What do you mean?*

"They always want something. She's no different." They passed unicorns, who looked him over and Noc. They didn't get visitors often, he guessed. If he had to find Bella—and he didn't—they'd probably seen where she'd gone.

Want something? Like the lifebond?

"Exactly like." Ahead, a unicorn ambled briskly toward the center of the meadow, where Gwydion stared into the scrying bowl again. "She thought she could manipulate me into one by telling me she loved me." He kept walking until he realized Noc had stopped, then looked over his shoulder. "What?"

You've been hearing her thoughts all this time and seeing her memories, Noc began.

"I have."

Did she ever seem to want anything from you besides pleasure?

From what he had seen and heard, no. Not that he could think of, anyway.

Well?

Dhuro shook his head. She could've still had something in mind.

She has both been so unskilled to have earned multiple rebukes from you, and yet such a cunning trickster that she managed to keep her malicious intentions from her own thoughts, dreams, and memories? Noc pawed the ground with a hoof. *Did it occur to you that she actually loves you?*

He puffed, averting his gaze. It had been just like with Janessa—attempting to coax commitment and affection out of him, all to serve her own ends.

If all she wanted was a lifebond, then Gwydion already offered one to her. Why would she need you?

Dhuro scowled at him. *Gwydion doesn't want to sacrifice himself if he can avoid it,* he thought back as loudly as he could, hoping Noc was listening.

Does she know that? Or are you just making excuses?

Dhuro opened his mouth, but then quickly closed it. Bella hadn't seemed to know that detail, but if she didn't love him, then what else was there? What was it she wanted so badly? His heart pounded harder, thundering in his tightened chest. *It doesn't matter. She doesn't love me.*

How do you know that? How?

Breathing hard, Dhuro spun away from Noc, but Noc darted in front of him and barred his path.

How do you know, Dhuro? How?

His pulse pounding in his ears, he invaded Noc's space. "How? *How?* You really want to know how, Noc? I'll tell you how. It's happened before, that's how. I just *know.* That's how." He'd kept it all in for so long, but the words tore out of him and wouldn't stop. "All of them want something from me. All of them take something from me. Because what am I? I'm not the strongest—that's Zoran. I'm not the smartest—that's Veron. I'm not the handsomest—that's Miro. Look anywhere in my bloodline, and anywhere you look is someone worth loving, worth wanting forever. How, you ask? *How?* There is a trail of women who've come to me, taken something, and left. A trail so damn long I don't even want to remember. Why should this one be different? Why? She sees what they've all seen. I'm the fool who nearly fell for some deceitful human's scheme and defied our queen. I'm the weakling who couldn't even earn a place as a kuvar. I was supposed to be her guardian—and I couldn't even protect Bella from one Darkness-damned macedda. She would have *died* if not for you. Dakkar was in my grasp, and you know what? I failed there, too. How do I know she doesn't love me? The same way I know no one ever has, and no one ever will. I'm not good enough. That's how. If anyone claims to love me, it's because they see a mark, and something to take."

All the movement in the meadow had stopped. Every one of the unicorns, including Gwydion, gawked at him.

He'd been shouting.

Darkness, damn it all. Shaking, he scrubbed a hand over his face and headed for the trees.

Something held him back, and he spun. Noc had the hem of his shirt between his teeth.

"Let me go. Now."

Do you want to add "coward" to that list, Dhuro? Because if you run away now, you might as well add it.

His hands went cold, frozen like ice. Did Noc want to just rub his face in it?

You are worthy of love, Dhuro.

His face twitched, moving against his will. He crossed his arms, avoiding Noc's gaze.

You love her, and you've reached the point in your relationship where you must choose whether you will be open and vulnerable, or whether you will stay behind your walls and let her go. If you stay behind your walls, you'll be hurt, just not by her—by yourself. But if you choose to be open, you might still end up hurt... or you might believe her and find that she truly does love you for you. Not for what you see missing. But for who you are, which is more than the sum of your mistakes.

That was easy to say. "Other than my mistakes, what else is there?"

Noc tossed his head. *You'll have to ask her. I'm not the one in love with you.*

Dhuro rolled his eyes, and as Noc dragged him toward the trees and away from prying eyes, he had no choice but to be strung along unless he wanted to lose his shirt.

Bella makes mistakes, Noc said. *A lot of them. Do you love* her *despite them?*

That wasn't the same. She was different. Although she made mistakes, she was special. His issue with her was that she was dangerous. He'd heard her thoughts and seen her memories, so he knew firsthand what kind of love she was capable of; but she'd already had that true love with Cosimo, so now, with him, what hope was there that he compared?

You mention becoming a kuvar and killing Dakkar and so on... But those are all things others expect of you, aren't they? Ignoring everyone else's expectations, what do you want, Dhuro?

If he didn't know any better, he'd swear Noc was a very strange-looking unicorn, because somehow he knew what Bella herself had asked him. At the healing glade, she'd asked, *But how would you feel if not for your mother's orders? Setting aside what you think everyone else wants of you... what is it that you want? What is most important to you?*

What did he want? What was most important to him? He'd never given much thought to either. A prince's life came with duty, responsibility, and obedience. Every one of his siblings had followed Mati's desires to the last detail. Miro and Zoran had made the Offering for Mati's reasons, and so had Veron. Vadiha had followed Mati's path to become her heir. And Amira, Zaida, and Renazi ran the volodari to Mati's specifications. His brothers had chosen between becoming kuvari or volodari.

Mati had expected him to become a kuvar, and he'd failed.

But what did he want?

There was nothing he wanted in Nozva Rozkveta.

From the moment Ata had taken him to the sky realm, he'd begun a lifelong addiction to its wonders. He liked seeing new places, trying new things, learning about the world. But none of that served Nozva Rozkveta's needs.

More than that, however, what did he want?

He wanted... He wanted his verbal sparring with Bella. He wanted her quiet comfort. He wanted her probing questions, her starkly different worldview, her challenges, and he wanted her kindness.

He wanted her.

Deep, Darkness, and Holy Ulsinael, he wanted *her*.

Even though she made mistakes, he wanted her. His sheihan, his only true match. And no one but her.

Well? Noc asked him.

"Her," he admitted.

Finally. Noc snorted. *Now what are you going to do about it?*

He did love her, but... Before they'd arrived at the Eternal Grove, he'd wanted her thoughts and memories to stop invading his mind. Yet by experiencing them, her private self had been comfortably open to him. Since arriving here, however, she'd been able to share the control she needed with the herd, and her thoughts had gone silent, closed to him. He hadn't realized how much he'd enjoyed seeing her genuineness until that had been taken from him. "I still don't know if I can trust her."

You don't? All right. Then don't waste her time. She may have a human form, but she has an equine form, too, you know. A woman like her doesn't come by every day, and I would risk a lifebond to win her hand for an eternity. Perhaps I should court her?

He wouldn't. Dhuro smirked.

Or I could take a human form. Before the Sundering, human women seemed to enjoy it.

He'd seen Noc's human form, and he wasn't wrong. He stood a little taller. "You wouldn't."

Wouldn't I?

Although Noc had to be joking—hopefully—but he wasn't wrong. Bella challenged him, opposed him, and infuriated him, in all the best ways, and she said she loved him. Risking betrayal was bad, but losing her was worse.

And Darkness, not only had he hurt her, but she'd run off, and he hadn't chased after her. There was no telling how far she'd gone or what state she was in now, all because of him. "I need to find her. Now."

Noc bobbed his head and lowered to let Dhuro onto his back. *What are we waiting for?*

CHAPTER 22

hen Bella came to, she was striding past a stone-pillared temple with a portico, that same one she'd seen in his first shared memory with Dhuro, in the cloak of a summer evening. She tried to stop walking, and when her legs simply continued on, it meant this could only be another memory of his. Wherever he'd been going in this moment of his past, it seemed she was now bound there, too. No matter what had happened between her and Dhuro, it seemed her unicorn powers weren't done with either of them.

The last thing she remembered was a fist to her face, and a black-masked stranger. Although she should be afraid, there was none of the cold fingers, pebbled flesh, or trembling limbs; Dhuro's body strode confidently, shoulders back, chest puffed out. He had purpose and seemed proud of whatever it was he was about to do.

As for her, there was no question that something horrible was about to happen, if it hadn't already. A stranger had hurt her, and if she was in this memory, then she wasn't awake—but she wasn't dead either. Maybe the assassins that had been hunting Renato weren't assassins at all, but bounty hunters.

Or maybe Dakkar had abducted her, in some attempt to gain an advantage over Dhuro? She could have laughed sadly, if she were capable. If Dakkar had hoped taking her would affect Dhuro in some way, he was mistaken. All this had done was remove a thorn from Dhuro's side, a threat waiting in the wings to betray him... because that was how he saw her.

I don't trust you. And now I never will, he'd said, as if she were some predator, some scheming, hungry wolf waiting for the first moment he'd turn his back.

If someone removed that wolf, there would be no revenge, retaliation, or rescue. Just relief.

If she was honest with herself, these were among her last moments. Soon, it would be all over.

Her heart wasn't there to hammer. Her eyes weren't there to cry. Her body wasn't there to allow her to feel even the grief of losing everything, the reality of this last breath of life. The gods had taken so much over these past few months, what were her last moments but a raindrop in a storm?

Her final exchange with Dhuro had been horrible. But he flashed into her mind unbidden—his embrace, his kiss, but also a pansy on her bedroll, his sleeping form keeping vigil, his hand extended to hers. It should have twisted her stomach, made her sick, but it didn't—maybe because this wasn't her body, or maybe because if these really were her last moments, then a few words spoken in anger still didn't erase what she felt. And it hit her that she'd never see him again, or spend another second in his arms, and although she didn't have tears to cry, they welled anyway in this space that wasn't hers but she inhabited nonetheless.

Dhuro's steps slowed as he approached a dense garden surrounding a well-kept home near the town's bustling square. His mouth curved in a slow smile, and he raised his arms, where he held a large bouquet of the most beautiful red roses she'd ever seen—

No, she'd seen them before, outside Nightbloom at their Gates, shimmering as if misted with diamond dust, radiant as if glowing with the vibrancy of life. The dark-elves called the tangled thicket of supernatural roses the Bloom, a natural guard that allowed only allies to pass.

Was it possible that he'd cut these? Or that they had allowed him to take them?

Either way, it was an important gesture, and that meant something big was about to happen.

BRIGHT OF THE MOON

Oh, no. No, no, no... Her mind swam with dread, but his face—that smile was implacable.

Voices carried on the night air from a small outbuilding nestled among the garden, a mill by the looks of it, and his smile broadening, Dhuro neared, keeping to the shadows.

"Oh, I have no doubt." Janessa sounded different, far from the hurt, fragile woman who'd retreated from their last tryst, licking her wounds. Her voice was firm, confident, a little boastful, even?

"I'm amazed. Playing them both against each other, and for so many months. You've worked so hard, and it's finally coming to fruition," another female voice replied, awestruck.

Playing them both...?

"If he doesn't come see me at the spice stall tomorrow, I'll be surprised," Janessa remarked with a mischievous laugh.

"You'll be one of the rare humans to live forever."

The bouquet descended slowly, along with his heavy hands. The spice of pepper dominated, what Janessa worked on, making Dhuro's eyes water and his nostrils sting, but he didn't move, lingering outside the mill.

"Mm-hmm," Janessa agreed dreamily. "And then I can abandon this trade and see the world on my own."

"And if he doesn't show up tomorrow?" the second woman prompted.

"That's the best part." Another laugh. "I have them *both* eating out of the palms of my hands. If one doesn't deliver, then I'll take what I need from the other. It doesn't matter which one—it's not as though I'll be spending my eternity stuck with either!" Janessa added in an excited whisper.

Take what she...?

Gods above, Janessa wanted to live forever on her own... She just wanted Dhuro for a lifebond. And it wasn't even just *him*. There was a second suitor. *Merciful gods and empyreal Veil threads...* Janessa had not only used Dhuro, but betrayed him. For months.

Tears welled in her eyes—but no, they weren't hers. They were Dhuro's.

Backing away, he dropped the roses on the ground. He kept backing away, more and more, eyes wide as he took in the mill, the garden, and everything he'd just heard, and then he retreated, vision blurring, cutting a path through the town. He didn't look where he was going, and although he bumped shoulders with strangers, he didn't stop, blinded by tears.

Her heart broke for him. He'd showed up here with hope, and was now leaving broken.

He'd showed up here... Wait, if his last conversation with Janessa had been about lifebonds, then if he'd come here with so grand a gift as the Bloom's roses, then... then maybe he'd been prepared to offer her everything.

He'd gone to her with no walls around his heart, ready to give her everything, only to learn she'd not only been using him for the chance at eternal life, but had been betraying him and... and had planned to leave him as soon as she got what she'd wanted.

If not for overhearing this one conversation, he might have done it, too, given her everything only to be destroyed in every possible way.

It was no wonder the prospect of love made him wary. If this had been his experience, then love wasn't just risky, but truly dangerous, and she knew that feeling, too, albeit in a different way. He was afraid to lose his heart, but more importantly, his *life.*

His life...

And she'd suggested a *lifebond* to him.

Gods... her heart sank. Janessa had made a fool of him, manipulated him, and nearly robbed him of a lifebond for her own ends, and... and...

And to him, I did the same.

Hot tears blazed trails down Dhuro's face, and although it wasn't her body, she was crying them, too. Gods help her, she loved him and had been ready to be with him for the rest of their lives, but to him, it must have looked as though she was doing exactly what Janessa had.

No, I would never, she wanted to say. But was he wrong in thinking so, when she'd been so ready to accept those terms willingly from Gwydion? She'd been ready to do exactly what Dhuro had feared, even if it would have been with Gwydion's permission.

And in the blink of an eye, she'd been confessing her love to Dhuro and suggesting a lifebond to him, too.

No, no, no...

Never had she wanted to wake up more than now, to leave this dream, this memory, and find him. Tell him she was wrong, and that she loved him, and even if she had to wear arcanir for the rest of her life, she would happily remain by his side with no promise of anything official or irreversible. She wanted him, and to be with him, but she wanted nothing more than he was willing to give. And she never would.

As his tears flowed, the night of Cosimo's death came to her in fragments, like daggers penetrating her heart, each moment a new sharp length of steel, finding new depths in her flesh and new blood to spill. That night had hurt immensely, and so had the following years. And yes, she'd vowed never to let it happen again, and yes, the shadow of the Belmonte family stalked her and those dear to her.

But death hadn't been the sum of Cosimo, or of her time with him. Dhuro had shown her that. What she treasured most had been his life, their joy together, their love. Cosimo giving her a flower, and his wit, his humor, and how he'd made her smile. She would have given anything to save Cosimo, and still would in a heartbeat. But she couldn't. With reality being what it was, the most important thing about him to her hadn't been that she'd lost him, but that she'd loved him, and she wouldn't have traded away her time with him to spare herself the sorrow, even knowing what those moments had led to.

Loss could happen. It could always happen. But wasn't the risk of loss worth the joy love could bring?

She loved Dhuro. It wasn't up to her whether or not he wanted to be with her. If the danger of her being a Belmonte was more than he wanted to face, that was his choice and she would respect it. But if he did want to face it anyway to be together, then she would respect that, too—and do everything in her power to protect him.

She couldn't protect Cosimo. She would have given anything to save him, but she hadn't been able to, as a mere human, as the sheltered and naive daughter and sister in a family of men who warred.

She wasn't naive anymore, and she didn't allow herself to be sheltered. Her eyes had opened to the river of blood her family spilled for coin, and she did all she could to stop it.

She wasn't a mere human anymore, either. She wasn't trained well enough yet, but someday she would be, and she would use every last bit of her unicorn powers to keep Dhuro safe, and to stop anyone who wished to do him harm. She would protect him. She would give anything to save him, and she not only planned to, but would most certainly be able to as a unicorn coming into her powers to stop even wars.

I want nothing but to be by his side, and to give him everything he needs.

That was what she would tell him. If she survived this, she would go to him with no demands or needs, offering him everything. If he truly didn't want her, then... then she would wish him well. But if he did want her, then she wouldn't abandon him out of fear for her own feelings. Because loving him was worth the risk of pain. He was worth the risk of pain.

Cutting through the woods, Dhuro approached the small hunting cabin she remembered from her first shared memory with him. Just outside, the tall, long-haired dark-elf who resembled Prince Veron swung an axe, splitting firewood. He paused in his work, facing Dhuro with a canted head and creased brow.

"Son? What's happened?" The dark-elf, Dhuro's father she now realized, jogged up to him and didn't let him pass, blocking his path.

Shaking his head, Dhuro swiped a forearm across his eyes, turning his head away. "Let me go," he rasped. "Don't look at me—"

"Come here," Dhuro's father said, and although Dhuro resisted, his father pulled him into a firm embrace. "You never have to feel shame with me, Dhuro. I love you whether you're smiling or in tears. Tell what happened, or don't, but I'm here for you in either case."

Darkness pervaded as Dhuro's eyes closed, and the tension lessened in his body as he surrendered himself to his father's hug, and his comfort.

&.

WHEN BELLA BLINKED, it wasn't Dhuro's father she saw, but a pair of familiar hazel eyes in her face. She gasped and tried to pull back, but something rough abraded her neck. She was—

She was tethered. A small, fortified camp surrounded her. Beneath her were four white legs and hooves, and before her was the dark-haired and dark-skinned woman who reminded her so much of Cosimo.

Isisa, she said—or, rather thought. What was Isisa doing here?

Her eyebrows creased together, Isisa held up a finger to her mouth, signaling her to be quiet. Isisa's thoughts, however, were loud. *They know you're Renato, and a unicorn, and they've taken you to collect the bounty. Whoever put the bounty on you goes by "B." and has a camp set up not far, working closely with this cell of hunters. I will try to free you if I can, but there is a dark-elf army not far from here and everyone is alert. Do with that what you will. You're responsible for my brother's death, but Cosimo would never forgive me if I sat by and did nothing. He did love you, and we were friends once.*

Isisa was... trying to help her? *I don't deserve it, Isisa. And I don't deserve you.*

Narrowed eyes bored into her from an inscrutable face.

But wait... *Dark-elf army? Do you know if it is Dakkar of Dun Mozg? Dunmarrow?*

"Did you put the arcanir on her?" a voice called from nearby.

Bella craned her neck but couldn't see past the fortifications. Isisa held up a long, thin arcanir chain, then unclasped it.

There is a dark unicorn wandering these woods, Isisa's thoughts said. *If he sides with the other army, then a lot of humans will die. I'm going to lure him away. Don't try to follow me.* Before Bella could reply, Isisa secured the chain around Bella's neck.

The burn was instant.

Close quarters in darkness flashed through her mind, unbearable agony over her entire body, and the laughter of Brotherhood soldiers. She tamped down on the memory—she'd become an old hand at doing so, after all—and stilled.

"Yes, sir," Isisa called out, and then with a final once-over, she held up the rope tether, raised her eyebrows at Bella, and then disappeared behind the fortifications as well.

A weight settled in the pit of her stomach as Isisa disappeared, but she tried to ignore it. Fear and panic wouldn't help her now. Isisa had said she would try to free her if she could, and Isisa had never been a liar or a coward. Gods above, Isisa had been here only a moment, and she already intended to somehow lure away a dark unicorn. From Nonna's books, it was a unicorn who had rejected pacifism and lost his powers of peace. If one was here, the reason couldn't be good.

Although if Isisa said she would lure it away, then her word was ironclad.

There was still the matter of getting free. While Isisa had said she would try, sitting and waiting wasn't an option.

There was an army nearby. It could be Dakkar, or someone else, but either way, she had to tell Dhuro. Who knew what this army planned to do, and who it would hurt? If Dhuro was at risk, she would die before she'd let him be ambushed. And Isisa had also said *other* army. The situation worsened by the second.

With the arcanir chain in contact with her, she couldn't use her unicorn powers. She couldn't Change either, although even without the arcanir to bind her, it was unreliable.

All she had was this unicorn body.

She pulled at the tether again, digging her hooves in, but it was secured to a large ancient oak. Even with the supernatural strength of the Immortali, which the arcanir bound, she wasn't certain she could rip a massive tree out of the ground.

She did, however, eye the rope tethering her. It was thick, heavy-duty rope, but... it was still *rope*. Isisa had held it up to her as if the answer were obvious. It was, actually.

These bounty hunters had known enough to use arcanir against her, but otherwise, they still seemed content to treat her like a horse.

That was their mistake.

She stepped into the shadow of the oak, out of view of the exit Isisa had taken, and then grasped the tether between her teeth. It was rough, it was hardy, but all she had here was time. As she gnashed her teeth, she tried not to think of what would happen before she could break free. She wouldn't be turned over to B. She wouldn't be killed. The dark-elf army wouldn't ambush Dhuro and the unicorns.

None of that would happen... because she was determined to break free, and she would. She had to.

CHAPTER 23

ith both his own vjernost blade and Dakkar's, Dhuro searched the woods outside the Eternal Grove for Bella, grateful for Noc's speed. Bella had run, but she couldn't have gone far. He and Noc had already scoured every bit of the Eternal Grove, and Gwydion had mentioned before that sometimes younglings accidentally crossed the bridge between realms. Perhaps Bella had done the same, but every moment he didn't find her, his worry grew. Darkness, she could be in tears somewhere, afraid, unable to cross the bridge again on her own, and it was all his fault.

She'd told him she loved him.

And he'd told her he didn't trust her. He'd been cold. He'd *hurt* her.

It was horrible, but he'd chosen this. He'd chosen pushing her away instead of holding her close, bringing her as close as possible, and never letting go again.

He ducked under a heavy-laden bough of an old oak, scanning the distance, but there was no sign of her. They should've encountered Gavri and the rest of the squad, too, by now. Where were they? Shrelia was helping, too, and had flown to search the southern part of the woods for both Bella and the squad. On his weapons belt, he had his dagger and both his vjernost blade and Dakkar's. Whatever she needed, he was ready to do.

I hear something, Noc said. *Stay quiet.*

Quiet? What is it? he thought back, but if Noc had asked him to stay quiet, then it couldn't be Bella. It was something else—a potential threat. Although dark-elves had great hearing, it didn't compare to that of a fey horse.

He dismounted but stayed close to Noc, who led him silently among the dense undergrowth toward an open area of sky. A cliff.

There, Noc said, tipping his head to indicate the edge.

Nodding, Dhuro crouched, slowly inching forward in the concealment of the leafy brush, myrtle bushes. Even he could hear it now—the barest hint of voices, footsteps, and other noises. In the thousands. His chest tightening, he peeked over the edge, just enough.

A sea of tents, soldiers, and beasts, Immortals and mortals alike. The soldiers included light-elves, dark-elves, goblins, and others, a mix of Immortals. An army.

Darkness help him, Dakkar was here. Bella and the rest of his squad were in the path of an army, if they hadn't been captured already.

Or worse.

He shook his head. No, Dakkar wouldn't, would he? He wouldn't hurt Bella.

You don't understand the disloyalty of humans, Dakkar had said to him. *They can't help themselves.*

Dhuro's blood ran cold. Dakkar would do it. If he got his hands on Bella, Dakkar might kill her, especially in her human form.

He and Noc had been unable to find her. There was a chance Dakkar already had—

An unusual man with long black hair strode among the rank and file, tall, pale, and well-muscled as if he were hewn from stone. He wore mere loose black robes, tied at the waist, and carried himself with unshakable confidence. On his forehead, a crescent moon tattoo came into view as the man turned his face toward this direction.

Dhuro pulled away with a shudder. Who was that?

Let's go. Noc's muzzle grazed his neck, teeth pulling on his collar. *Before we're detected. That man is a dark unicorn, the night to Gwydion's day. Rhain. Pray that his curiosity takes him elsewhere.*

Their best hope was a prayer?

Everything inside of him demanded he go down there and find

Bella, but it would be suicide. And if she wasn't there, he couldn't help her if he was dead.

He backed up through the thicket, following Noc back toward the Eternal Grove. A small glow shone among the oaks—a pixie. He and Noc closed the gap toward Shrelia, pushing through the shrubs. Had she found Bella?

But no, Shrelia was alone.

Shrelia rushed toward them, then landed on Noc's nose.

"What is it?" he whispered to Noc impatiently.

Noc eyed him. *She spotted a small camp not far from here, well fortified, but she was detected by a sentry before she could investigate further. But I've tried reaching out to Bella's mind, and I hear nothing.*

Dhuro bolted upright, heart racing. *That's it. That's where she is. Tell her to take us there.* He tried to ignore the rest.

Noc bobbed his head and turned to Shrelia, and in an instant she flitted up from Noc's nose and took off toward the south. *Get on*, Nod said, glancing back.

Dhuro mounted up, and as soon as he had a fistful of Noc's mane, they sped among the trees, rushing past a blur of greens and browns. A small camp separate from the army in the valley meant this was another enemy—the human assassins who had ambushed them in the foothills among the janas' domus. If these assassins had her, who knew how long they would keep her alive?

Darkness, please let her be alive.

Leaves and twigs struck his face and his body, but he didn't care. Time was running out, and he prayed it hadn't already.

Bella, please, if you can hear me, don't be afraid. I love you and I'm coming for you.

At last, the final thread of the rope snapped. Bella took a quick glance around the large oak. No one paid her any mind—the nearby army was as much a blessing as a curse, at least right now. And she needed to get to Dhuro and tell him as soon as possible.

The arcanir chain around her neck stung, and as long as it was there, she wouldn't be able to Change back into her human form or do anything more than a horse could. Her choices were either to attempt sneaking out of here or charging away at full speed.

While she'd avoided attention until now, a swift escape could change that in a heartbeat.

Gaze carefully fixed on the camp, she crept out of the oak's conceal-ment, head hung low, toward a dense thicket of wood-rose shrubs. She kept them between her and the camp, hoping to stay hidden, gulping down her breaths to stay quiet. As much as she'd struggled with her powers, what she wouldn't give to hear the thoughts of her captors now.

Voices rose from the camp.

A snap. The remnants of rope yoking her neck caught on a wood-rose branch, breaking it.

Her legs trembled as she tried to pull free, but the shrub, so tangled with the rope, pulled with it. The cracks and rustling only worsened the more she tried to untangle herself. The branches wouldn't break. Gods above, this was the last thing she needed, to barely escape only to be caught.

The voices in the camp grew louder.

She jerked to the side, thrashing and twisting her head to bend the branches, to weaken them, so they would snap. A few cracks, and then a shout rang out, followed by loud replies.

She tossed her head, yanking on the rope away from the wood-rose shrub. A black-clad man bolted toward her from the camp some fifty yards back.

Shying wildly, she dragged clumps of leafy branches knotted up with her yoke. *Yes!* They were finally breaking away.

Her trembling legs nearly buckled under her as she broke free. An aggressive swipe of an arm missed her just barely.

She ran. Darting through the oaks, she avoided the bushes as best as she could, cantering wildly, too frantic to pick a careful path.

Please be clear... Please be clear...

This was her one chance to escape. Her one chance. Her legs trem-bled beneath her, and she had no choice but to trust them to take her to safety.

Hot on her tail, the man chased her, joined by a few other sets of footfalls farther behind him. She pushed harder, faster, leaping over gnarled roots in the undergrowth.

She could lose him—she had no other option.

Weaving her way among the trunks, she took a chaotic path, placing distance between herself and her pursuers. She didn't know where she was going, but it wouldn't be the camp. Not if she had anything to do about it.

§•

DHURO RACED into the forest with Noc and Shrelia. If because of his actions Bella had come to harm—he'd never forgive himself.

His life had been full of frauds, liars, and users, and the first time in a long while that something good had come into his life, he'd pushed it away, crushed it, nearly destroyed it. And if she was alive—and he prayed she was—he would do everything in his power to save her, and beg her forgiveness, and love her if she'd only let him, anything she wanted as long as he didn't lose her.

Up ahead, flashes of white broke the span of oaks. Had the unicorns sent help?

Shrelia changed direction, and Noc followed, his sure-footed hooves tearing up the forest floor. The unicorn had turned toward them, too, wearing a chain and a rope around its neck that led to frayed ends and leaves—

It's Bella, Noc said, and he needn't have, because Dhuro would know her anywhere.

A human chased after her, clad in black.

He leaped off Noc's back and ran past her, catching her wide-eyed gaze as he drew both vjernost blades.

The human pulled a sword free of its scabbard and swept it upward. With a parry to right, Dhuro struck with his left blade—pommel end to the head.

The human fell to the forest floor, unconscious.

As much as instinct demanded he kill this man, Dhuro only kicked the human's sword aside. Bella's passion for non-lethal means had to be getting to him.

Her big green eyes snapped from Shrelia to Noc to him as she shuffled frantically, tossing her head.

The arcanir, Dhuro, Noc said, stamping at the ground beside her.

Dhuro grabbed the sage-tinted chain. Not only did it bind her abilities, but it also had to hurt, and he wouldn't let it burden her a second longer. If there was indeed another way for her to control her powers, then he'd never want her to feel arcanir's sting ever again. As soon as he removed it, he began working on the rope, too, enraged that someone had dared tie her up. "Are you all right?"

Turning her horn aside, she rested her head against him for a moment. *Yes, I'm fine.* She looked up, meeting his eyes, and Shrelia landed between her ears. *Dhuro, there are more of them out there. I've lost them in the forest for now, but we need to return to the Eternal Grove right away.*

Noc gave him a shove. *Get on. Now.*

Wasting no time, Dhuro did as bidden. Noc and Bella raced through the trees, their trunks and leaves a blur of browns and greens and golds.

Ahead, through the tunnel of gnarled autumn trees and gliding leaves, a pale light shone, glowing brighter and brighter as they neared.

The bridge between realms.

If the unicorns allowed them to enter, they would cross.

The golding woods greened, from autumn to eternal spring, and in the blink of an eye, all that surrounded them was an impossibly verdant paradise.

On the other side, they came to a stop. He dismounted, giving Noc a pat before reaching for Bella. "They can't get in. You're safe."

She rested her head against him. *I saw another memory, Dhuro. And—and about the lifebond, I... I'm sorry. I would never want anything more from you than you're willing to give, Dhuro. I'm so sorry I ever made you feel otherwise. I had no idea what happened between you and...*

"Janessa," he finished for her, the name venomous on his lips. "You're not her, and I'm sorry I ever thought any different," he said, stroking a palm across her head's soft white coat. "You challenge me, you oppose me, you infuriate me... and yet I must have you, sheihan, or no one at all. I don't know what you see in me, but I love you. And I will gladly give you whatever you need to keep you safe, happy, and by my side."

I love you too, Dhuro. And we can figure things out. Her tail swished, and if his eyes didn't deceive him, something glimmered in her gaze. She meant it—he could feel it in every corner of his being. *But I have some bad news I need to tell you.*

Swallowing, he canted his head.

There's a dark-elf army nearby. I don't know who they are or what they want, but it can't be coincidence that they're where we are.

He froze, the words like an ice arrow to his core. *A dark-elf army? Are you certain?*

Yes, that was how she said it. Isisa—she was there and warned me.

Isisa had?

He shook his head to clear it. If she had specifically said a *dark-elf* army, then there was a likelihood that something devastating was about to happen, regardless of whether it was from Nozva Rozkveta or Dun Mozg. "There's a second army."

Join us in the meadow, Gwydion's firm baritone cut in.

Dhuro grabbed his own head. Darkness, that never stopped surprising him.

Come, Noc said, moving ahead of him with Shrelia fluttering above.

Exchanging a look with Bella, Dhuro nodded and followed him.

IN A CIRCLE OF UNICORNS, Gwydion stood at the center in his billowing white robes—but so did a trio of dark-elves. Two of them wore black leather kuvari armor, one with a long thick braid and the other with innumerable beaded braids—Gavri and Kinga. And between them, armored in a similar battle-worn set, was their queen, only the fine jewel beads in her voluminous cascades of platinum hair marking her status.

"Mati," he gasped under his breath. The dark-elf army was from Nozva Rozkveta.

Gwydion spread his arms wide, his billowing sleeves opening like wings. "We are rich with visitors today."

Mati spun, following Gwydion's line of sight with slitted eyes, and strode to him. "Dhuro," she spat, her diamond-shaped face contorted with rage. "You disobeyed a direct order."

She'd ordered him to take Bella to Gwydion, forge an alliance sealed with an Offering, and to kill Dakkar.

Mati hadn't believed he'd accomplish the mission, and if Kinga was with her, then she must've gone back and reported. If she was here, then Mati would do no less than kill Dakkar herself, and there would be all-out war between the two armies. And once Queen Nendra learned of her son's death, there would be another between Dun Mozg and Nozva Rozkveta. Zoran had been right.

Bella stepped up next to him, planting her hooves firmly beside his booted feet. She'd asked him before, *Setting aside what you think everyone else wants of you... what is it that you want? What is most important to you?*

Dakkar had been used by Janessa, and but for one chance conversation, it could have easily been him. Dakkar had been tricked into sharing his life force with Janessa—if either of them died, so would the other; Dakkar could never rid himself of her, and somewhere out there, she was a liability, a deadly one. Janessa's betrayal had twisted up Dakkar, whom he'd grown up with, who was family to him. And just as he wouldn't want Ata or Veron or Vadiha to die because they were twisted by pain and betrayal, he didn't want to kill Dakkar. He wanted to *save* him.

But wanting to and telling Mati so without her dismembering him were two very different things. But he stood his ground, taking a fortifying breath. "Mati, I won't give up on trying to stop him. He will see the error of his ways, or I will die trying to show him. But I won't kill him."

Mati's eyes widened, the corner of her mouth twitching almost imperceptibly. It was a rare few who dared defy her, and of those few, most did so to their peril.

She leaned in. "Vadiha said you were ready, that it was finally time to let you prove your leadership," she hissed. Vadiha had said that? "But I can see she was wrong. You still believe in the fancy of hope and love, after all. You think *hope* and *love* will keep the serpents from the cavern? That is not our way."

"It is my way." He held her unrelenting gaze. "There will be times I will have to draw my sword. But I don't need to draw it for everything."

Raising her chin imperiously, Mati stared him down with fierce eyes that grew hotter by the second, her entire body going rigid. Her claws twitched.

Bella stepped between them, her gaze fixed on Mati, who snarled.

"Queen Zara," Gwydion called, his usually lofty voice firm, "your son has negotiated an alliance between our peoples, pending final wording."

Over Bella's head, Mati glared at him, then looked back to Gwydion slowly. "You will fight with us against our enemies?"

Gwydion inclined his head. "In exchange for access to territory above your queendom, we will bring peace to any conflict to prevent loss of life."

Lowering her gaze, Mati narrowed an eye. It wasn't exactly what she'd wanted, but she had expected something the unicorns would never agree to.

"Should the worst, as you fear, happen," Dhuro cut in, forcing a confidence into his voice he didn't feel, "then the serpents at the cavern will leave in peace."

Mati didn't acknowledge him at all.

He didn't need her praise. He'd helped his people and Gwydion's, and she knew it.

"If there is an agreement," she said to Gwydion, "then my son is making the Offering to one of your line."

Gwydion glanced at Dhuro. They were out of time, but more importantly, there was only one woman he could ever walk his life with for as long as the Deep would allow.

Bella craned her neck back to eye him.

He winced. "To Bella," he said, answering Mati but keeping his eyes locked with his sheihan's. "If she'll have me."

Those vivacious green eyes widened, reflecting his face in them. But she didn't speak a word into his mind.

"You would bond your life to hers?" Gwydion asked.

A shiver rippled Bella's snow-white coat, but she didn't look away from him.

"Yes," he said to Gwydion. And to her, "Not how I wanted to ask you."

Her mouth dropped open, and she breathed hard.

This is sudden, and I... I need to think. Before he could open his mouth to say anything more, she retreated.

CHAPTER 24

*B*ella grabbed for a sheet off the canopied bed in the small glade; she had willed herself to Change to human form, and she had, but whoever had helped her last time had been able to give her clothes. Something she didn't seem capable of.

She wrapped the sheet around herself and fixed it tight with trembling fingers. Dhuro had said he would lifebond with her.

He couldn't just offer that, not when she needed so much more than he could ever give. In the hunters' camp, she'd seen exactly how the pieces of him had shattered. And after what Janessa had done to him, he'd been justified in being wary of commitment, in abhorring the idea of a lifebond. He had good reason, and if he didn't trust her enough yet, or if he wasn't ready, then he shouldn't enter into it for her sake or to appease Gwydion and Queen Zara.

Dhuro had helped her look beyond what was in front of her, and she would keep trying. This wasn't just about what she wanted; it also had to meet Dhuro's needs and respect his boundaries. There had to be another way. The alliance didn't require a lifebond, but a marriage—an Offering.

To help control her powers, Gwydion had suggested either staying with the herd or forming a lifebond. Was there a way for her to remain with the herd but married to Dhuro? Then she'd never be able to leave, lest she risk her powers manifesting out of control. But wouldn't Dhuro want to leave? He wouldn't want to stay in the Eternal Grove either, even as beautiful as it was.

Could she still accept Gwydion's offer to lifebond, but marry Dhuro? Would that upset him?

Although, after seeing what Janessa had planned to do and the impact it had, a loveless lifebond looked different to her, even if Gwydion offered it willingly. It was cold, cruel even.

There was the arcanir.

It always took her back to those months spent netted by the Brotherhood, in fear and in pain, and she didn't know if their hold over her would ever abate. Could she spend the rest of her life bound by arcanir, endure the flashes of trauma?

But then, she'd never be able to use her abilities to help stop wars. Even removing the arcanir, she wouldn't have the necessary control to ensure her powers would only do what she wanted them to, or even over her form, or her thoughts. It would require years of training, or maybe decades, for her to acquire the requisite skill.

What options did that leave her with? Because she wanted to be with Dhuro—she was firm on that. But she also wouldn't accept anything more than he genuinely wanted to give—she was firm on that, too.

There had to be an option.

Dhuro ran into the glade and stopped as soon as he entered, looking her over, eyebrows raised. "That's a different look."

She ignored her desire to laugh, shaking her head.

As he approached her, she turned away, but he took her hand regardless and brought it to his lips. She didn't want to give in to this, not when he felt forced to offer more than he was comfortable with.

"Come back to the meadow, sheihan." He kissed the inside of her wrist. "Everyone is waiting for us."

Gods, his touch made her melt, but how could he act so unperturbed by all this? "Dhuro, you don't have to do this. I don't want you to."

"This is what you need." He dropped another kiss higher up on the inside of her forearm, and her gaze meandered toward him. His sensual eyes locked with hers, he lowered his lips to the inside of her elbow, pressing their warmth to her skin as he watched her, making her shiver pleasurably.

Her mouth went dry, and she swallowed past the lump in her throat. She was trying very hard to have a serious conversation, and it wasn't fair, him using his seductive wiles on her. "But after everything that happened with Janessa, you hate the thought of a lifebond."

"Not as much as I'd hate losing you, or seeing you suffer." He kissed the inside of her upper arm, a place almost no one had ever touched, and she tensed as it tickled. A sly grin played around his mouth. "I want to give you everything you need, always."

"That goes both ways, Dhuro. I want you to have everything you need, too," she said, making a half-hearted attempt to pull away as his lips moved to her shoulder. "And I know you need to be free of a lifebond to trust your partner."

He rumbled a sound of disagreement in his throat as his kiss pressed to her neck. "You're not Janessa."

As his lips passionately met her neck, her thighs began to tremble, her knees buckled, but just as she began to lose herself, his arms wrapped her like a vine. "Sheihan," he whispered in her ear, sending a pleasant shiver through her, "let me be what you need."

"Sheihan," she repeated, and he groaned deeply, leaning to her. "You've said that before... What does it mean?"

Smiling warmly—a rare treat that was becoming more frequent now—he drew away only enough to meet her eyes, searching them. "The perfect match to a warrior, a mind, a heart. We have a word for this in the dark-elvish tongue." He lowered his mouth to hers, brushing it with a kiss before pulling back once more. "You're my true match, my sheihan, and I understand all that it means now. Every time I pushed you away, you could have given up on me, but you fought for me. When everything around me wanted to control my life, you asked me what I wanted and fought for it. Darkness, you got in my *mother's* way. And I know you don't need a lifebond with me for an immortal life—you already have it."

"But I *do* need one, to control my Change."

He cupped her face in his hands. "And you could have it with Gwydion. But I count myself lucky that you love me, and you want me." Then, his voice dropping an octave lower, he added, "And you *do* want me, sheihan. You've made that clear."

Her chest rose and fell faster as her heart began to race. "You're not afraid?"

"I am," he said softly, his gaze on her lips, "but my love for you is greater than my fear of betrayal. And I want this." He slipped a claw between the sheet and her chest, slowly tracing its edge along her skin, and she clutched it a little tighter, even as heat pooled low in her body. "The things I would do to you, sheihan, if there weren't a war about to happen"—he tugged the corner of the sheet—"and I'd be lying if I didn't admit I am very tempted to anyway."

With a gulp, she re-tucked the sheet's corner, stepped away, and cleared her throat. None of that helped tame the fire simmering in her blood. "Are you sure you want this, Dhuro? Because it completes me just to be with you. The rest we can figure out."

"I want this. Do you, sheihan?" He smiled, fully, happily, and extended a hand to her. "Will you share your life with this cave troll of a dark-elf?"

Rolling her eyes, she laughed.

He tilted his head, and that full smile of his twitched. "To spend eternally arguing with me, telling me how wrong I am, and maddening me in the best ways possible?"

She laughed again and placed her hand in his. "It would be my honor and joy."

"Then my people have a tradition. I'm not prepared, but I have never been more ready." Holding her hand, he lowered to a knee, bowed his head, then looked up into her eyes while her heart threatened to burst. "Arabella Belmonte, heir to Gwydion of the Eternal Grove, I, Dhuro of Nozva Rozkveta, offer you control"—he placed a hand over his chest—"protection, support, never-ending amusement, and love"— then on his vjernost blade, his ear, his lips, and he took her hand once more—"to harness for your ends or ours, as we walk our lives together from this day forward for as long as the Deep allows."

He didn't look away, and gods above, a madness came over her and she jumped into his arms, kissing him deeply as his arms encircled her and a laugh rumbled in his mouth. "I accept," she breathed between kisses.

"Dhuro of Nozva Rozkveta, I, Arabella Belmonte, offer you my love, my protection, my support, and my loyalty, to harness... for your ends or ours, as we... walk our lives together from this day forward." Hoping she'd remembered the words, she kissed his smiling mouth. "Did I do it right? I wanted to add one more thing, but it might be a little too obscene for the moment—"

A hearty laugh broke free of him, and he kissed her again. "I think I've already accepted that particular Offering with enthusiasm."

"Oh, you have," she said playfully.

"And I plan to again tonight. Thoroughly," he said slowly, his voice an octave deeper as he held her gaze. "But first, we have a war to stop."

Nodding, she nevertheless leaned in to claim his lips once more. Nothing made her happier than the notion of stopping a war and saving lives from needless violence. Except maybe what Dhuro would do to her tonight.

He rose, her hand still in his, and sharing an affectionate look, he led her back to the meadow.

※

HOLDING Bella's hand in his, Dhuro entered the Eternal Grove's central meadow, where Noc and Shrelia approached them from the flower-lined edge.

The queen and her kuvari left, Noc told him while Shrelia flew up to Bella and chimed excitedly, fluffing her hair.

Gwydion awaited them, his head bowed over the scrying bowl on a table.

"You will want to visit your family soon, Arabella," Gwydion said, without looking up from the water's surface.

"Is everything all right with them?" Bella asked, and Gwydion only beamed a serene smile at her and returned to his scrying. "Queen Zara leads her army at dusk," Gwydion added, changing the subject. "Although she has said it is to push for peace."

"We have to stop the battle," Dhuro said. "No matter what she agreed to here, she'll want to kill Dakkar." Unless unilateral violence by Nozva Rozkveta would nullify the alliance, which Mati would never have agreed to, she would try to eliminate any threats to the treaty with the humans.

"We have been asked to mediate the negotiations," Gwydion added, "and that includes you, Arabella, as my heir."

She nodded. "I will help in any way I can, in any way you see fit."

Next to the scrying bowl lay a small, bright metallic cluster shaped like a crystal. A *kryzi*. It was the sacred item that dark-elf mystics used during lifebond ceremonies. Had it only just appeared? Had Mati brought the kryzi from Nozva Rozkveta?

"It is not the same one," Gwydion said, once again eerily reading his thoughts. He wondered now just how thorough the unicorns' mind-reading had been, because he'd had some vivid, graphic, extremely private thoughts recently. But if they'd overheard any of that, they gave no sign. Praise the Dark for that, at least. "It is not a thing created by your people, but handed down from mine."

"Unicorns?" he asked, raising an eyebrow. He'd never heard of unicorns using a kryzi.

Gwydion rose and faced them, hands clasped behind him. "Dragons."

Dragons? Next to him, Bella's mouth fell open.

"My people are shapeshifters, but I and my kin were exiled when we pushed for a peaceful regime. All knowledge of the dragon form was taken from us by the Dragon King, Nyeris. Since then, we have claimed a new form as our chosen one." Gwydion said it as if he were relaying a cave wine recipe, as there were nothing shocking about it at all.

A lofty laugh, and Gwydion's eyes shuttered to half-moons. "How amusing," Gwydion said to him, then gestured toward the kryzi beside him. "Have you both come to a decision?"

Surely Gwydion knew the answer. Bella gave his hand a gentle squeeze and glanced from him to Gwydion and back again with a smile.

"We have. Bella and I have made the Offering, and we wish to seal it with a lifebond." Saying it aloud had a power to it.

"We do," Bella added, nodding her agreement.

You do? Noc asked, with a pleased swish of his tail. *Congratulations to you both.*

Shrelia flittered before Bella's face, chatting. She must have said something funny, because Bella laughed heartily.

"I am pleased to hear it." Gwydion glanced between them, then looked Bella over. The sheet she'd wrapped around herself became the pink velvet gown she'd worn the day before. She gasped, running her palms over the skirt.

Gwydion retrieved the kryzi. "I don't know your people's customs," he said to Dhuro, "but the bond will work all the same."

The dark-elves made lifebond ceremonies elaborate banquets, with all their loved ones present, abundant food, games. Despite all the fanfare, the lifebond act was very simple.

Although he wanted to shout into every corner of the deep realm and this one that Arabella Belmonte had chosen him, what mattered most was *that* she had, not shouting it to the world. What mattered most was right here beside him, and even if there was no large crowd, no abundant food, and no games, there was her, and him, and the incredible, enormous, exhilarating step they were about to take together.

He'd only ever seen Nozva Rozkveta's elder mystic, Xira, perform lifebonds, and he knew enough in order to do this properly. He opened his palm to Bella, and looking up from her magically conjured gown, she mirrored his movement with hers.

Gwydion placed the kryzi between their palms, and they squeezed it together. A pinprick stuck his palm, and Gwydion took their joined hands between his and closed his eyes.

When he opened them, he let their hands open.

There was no mark, nor blood on their palms.

"You are now lifebonded," Gwydion said, taking back the kryzi, which instantly disappeared.

"Joined in life and death," Dhuro added, holding Bella's radiant gaze, reciting the same words he'd heard Xira recite so many times before, "able to sense each other, draw each other, call to each other. What Offerings made and accepted today before the Deep, Darkness, and Holy Ulsinael, let no other pursue. We swear this by the Darkness."

By the Darkness, Noc replied, no stranger to dark-elf Offering ceremonies himself.

"So let it be." Gwydion inclined his head and took his leave.

Well done, Noc said, nudging him with his nose, while Shrelia sat between his ears.

"Thank you for your wisdom and your support, old friend." He might not have been here right now without Noc's guidance.

With a bob of his head, Noc followed Gwydion with Shrelia.

Holding Bella's hand in his, Dhuro pulled her to him, and she fell against his chest, giggling. "Now you're stuck with me, sheihan."

"I believe you have that backwards, my husband. I hope you're sure you want me annoying you for the rest of your life, because there's no turning back now."

Raising her chin, he kissed her, stealing her away into his embrace, letting his mouth and his tongue tell her everything his heart sang to him.

"Is that a yes?" she whispered, her breath warm on his lips.

"An enthusiastic one," he said, grinning. "Verbal communication isn't one of my precious few skills, remember?"

He gave her a playful wink, and she pushed him away jokingly. The moment faded in quiet affection.

"So now, instead of my wedding night, we go to war," she said with a grave sigh.

He nodded. "Help me, sheihan," he said softly. "Help me before my mother kills my best friend."

CHAPTER 25

*H*olding Bella's hand securely in his, Dhuro followed
Gwydion and his herd through the bridge between realms,
across its iridescent blur and into the sky realm's dusky woods, with
Noc and Shrelia beside him. Only the younglings and the pregnant
females had remained in the Eternal Grove, while the rest joined
Gwydion, who still wore his human form.

Even on the other side of the bridge, Bella retained her form as well.
Her face aglow, she rested her head on his shoulder for a moment,
closing her eyes and taking a free breath.

The lifebond had worked. She didn't need to be in the Eternal
Grove to have control over her Change and her powers now—or maybe
it was that she was still with the herd. In any case, the thought that he in
any way nourished her with his life brought him a joy he'd never imagined possible. All this time he'd feared others taking from him, and it
turned out that giving to his sheihan made him happy beyond measure.

As he held Bella's hand, he couldn't help but think that the very last
place he wanted to take that which he held most dear was a battlefield,
to a clash between two armies. He still might have questioned the
soundness of following Gwydion, even with most of the herd doing so,
until he recalled that Gwydion had claimed to be a dragon.

He should've laughed at the very notion, but there were things he'd seen in the past few days that he couldn't explain. It was widely known that unicorns had magical abilities, but the power Gwydion possessed was as impressive as it was eerie. If any deadly threats did arise, there was no question Gwydion could quell them.

Perhaps that was why Gwydion had revealed his origins. To set them at ease, to give them confidence.

He looked at Gwydion as he strode through the myrtle and the oaks, but Gwydion gave no indication of hearing him.

It's going to be all right, Bella spoke into his mind, her voice reassuring. *Nothing's going to happen to you. I won't let it.*

Don't tell me you heard all that? He winced.

Fine, then I won't. She gave his hand a squeeze.

There really won't be any secrets between us. Although it was strange to have his thoughts heard, it didn't displease him. If this was an incidental benefit of their lifebond, he didn't mind it.

Bella studied the undergrowth ahead, where creepers of colorful flowers had entangled the oaks. *Secrets are like vines of autumn bittersweet... Alluring at first bloom, but as it wraps everything, the vines smother all in their grasp.*

She was right, and he didn't want to keep any secrets from her.

I'd like to take you to Roccalano to meet my mother, Bella added thoughtfully. *I want to introduce you, and I want to tell her and my brother Luciano the truth. Neither of them know about my activities as Renato... Just because someone doesn't know the truth doesn't mean they're not endangered by it. I want to live an honest life. If these past weeks have taught me anything, it is that you can only truly love someone when you can see them clearly. And that can only happen when we let each other in.*

He nodded. Bella's unusual abilities as a unicorn had allowed them to become closer than he ever could have imagined. What had started out as an inconvenience had become a gift. *I would be honored to meet your family.*

When Gwydion led them out of the woods, sprawling plains awaited them beneath the banked fire of the setting sun. On each end lay a sea of troops in the thousands, darkening the edges of the field to the horizon, and between them a thick swath of grass. Gwydion took the middle way, guiding a ribbon of white down the center.

As they came between the two armies, a small squad rode out from each toward them like arrows.

Darkness willing, there would be no crossfire, but he was glad he'd brought his weapons.

Bella leaned against his arm, intertwining her fingers with his.

Fierce in her kuvari battle armor, Mati approached on horseback, with Gavri bearing the black sun flag and Captain Riza with her. Her hair tightly pulled back and her face cold, Riza gave nothing away. But as captain of the royal guard, there was no way she'd disobey Mati, even for the sake of Nozva Rozkveta's best interests; her loyalty had always been stoneclad.

From the other army, Dakkar rode in with a flag-bearing light-elf warrior and Zoran. Even in the beginning, Zoran had never wanted Dakkar dead, just dissuaded and returned to Nendra in Dun Mozg. Judging by this, Zoran hadn't succeeded in either, so now it fell to him to defend Dakkar's life to prevent angering Nendra.

When both squads stopped within ten feet of them, Gwydion held up a hand, his robes catching in the wind. "We are here to witness a peace between Queen Zara of Nozva Rozkveta and General Dakkar of the Immortal Army."

The Immortal Army? Was that what Dakkar called it? And did he now introduce himself as a general rather than a prince, renouncing his title?

Mati steered her horse to the side, sizing up Dakkar and glaring at Zoran. "Disband your army and return to Dun Mozg, and we will have peace," she bellowed. "That is my offer."

Dakkar stared at her with an even gaze. "Join me in conquering the humans, and share in the spoils equally. That is *my* offer."

Mati puffed derisively. "You do not dictate terms to me, child."

"Then take your army and leave. Don't trouble yourself with the humans. You have my word I will not harm your kin," Dakkar declared.

"You ask me to break my word to the Sileni king, and in the next breath you offer yours." Mati stilled, eyes narrow. "Nendra neglected to teach you that to produce food, there must be agriculture. Conquer the humans and we shall all starve, lest you plan to eat them."

"I'm well informed. We will take whatever our people require." Dakkar sneered. "But have it your way, Your Majesty."

Negotiations were over.

Dakkar signaled to the light-elf, who lowered their flag, a black griffin on a purple field. Mati did the same, locking gazes with Gwydion before she turned back. Gavri and Zoran shared a look across no man's land and followed their leaders.

Just like that, his mother would cross swords with his brother and his best friend? What had been the point of coming out here between them, when Gwydion and the unicorns had done nothing?

"We cannot force others to change their minds, Prince," Gwydion said, showing no sign he planned to move, let alone quit the battlefield.

"You didn't even try," he shot back. A few faces turned toward him, and even Bella flinched beside him. The herd parted, creating a clear line of sight to Gwydion.

"Each of them tried. We do not force minds to bend to our will." Gwydion's gaze wandered the herd. "But we also will not allow innocents to be killed."

Gwydion wouldn't allow—?

He and the unicorns planned to use their powers?

Yes, Bella answered for him. *And so will I.*

A tremor shook the ground. Cavalries charged from both ends of the field.

Here, he and the others were in the worst possible position.

Don't be afraid. Next to him, Bella faced the Immortal Army with a determined look. Unicorns took up positions around him, Noc, and Shrelia.

The ground quaked harder. Battlecries warred in the air. Front lines tore up the grass between them, clashing on the far ends and sealing the gap toward the center.

He moved to shield Bella when the cavalry split.

All around them, horses, riders, and warriors flowed around them and froze, mid-step, mid-strike. Gwydion's gaze roved over all those around him. Every soldier who raised a weapon to kill another was paralyzed by Gwydion's look. And every unicorn did the same—even Bella's gaze stopped every clash it sighted.

Her eyebrows creased together as she glowered at individual warriors. Each of them gasped, as if set free from some spell, and then spun to quit the field.

She's willing them to leave, Noc said, standing beside him. *They're dispelling the negative emotions, commanding them to stop, and then willing them to leave. They're pacifying the battle.*

He wanted to ask how that was possible, but it wasn't so long ago that Bella had charged into a battle between his squad and a group of light-elves on griffins, and she'd done the same then.

The black silhouettes against the fire-red sky began to fade, dissipating as warriors left the field, one by one.

With a groan of effort, Bella took a few steps outward as the armies dwindled and dwindled, until less than a hundred fighters engaged each other. He followed her, keeping a watchful eye on the periphery; she was strong and well supported by her people here, but he'd recently been reminded that unicorns weren't indestructible.

She froze two dark-elves mid-strike—Mati and Dakkar, her jaw clenching, her face tightening. *Their wills are too strong—I can't hold them much longer, Dhuro.*

"Kill him, Dhuro," Mati gritted out, although she didn't move. "Kill him now, or you will never have a place in Nozva Rozkveta again."

"Why would he want a place in a queendom ruled by a coward?" Dakkar hissed, and the fingers curled around his blade's hilt twitched.

Hurry, Bella's voice implored.

"I'm not going to kill you, Dakkar." Ignoring their wild eyes, Dhuro disarmed them both, throwing each of their swords far away, and then faced Dakkar. "Janessa deserves to be brought to justice, but you're not just hurting humans with what you're doing. You're hurting your own people, too, and in your heart, you know it. When the mages unite against us and crush our people, will your vengeance have been worth all that loss of life?"

Dakkar's eyes stared into space, into nothing. "You don't know that—"

"I know, and so do you."

I can't— Bella's voice broke off.

Drawing both of his vjernost blades, Dhuro blocked Dakkar's sword as it came down on him accompanied by a loud vykrikovat.

"You chose the wrong side," Dakkar growled, unleashing a torrent of strikes. Dhuro parried each one as the unicorns thinned the field around them.

Dhuro, your mother—I can't hold her much longer—

Under a relentless assault from Dakkar, he didn't dare look over his shoulder at her.

"Fight me," Dakkar snarled, cutting his arm with a well-placed blow. "I don't want your pity!" he gritted out, each word punctuated with a strike.

Evading a cut, Dhuro swept Dakkar's legs out from under him. "I won't kill you."

Dakkar rolled. *Toward* Mati, who was immobilized, roaring an ear-splitting vykrikovat.

His heart thundering, Dhuro lunged after him, but Bella released her instantly.

In a deadly torrent, Mati lashed out with her blades, faster, stronger, fiercer than Dakkar, putting him on the defense and forcing him to fall back. Glittering with battle rage, she set upon Dakkar like a storm, leaving him to flail in the violence of her advance.

Dakkar roared a call. A sharp griffin's call rent the air, followed by the flapping of wings. As Mati lunged, Dakkar leaped away toward the waiting claws of a swooping griffin, who snatched him up.

Mati sprang up after him, but not close enough to catch him. She landed with an anguished, infuriated cry. Looking over her shoulder, she turned her anguish and fury at Dhuro.

Dhuro! Bella's shrill voice cried out in his mind.

Blades drawn, Mati charged toward him. He faced her with his own twin vjernost blades, his throat tightening but his stance ready.

Bella jumped between them.

In a flash, Gwydion was in front of them both and caught Mati's wrists with his palms, tightening his grip until she dropped her weapons. Her gaze went wide as he splayed his fingers open with a blast of blurry power, sending her flying backward. Skidding in a deep muddy furrow across the field, she at last speared a clawed hand into the dirt and stopped.

"You," she spat, glaring at Gwydion. Ethereal runes sprouted from his back in the shape of massive phosphorescent wings.

"*Queen Zara,*" Gwydion replied, his voice the choir of a thousand deep eldritch creatures, "*we bring peace to any conflict to prevent loss of life. Even against our allies. You were warned.*"

Mati's face drained of blood as she stared, her eyes so open that the whites surrounded her amber irises entirely. Tears burst and trailed down her cheeks, as if she had seen the face of Holy Ulsinael.

"Return to your queendom," that bone-chilling choir of voices commanded, and without a breath in protest, she receded, spun, and fled, just as both armies had already.

Dhuro's blood ran cold; he'd never seen Mati afraid in his life, much less fleeing.

Gwydion twisted, his face a mosaic of glowing rune-like pearlescent scales, his eyes burning a luminous violet like miraculous starlight. He would have been sublimely beautiful if not for his too-wide mouth, overly full of needle-sharp teeth.

Dhuro moved in front of Bella, standing between her and Gwydion, before he even realized what he was doing.

Gwydion's runic wings enfolded him, and slowly, his radiance diminished until his appearance returned to his simple human form, with a sun rune on his forehead and waves of snowy hair. The battlefield around him had cleared of both armies, and the herd of unicorns trickled in to surround them.

Whatever Dhuro had just seen, it had dispelled a battle and not only disarmed but terrified two of the strongest warriors he'd ever known. Whatever Gwydion was, or whatever monstrous wraith had possessed him, he had ended a clash with no loss of life.

Bewildered, Dhuro looked about the empty field, attempting to piece together what this meant.

Mati had been unequivocal in her banishment; he would not be allowed to return to Nozva Rozkveta. The unicorns had delivered on their alliance terms and had brought peace to the conflict. And Dakkar's army had been disbanded.

Dakkar lived, and as Gwydion had said, there was no forcing his mind to bend to their will, but without an army, he was now a toothless wolf. Hopefully Dakkar would use this peace that had been imposed upon him to search his soul for the truth.

"Come," Gwydion said serenely, himself again. "Let us return." He led the way back to the woods, and the herd followed.

Noc and Shrelia waited beside Dhuro, and he glanced toward Bella. "What about us? What should we do, sheihan?"

She took a deep breath, scouring the horizon with a far-seeing gaze, then looked back to him with soft eyes. "Let's go home."

CHAPTER 26

*A*lthough a part of him had wanted to return to the Eternal Grove, Dhuro didn't object when Bella led him, Noc, and Shrelia east instead in the night. Gwydion and his herd would be traveling west to Nozva Rozkveta, where new territory now awaited them. Still, it would've been nice to have supplies.

There had been no sense in going with Gwydion, considering Mati had banished him from Nozva Rozkveta. Returning there would be asking for imprisonment or worse, and he very much liked his freedom. Someday he would find a way to reconcile with Mati, but given her rage, it wouldn't be anytime soon.

"We'll both find a way," Bella corrected as she pushed aside a sapling's branch. It would still take some getting used to before he'd grow accustomed to having his thoughts heard, but it *was* growing on him.

If he was honest, he did enjoy the sky realm. Janessa's betrayal had soured it for him somewhat, but her ugliness couldn't destroy the freshness of the air, the vibrancy of the trees and plants, and all the strange creatures and things that could be found here, new ones he had yet to see and learn about.

What he would miss, however, was his family. His sisters, even Vadiha, and her daughter, Dita. He'd even miss Mati. At least he could still visit Zoran in Dun Mozg, if Queen Nendra didn't take his prior attempt to kill her son too poorly.

Bella had been keen on them returning to Roccalano, to stay there at least for a while, and he did want to meet her family. Perhaps that place would feel like home in time, too.

"Trust me." Bella smiled over her shoulder at him as they cut a path through a small birch woods. It was nearly dawn, and they'd been walking for some time, but she wouldn't tell him more except that there was a surprise.

The hum of rushing water came from the area ahead, and he exhaled a sigh of relief. With no supplies, a river was a welcome gift. Still, judging by her coyness, he'd expected a hot bath, a lavish feast, and a comfortable bed to await them. They'd just survived a battle, after all.

A fire flickered among the birches. He canted his head.

"Surprise," Bella said, extending her arm toward the fire. Leaves littered her hair and her dress was torn in places, but with that beaming grin and her face aglow, she was adorable. Shrelia perched on her shoulder, while Noc eyed him, tail swishing mischievously.

You'll like this surprise, Noc said, tossing his head.

Emerging from behind a cluster of birches was none other than Zoran, still wearing his battle leathers, his long hair unbound. Before he could say anything, Zoran already charged for him, arms wide.

"Brother!" Zoran called out with a broad grin before wrapping him in a huge hug. "It's so good to see you alive."

Although he pushed Zoran away, he had to admit it was good seeing him, too. "Same to you."

"And you," Zoran said, circling Bella with a hug while she giggled. He ruffled Noc's mane, receiving a head bump in reply. "Old friend."

Dhuro crossed his arms. "You didn't seem pleased to be by Dakkar's side."

Turning back to him, Zoran pressed his lips tight in a rare frown, then leaned a hand against one of the birches. "His forces showed up to stop me before I could subdue him. When I found out Mati had come with the army, I had to stay to protect him. For Karla."

Dhuro nodded. "Do you know what happened to everyone after Gwydion and the unicorns sent them away?"

With a heavy sigh, Zoran let his back rest against the tree trunk while Bella passed him with a smile, heading for the campfire with Noc and Shrelia. The surprise had been worthwhile indeed.

I did say to trust me, she replied with a wink.

"After the unicorns pacified the field, everyone went their separate ways. Without a headquarters, Dakkar's army is scattered to the four winds. As for Mati's forces, no doubt they'll all find their way back to Nozva Rozkveta," Zoran answered with a shrug.

He wanted to tell Zoran he'd been banished, but with the tight-fisted control Nendra kept over Zoran, he'd already been living a banishment in effect, too. "Do you think Mati will leave it be?"

"Dakkar?" Zoran asked, quirking a thick eyebrow. "Probably not. But neither will I. I'm going to find him and bring him back to Nendra, just as she commanded."

With Zoran's access to his own daughter at stake, he wouldn't give up. "Find me in Roccalano if you need help."

Zoran gave him a wink. "Already planned on it, my brother."

Clapping him on the back, Zoran urged him toward the campfire, where he'd enjoy his brother's company before setting out for his new home with Bella tomorrow.

ALTHOUGH BELLA HAD RETIRED to their tent, sleep proved elusive even as the night wore on. Outside, Dhuro's and Zoran's voices rose and fell in peaks of excitement and valleys of whispers, and she couldn't help but smile to herself, tucking the wool blanket closer around her body as she teased a vine-patterned silk scarf between her fingers. As grumpy as Dhuro seemed, he really did enjoy his brother's company, and she was glad to help give him this evening, especially considering his banishment from Nozva Rozkveta.

Queen Zara was angry about Dhuro's disobedience, but he'd accomplished the tasks she'd set before him, just in his own way. He was his own person, with his own values, and his mother's anger would fade with time. Surely she wouldn't keep her own son in exile for wanting to save his best friend, especially when he'd prevented unthinkable loss of life.

But if she did, that wouldn't be the end of it. Bella clutched a small sachet tightly in her other fist. She and Dhuro had overcome the janas, the maceddas, Dakkar, and the ghosts of their own pasts. They would overcome this, too, or else she'd never stop trying to heal the rift between him and his mother. Even if it took something so massive as finalizing peace in Silen.

Gwydion, who'd claimed to have been a dragon, had done great things before her very eyes. If, as his heir, she was capable of even a fraction of that greatness, then she would do all in her power to achieve that peace.

The tent flap rustled open, letting in playful firelight and the autumn chill. Dhuro poked his head in, slicking back his pale hair from his face. His eyes widened, and he blinked over their warm gold. "You're still awake."

Setting aside her scarf, she sat up, propped on her elbows, and nodded as he entered, securing the flap shut behind him. "How was it?"

Although their voices had carried some, she wanted to hear him talk about it. She loved hearing him talk. Shimmying, she shuffled over as he sat down next to her and began pulling off his boots.

"He's fallen out of favor with Nendra. Her other consorts have her ear and her attention, and he thinks she'll limit his time with his daughter," he said quietly.

It was a dark-elf tradition for queens to take multiple consorts to build alliances, and although they were marriages, which should be loving and strong, they didn't avoid falling victim to politics.

"Is there anything we can do to help?" She rested a hand on his arm, and he covered it with his.

"He wants to find a way back into her good graces." Dhuro set his boots in a corner of the tent. "He plans to track Dakkar, and I let him know that if he needs me, I'll be waiting at Roccalano."

"We." She sidled closer as he leaned back onto the bedroll.

"That's right," he said, and she could hear the smile in his voice. "My sheihan is a force to be reckoned with."

"Thanks to you"—she kissed his cheek—"I can control my abilities. I'll keep learning, too, and I won't stop working toward peace. But, Dhuro..."

She'd seen what great things Gwydion could do. She'd also seen the frightening power he was capable of.

Dhuro rolled onto his side, facing her, and brushed her cheek with the backs of his fingers. "What troubles you?"

She raised her hand, the one clutching the small sachet, and opened her palm. Within was the arcanir earring they'd risked so much to find. She had control over her powers now, and she'd never felt stronger. And that was why she needed this arcanir now more than ever. Why she needed to give it to Dhuro. "Power tends to corrupt—"

He laughed under his breath. "Not you, Bella."

She shook her head.

"Listen," she said, and waited until the faint smile faded from his lips in the dimness. "When we lifebonded, you trusted me with your life. I trust you to give me this if I'm ever not myself."

"Bella—" he tried to argue, but she placed the sachet in his hand and closed his fingers around it.

"For me." She pulled aside the blanket and sat up, then slowly swung a leg over his hips to perch on top of him. Her fingers busied themselves unfastening his shirt.

"For you," he agreed seductively, with a nod and a grin. "But I know what you're doing."

She shrugged a shoulder in mock innocence. "What am I doing?"

"Distracting me from the subject."

Once his shirt was open, she pulled her nightgown over her head, fighting a smile. "Should I stop?"

"No." His gaze fixed on her chest, he slowly swept his palms up from her hips, over her ribs, to her breasts. His touch, just the sensation of his skin against hers, made something tighten in her lower body.

"Good, because there's something else I want to ask you for." She moved on to unfastening his trousers, finding him ready.

"Yes," he answered.

"I haven't even asked you yet," she teased.

He grabbed ahold of her and rolled her onto her back, a hand bracing her head as he laid her down. He leaned in, his lips an inch away from hers as he fixed her with his intense gaze, and then kissed her.

"Tell me," he said, his voice deep, sultry.

Asking for what she wanted had almost never been an issue for her. Although she and Dhuro hadn't been wed in front of his family, and the wedding at Roccalano would probably be a year from now, they *had* married in the Eternal Grove with their Offering. She'd wanted a night of baring their souls to each other, but instead, they'd had a battle. Somehow, asking for that, even from her husband, heated her face.

Ignoring her racing heart, she rested a hand against his cheek, meeting his wanting eyes in the dark. "We never did get our wedding night."

He raised an eyebrow and flashed a sly grin. "Is that what you want?"

Gods above, he only made her face burn hotter. She nodded hastily. "Quietly."

The last thing she wanted was Zoran, Noc, and Shrelia subjected to it. She preferred not to cut short her immortal life by dying of embarrassment.

"No promises." He pulled his open shirt off, then his trousers, undressing until he was as bare as she was. All of him was firm planes and hard lines, as if he'd been made in the image of Forza, god of war, and sculpted from the stone of the dark-elf queendoms. She stroked a hand up his strong body and brought her palm to the black sun tattooed over his heart. She'd seen him naked, taken in his form for hours at a time, but it would never be enough. She'd never tire of looking at him, of being with him, of loving him, her husband.

I love you, sheihan. His thought, powerful and true, filtered into her head. Warmth spread through her chest, and she took his hand, intertwining her fingers with his.

I love you, too, she replied, and a glimmer shone in his eyes as he lowered his face to hers, covering her mouth with his. Locks of his hair brushed her forehead, her nose, her chin as he traced a path down her body with kisses.

She squirmed beneath him as his lips awakened her flesh, trembling as he parted her thighs and touched her tenderly, caressed her with ardent strokes that made her throb with need for him. She reached for him. "Dhuro—"

Soon, sheihan, I promise. And with that thought, he descended to her, his kiss replacing his tender touch, his mischievous gaze fixed on hers. She bit back a moan, and he raised a hand to her face to rest a clawed finger gently against her lips.

You did say "quietly," his amused thought spoke.

Her spine arched off the bedroll, as his wet, hot pressure coaxed her to the edge, everything in her lower half tensing to a fine point. She pushed against that tension, forcing it out to him, and her need grew and grew as he made love to her with his mouth, until her entire body seized with pulsing pleasure. He didn't stop, didn't let up, taking her over that edge.

The cries she stifled in her throat escaped as tears from her eyes, and she threw her head back against the pillow, reaching for him. He took her hand and pinned it to the bedroll, rising to meet her with a cocky smile as she whimpered.

He held a finger up to his lips, but no, she would be hopeless. She glanced at the scarf she'd set aside, and he followed her gaze, raising an eyebrow mischievously.

Yes, she thought to him. Maybe it would muffle her and spare their traveling companions from hearing all of this. But more than that, the prospect was exciting.

He snatched up the scarf and tied a big knot at its center. Leaning over her, he feathered the silk between her breasts and upward, awakening and pebbling her sensitive skin, and trailed the fabric slowly over neck and chin before guiding the knot into her mouth. She took it between her lips, gazing up at him as he visibly contracted, all of him going rigid.

Darkness, you do things to me, sheihan, he thought to her with a hard shudder, a fang pinning his lower lip as he tied the scarf around her head.

She looked up at him, blinking innocently, hoping to provoke him. He pulled away, but before she could pout, he grabbed her hips and dragged her to him, flush against her core. She moaned at the contact, muffled through the knotted silk, but the sound broke when he pushed into her, became one with her, and all the sound she could manage became a sharp inhalation.

His hand stole under her head, where he grabbed ahold of her hair, keeping her in place, her eyes locked with his, as he took her. Every thrust felt divine, and she clamped down on the scarf, squeezing her eyes shut. He tugged her hair back, and she opened her eyes to face him.

I waited thousands of years for you, sheihan, he thought into her mind, *during the Sundering, petrified to stone. I didn't think I'd be grateful for those millennia, but I am. They led me to my mate. To you.*

She wrapped her arms around him, urging him closer. All that had happened in her life had brought her here, and although there had been pain and anguish and loss, it was the gods' own blessing that it had led to Dhuro. They'd seen each other whole—not just what they'd chosen to present, but their innermost thoughts—and he'd not only accepted her but embraced her, loved her, and she him. They'd seen one another in perfect clarity, and she wanted him, all of him, and would hold on to him with both hands for the rest of their lives.

Longer than that, sheihan. He pulled the knot out of her mouth and down, then brushed her lips with his before returning with a firmer, deeper kiss. She welcomed him, taking his mouth with hers as he claimed her with slow, powerful strokes. Need rose within her, bit by painstaking bit, leaving her eager for more, aching for a faster rhythm. Her hips bucked against him, but he pressed her down into the bedroll, keeping his steady pace, holding her gaze locked with his.

She wanted him, more of him, all of him right this moment. The anticipation made her writhe, but his grip on her hair kept her in place, and each thrust fed her anticipation and starved her need until she wanted to weep, gasps tearing out of her. He grabbed the scarf, holding her gaze as he shoved it back into her mouth, two fingers lingering on her lower lip.

He inhaled a sharp breath, and she knew that sound, knew what it meant, drawing him closer, as close as she could, as he thrust deeper, harder, the intensity of his eyes spearing hers. He was close. The throb at her core intensified, and as his body tensed, as his breathing turned ragged, her need pounded stronger, stronger, stronger, until he hissed a breath and she shattered, waves of pleasure breaking with his every movement as he finished, as she bit down hard on the knotted silk, only muffled whimpers of surrender escaping her throat. Arms tight around him, she pulled him to her as much as she could, and he let her, but he watched her face in the throes of pleasure, his eyebrows drawn tight.

When they were both finally spent, he untied the scarf, tossed it aside, and claimed her mouth with a hungry kiss. Gods above, she loved him, and his satisfied expression was a sight she wanted to commit to memory. With that look alone, he could melt her, and he had. He thoroughly had.

That was fun, he thought to her with a wicked grin.

She'd trusted him completely—with her thoughts, with her heart, with her life; trusting him in bed was a given, and gods above, had he rewarded her for it. She'd asked him for a wedding night, and he'd most certainly delivered.

Yes, she thought to him. *This was a beautiful night, Dhuro.*

Was? He pulled back a little, laughing darkly. *No, sheihan. You asked for a wedding night, and it should be unforgettable. You'll remember tonight for the rest of your immortal life.*

With that, he wrapped her thigh around him and took her mouth with his once more. Her eyes widened, but a thrill wove through her. Oh, yes. She'd hold on to him. She'd hold on to him with both hands for the rest of their lives.

BELLA TOOK a deep breath as she sat on a sofa across from Mamma and Luciano, who'd listened to her entire story and openly stared between Dhuro and Shrelia on her shoulder. The entire castello buzzed with every new bit of gossip, not just about her return but her surprising dark-elf husband, with occasional dumbstruck stares. The Roccalano children had been best of all, running up to him and bashfully demanding to touch his claws, fangs, and ears. Despite his sheepish look, he'd allowed it all—except the hair. But then, he never liked anyone mussing his hair.

When they'd arrived, the valet had presented him with some things of Tarquin's, the only clothing that would fit his large, muscular frame. As he sprawled, muscle straining against gleaming black floral brocade fastened with wood toggles, an embroidered white linen shirt, and tightly fitted black trousers, she'd never been so grateful for Tarquin's sense of style.

Servants came with cups of steaming coffee and departed with them just as full, except for Dhuro's, since he didn't seem to be done smelling it. *Gavri will want to smell this.*

It's meant to be drunk. She rearranged her skirts over her knees with one hand, while still joined with Dhuro by the other.

He rolled his eyes at her. Neither Mamma nor Luciano had said a word. They'd both dressed in the most elegant of finery in time for her return, but now they painted a strange picture—Mamma in her deep aubergine gown, jewels about her neck and ears, her hair pinned up voluminously, and Luciano, clean-shaven with his dark shoulder-length hair perfectly coiffed, in a well-tailored doublet trimmed in exquisite gold. Neither of them speaking, their faces pale, as if frozen in some dream rather than an elaborate banquet of some sort.

I think you broke them, Dhuro thought to her, and she laughed inwardly.

Shush. It's a lot to take in. She cleared her throat. "Is it really so hard to believe?"

Luciano answered "No" at the same time Mamma answered "Yes."

Covering his mouth, Dhuro looked away, doing a terrible job of pretending to cough. A maid brought him fresh coffee anyway.

Bella tilted her head. "What's so hard to believe?"

Mamma's perfectly manicured eyebrows hovered nearly at her hairline. "You stopped a war? Bella, that is..."

"I told you. I have been the one writing as Renato. It isn't so drastic as you believe."

Luciano raised his index finger. "About that. I might have taken out a bounty on you."

Mamma turned those raised eyebrows on him and swatted at his elbow. "Luciano! You did what? How could you?"

He held up his palms. "I didn't know Bella and Renato were one and the same, only that it was bad for business."

All this time, it had been Luciano who'd sent people after her? "You're *B.*?"

His mouth fell open, but then he nodded. "Yes. Bianca took out the bounty for me."

Bianca... His wealthy princess-wife had taken out the bounty—*Bianca* was *B.* The bounty hunters who'd captured her and taken her to their camp outside the Eternal Grove had done so at her brother's and his wife's behest.

She fought a grimace. At least Isisa had been there, by a stroke of the gods' own good fortune. With any luck, Isisa had succeeded in luring away the dark unicorn, but Bella would write to Isisa's mother anyway and inquire about her. Isisa may have hated her now—and had every reason to—but Bella still loved her.

"Don't slouch, dear," Mamma reminded her.

Bella sat up straighter but stared down Luciano. "I would very much appreciate it if you would cancel the bounty on me."

He gestured his agreement. "That goes without saying. But you need to stop this Renato business as well."

"No."

Shrelia giggled on her shoulder, covering her mouth, and Dhuro's knowing eyes darted to her face, for just a moment. *Oh, this is going to be fun*, he thought to her.

She ignored him. "I'm not going to stop. I've wanted to say something for a long time, but no one has ever listened to me. But you'll listen now. Because of our family business, Tarquin has been exiled. Papà was killed. Cosimo was killed. And so was Nonno Silvio and Prozio Erminio. And their fathers, and theirs, and so on. We deal in blood, and we are awash in it, too. We are going to start a new family business."

"Bella—" Luciano began with a sigh, but this time she held up *her* index finger.

"No, Luciano. I will not lose you or Mamma or a single person more simply because it is tradition." Dhuro's hold on her hand tightened in support. "From now on, we will offer peaceful conflict resolution. Bloodless."

Luciano exchanged an incredulous look with Mamma before turning back to her, scowling. "You think you can just show up and dictate how I will lead this family?"

A slow grin stretched her face. This next part would be fun indeed.

Yes, she thought into his mind, canting her head as he started, his face blanching. *I can dig in your mind to my heart's content. As much as you'd love that, it's only the beginning of my powers.* As he froze, her grin only widened. *For too long, being the oldest male has meant power in our family. From now on, power will determine power. Mine.*

Sitting at the edge of his seat, he continued to scowl. She turned her attention to the vase on the table beside him, and wished it to rise. It floated up into the air, hovering just over the table's surface.

Luciano glanced at it and started, then shifted back into his seat, his scowl fading.

She wished the vase back into place.

I could watch this all day, sheihan, Dhuro thought to her with a conspiratorial grin as he sipped the coffee.

She didn't like forcing her brother's hand, but he and Tarquin and Papà and Nonno and countless male Belmontes had done the same, to force the family into the business of war. If she had to use their tactics, at least it was to force the family into a new bloodless era.

"This will be the new Belmonte legacy," she began. "I'll go where I'm needed to bring a stop to violence and hostilities. We'll employ scholars in diplomacy and dispute resolution to train new recruits so that we may have professionals ready to help our clients." When they said nothing, she added, "You don't have to agree now, but think on it. You'll realize it's the best course for both our family and everyone. I'll begin preparing plans and contacting the appropriate scholars."

This was far from over. The Belmonte family had dealt in war, but at home, victory was determined by finesse. She wasn't anywhere near done—this was just the opening salvo.

With that, she rose from the sofa and made a show of dusting off her skirts, and they all rose. She'd told them everything, had been completely honest, and now she would work openly to accomplish the things she'd once hidden as Renato. Once upon a time, those secrets had led her to chase fantastical creatures and had changed her fate.

It had been an ordeal, and although she was thankful for where it had taken her—and to whom—the time for secrets and intrigue were past. She wanted to go hand in hand with her family, old and new, into the light. "Now, if you'll excuse me, I'm taking my husband to the courtyard garden."

Looping her arm through Dhuro's, she inclined her head to Mamma and Luciano, who looked dumbfoundedly at each other and her, then she guided Dhuro outside.

"I think I really did break them," she murmured to him.

Dhuro laughed, patting her hand. "In the best possible way, shei-han. They don't realize it yet, perhaps, but you've blown in here like the wind of change, and you're sweeping out everything that they didn't know was holding them down."

That sounded good, but judging by Mamma and Luciano's expressions, they were resistant. "And if they don't?"

"Then we won't give up." A warm smile. They'd only become more frequent since the Offering, and as much as she loved her bitter porcupine of a husband, she loved seeing him smile, too.

In the courtyard garden, Cosimo's unicorn sculpture remained intact among the manicured shrubs. The sight of it squeezed her heart. Newly Changed, she'd once come here frantic, desperate, only to be captured by her own brother and his men for months of torture and fear. This beautiful place, with a gift from someone she'd loved, had had its memory stolen and tainted.

This place had been taken from her, but she was with the man she loved, and she would take it back and make new memories here. She'd run from her feelings about Cosimo's loss, but she'd stopped. She wouldn't run from this either, nor from saving her family from the dreaded Belmonte legacy. Those she loved were worth the effort.

Shrelia bolted off her shoulder and toward the plants, flitting over them excitedly.

A sparkle emerged from a rose bush. A little pixie clad in acorn shells, wielding a needle in a mad fury.

"Witam?" she asked, and he halted, flying up toward her face.

Unicorn? he asked, tilting his emerald-haired head.

Who is this crazed pixie? Eh? Shrelia demanded, tiny arms crossed over her leafy dress.

"Witam. He fought for my life once." The last time she'd seen him, a soldier had stomped on him in this courtyard. She'd thought him dead. "I never thought I'd see you again!"

You nearly didn't! But the human lady of the house found me and nursed me back to health!

She raised her eyebrows. Mamma had? If Mamma had softened toward the Immortali at all, no matter how small, then there was hope.

More sparkles popped up from the plants and fluttered toward Shrelia and Witam with excited chatter.

"Care to explain?" Dhuro asked with a smile.

"Someone I thought dead is alive, and someone I thought hopeless gives me hope." Tears welled in her eyes, happy ones.

It had been a long journey, and although she'd ended up back where she'd started, she'd both Changed and changed. Standing here with Dhuro, now and together, just felt right, like she'd been meant to return. She indicated the stone bench before the sculpture to Dhuro.

"Join me if you like," she said to him playfully, remembering a certain night by a lake. "I won't bite."

He cracked a grin, brushing clawed fingers gently through her hair as he peered down at her. "What if I want you to?" He rested his palms on her waist, then slid them down over her hips, his fingers tapping a light cascade.

She slipped her arms up over his shoulders and around his neck. "The night is still young," she whispered, eyeing his lips as he leaned in, "and our big new family isn't going to make itself."

"It would be my honor and joy," he said, his voice low and seductive, and then he kissed her.

THE END

Thanks for reading *Bright of the Moon*! If you enjoyed the adventure, please consider sharing about it on social media and leaving a review on Amazon or Goodreads. The review rating determines which series I prioritize, so if you want more books in this series soon, review this one!

Ready for the next installment in the Dark-Elves of Nightbloom series? The next book is called *An Ember in the Dark*!

AUTHOR'S NOTE

Thank you for reading *Bright of the Moon*, the second fantasy romance in the Dark-Elves of Nightbloom series. If you've read my Blade and Rose romantic epic fantasy series, you'll notice that those books and these interweave. Aless and Veron will be showing up again in *The Dragon King*, coming soon. And the next book of The Dark-Elves of Nightbloom will feature Dhuro's rogue warlord best friend, Dakkar, and will be coming soon as well! (I'm moving it ahead of Mirza's book, *Crown To Ashes*. Don't look at me—Dakkar made me do it!)

If you'd like to keep up with news about my books and other updates, you can sign up for my newsletter at www.mirandahon fleur.com. As a thank-you gift, you'll get the prequel story to the Blade and Rose series, "Winter Wren," featuring Rielle's first meeting with a certain paladin.

If you enjoyed this book and would like to see more, please consider sharing your thoughts about it on social media and leaving a review—it really helps me as an indie author to know whether people like my work and want to read more of it. Sharing is probably the most important way readers can show support for their favorite authors, especially independent authors like me, who don't have the help of a big publisher.

If you're familiar with Italian or Sardinian folklore, you may have noticed some special guests in this story. Also, both the Lago dell'Arcobaleno and the Parco dei Mostri are real places in Italy, so if you enjoyed them here, be sure to look them up!

All my books are only possible with the help of many people. *Bright of the Moon* is no exception! I owe a huge debt of gratitude to my friend Katherine Bennet, whose encouragement, support, and midnight chats helped keep me sane and on a good path, in addition to her invaluable insight on this story. I'd also like to thank Elise Kova for her lovely critique and helping me work on Bella, as well as Alisha Klapheke especially for her help on the early chapters. Thanks also to the ladies of Romantic Fantasy Shelf and NOFFA for their friendship and support.

The production of this book wouldn't have been possible without Mirela Barbu's gorgeous art, Lea Vickery's support and help as my personal assistant, Mel Sterling's and Jessica B. Fry's critical editing eyes, and Nic Page's and Anthony S. Holabird's keen proofreading, not to mention his paella and best husband hugs ever. Also, a big thanks to Melissa Wright, a talented author and kind soul who created the initial hardcover under-jacket design for this book!

And as always, to my mom. Your love and support have meant the world to me as I pursue this passion that impossibly is also my career.

Thanks go to my amazing street team, the Queen's Blade, as well for helping spread the word about my books and bringing a smile to my face! I am so happy we found each other, and I'm excited to keep having fun in 2021!!!

And you, my readers. Without your support, I wouldn't be releasing a ninth book. Thanks to your messages, reviews, and sharing the word about my work, I get to do my dream job and be an author. I love hearing from you, so please feel free to drop me a line on: www.miranda honfleur.com, Facebook, or Instagram. Thank you for reading!

Sincerely,
Miri

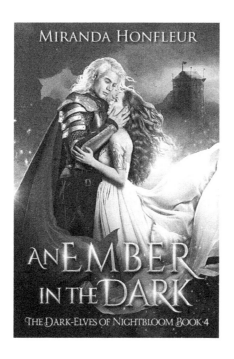

The war cut him in two. Only she can stitch his torn soul, if he'll let her in...

Born to a family of poor tailors, Lucia Perona has two talents: sewing and looking nearly identical to Princess Bianca of Silen. When a dark-elf warband begins to tear the kingdom apart, the princess and several highborn ladies are to be sent to a monastery for their safety. But to protect the princess, Lucia is sent in her stead. If only the dark-elf warlord leading the enemy forces didn't see the value of trading hostages for territory... and cared to respect the holiness of a monastery.

Dakkar grew up the son of a queen, raised to honor strength, the ways of the Deep and Darkness, and the power of his royal mother. A human once stole his immortal life, yet the queen-doms form a peace with an entire kingdom of selfish and untrustworthy humans, transgressions seemingly forgiven. Appalled, Dakkar leaves everything he knows to avenge victims like him and lead a warband of like-minded dark-elves to reclaim their dignity. After a few successful raids on human territories, he learns of a way to acquire more, bloodlessly: collecting valuable hostages to ransom. If only the most valuable of these hostages wasn't so troublesome. If only she didn't disprove his assumptions about humans at every turn...

As the humans and the queendoms negotiate for the women's freedom, Lucia continually chafes against her bonds and attempts to free herself and her friends, so much so that Dakkar shackles her to him. Forced to endure his presence, she seeks to demonstrate her people's strength at every opportunity—and find a way to end her captor. Only... when the time comes, she thwarts an attempt on his life. Hated by her fellow captives and looked upon with suspicion by Dakkar, she becomes responsible for their continued imprisonment...and devising a way to end it, without the aid she spurned.

The might of the allied queendoms and a human king threaten to rip the warband—as well as Dakkar and Lucia—apart, and if she can't repair the damage she caused, she'll lose everything she never knew she wanted, and he'll lose the half of his soul he never knew he needed. Can Lucia help a warlord see hope in the darkness, or will they lose each other... and the people they've hopelessly trapped along with them?

If you like the fantasy and romance of Elizabeth Vaughan's Warprize *and a marriage of* The Prince & the Pauper *and* Beauty & the Beast, AN EMBER IN THE DARK *will grab you and not let go.*

Preorder *An Ember in the Dark* today to journey into a medieval world of magic and Immortals, princesses and paupers, blood and passion, and enemies who could become lovers...

ABOUT THE AUTHOR

Miranda Honfleur is a born-and-raised Chicagoan living in Indianapolis. She grew up on fantasy and science fiction novels, spending nearly as much time in Valdemar, Pern, Tortall, Narnia, and Middle Earth as in reality.

In another life, her J.D. and M.B.A. were meant to serve a career in law, but now she gets to live her dream job: writing speculative fiction starring fierce heroines and daring heroes who make difficult choices along their adventures and intrigues, all with a generous (over)dose of romance.

Her current series include Blade and Rose, a romantic epic fantasy spanning six books, and The Dark-Elves of Nightbloom, a series of fantasy romance standalones. With over 250,000 books sold, Miranda has been toying with readers' hearts and apologizing for crushing them since 2017.

When she's not snarking, writing, or reading her Kindle, she hangs out and watches Netflix with her husband, gets constantly tackled by her dogs Gizmo and Luna, and plays board games with her friends.

Reach her at:
www.mirandahonfleur.com
miri@mirandahonfleur.com

instagram.com/mirandahonfleur

amazon.com/author/mirandahonfleur

facebook.com/MirandaHonfleur

bookbub.com/authors/miranda-honfleur

goodreads.com/MirandaHonfleur

patreon.com/honfleur

tiktok.com/@mirandahonfleur

twitter.com/MirandaHonfleur

pinterest.com/mirandahonfleur

youtube.com/mirandahonfleur1